Ralph Ashton gets more than he bargained for when police question him about the death of his ex-boyfriend Elijah Ray, whose body is discovered at the edge of the Saranac River.

When the local police visit Ralph and ask him about a critical piece of case evidence, Ralph becomes a prime suspect. He sets out to learn what happened to Eli the night he left his apartment and is startled to learn about his former boyfriend's shady past.

As Ralph pursues a dangerous investigation, he discovers things about Eli he did not know while they were together.

Ralph's life starts to unravel when he loses more people close to him as his mother lies in a hospital bed dying of cancer. Is learning about the truth of Eli's death worth jeopardizing his safety?

SCARS AND SECRETS

Thomas Grant Bruso

A NineStar Press Publication
www.ninestarpress.com

Scars and Secrets

First Edition, December 2024

ISBN: 978-1-64890-828-6

Also available in eBook, ISBN: 978-1-64890-827-9

CONTENT WARNING:

This book contains sexually explicit material, which may only suitable for mature readers, and depictions of the death of a prominent character, cancer/cancer death, incarceration, references to the abuse of a child by a parent, references to domestic abuse, homophobia, homophobic slurs, suicidal ideation, alcohol abuse/addiction, and attempted assault.

To Mom. I miss you.

Chapter One

THE SARANAC RIVER empties into the mouth of Lake Champlain and a sliver of late-evening sun shimmies and slices across shavings of broken ice like a school of shiny fish.

I straighten the blue-and-white striped silk tie my last boyfriend gifted me and stare out at the early November landscape. The ground is dusted with newly fallen snow, and the river, a swollen malignant serpentine of icy water, snakes through a vista of evergreens and sycamores.

I catch my hard stare in the reflection of the large picture window of my therapist's office.

Dr. James Matheson, basketball tall with peacock-blue eyes and warm brown skin, dressed in a rosy-pink dress shirt and charcoal-gray suit, coaxes me back to the present. His voice is butter soft and attractive, musically inclined and bilingual. Spanish on his mother's side, I think.

My thoughts unravel like vines on a branch, disoriented, a broken fuse box with faulty wiring. I blow out a loud breath and turn to the long-legged and handsome therapist, my hands packed in the pockets of my khakis so he won't see them shake. Men make me nervous and weak-kneed.

Dr. Matheson is patient and smiling, waiting for me to speak, to say something, since I've been standing in silence for the last fifteen minutes, staring out at the dismal day passing by.

I think about my mother who lies in the hospital dying. I've just come from visiting her, before my scheduled therapy session. Dr. Matheson wants to discuss it, from his stone silence and sensitive stares.

I glance at my wristwatch. I've been in Pretty Boy's office for almost an hour, and I haven't said much or given the good old doc enough to judge or dislike me or cancel my next session. I am surprised he has not asked me not to come back. Maybe he'll call County Hospital and admit me to the psych ward on the fourth floor if I open my mouth and let him into my dark, sad life.

He does not reach for the phone. He sits poised in the high brown leather chair behind his polished cherry wood desk, with many medical certifications on the wall behind him.

He stares across the room at me, grins, keeping a professional manner, waiting for me to give him his money and time's worth.

I drag myself toward the overstuffed leather chair across from his desk and collapse into it, as if it is my home base.

I find it hard to hold Dr. Matheson's gaze. Shyness overcomes me and I wring my hands. My anxiety levels heighten. My stare darts across the room at the sudden arrival of hard balls of sleet beating the glass and the braying wind cutting through the tops of snowcapped trees across the lake.

My breath catches, and I hear Dr. Matheson talking, his voice muffled, the tail end of his last words: "…do you want to talk about it?"

I cringe and feel his eyes on me when I turn away to the ice-crusted window on the far wall. My eyes close, and my lips clamp shut in a jagged line as rage seethes under my thin layer of vulnerability. My gut clutches.

"Ralph?" he says.

My name means nothing to me. Foreign, a stranger, someone I left in the past.

I lift my head slowly, and it is as if an unseen, supernatural force presses down on my shoulders, forcing me to keep quiet.

I am guarded as the walls go up around me. A nerve twitches under my right eye. Maddening!

Dr. Matheson shifts in his chair, and I sense that I have kept him waiting too long; his displeasure is like a bulldozer digging through the tendril of roots and dead zone of my brain, demolishing my thoughts. He's got to get home to his girlfriend, wife, whoever. Maybe it's a blind date, I imagine, invoking vulgar and naughty thoughts of Dr. Matheson in a heavy-duty threesome. One of the bottoms is me. I lift my dreamy gaze to his masculine, model-thin face, chiseled jaw, and rugged handsomeness. I can smell the citrus scent of his cologne ten feet from where I sit. Heat crawls into my face, aroused, my interest and other unmentionable areas proudly piqued.

I want a man like James: Built like a Greek God, Zeus or Ares. Tough. Striking. Dominant.

"What are you thinking about?" he asks, curling his small puckish lips. "You seem far away."

Clingy cobwebs of darkness thicken inside my head, gauzy and wet, sticking to the wall of my brain like silly string. "Deadness," I say, uncertain where this conversation is heading.

The face of my mother flashes in my mind, and I think about running back to the hospital and staying by her side.

James uncrosses his leg from left to right and changes positions so the side of his face illuminates in a shaft of soft glow from the floor lamp hanging over his shoulder. I want to tell him he looks fucking sexy that way, but I keep quiet. He holds his yellow writing pad, the tips of his fingers turning white, and I dream about what he can do to me with those meaty hands. Touch me in my favorite place, I want to tell him. But I don't.

I picture him holding my face in his sweaty palms as we lock gazes, staring haughtily into each other's eyes. The stiffness of my erection knocks against the fabric of my pants. I squirm in my chair.

"What do you mean?" he asks. "Deadness?"

I force myself to blink a few times, snap out of my hazy dream, and look up at Dr. Matheson. His expression is alarming, unblinking. He stares at me, bordering on the threshold of a stalker.

I find a way out of my rut, clawing, digging, and rummaging through a labyrinth of unfathomable responses. "All I want to do is listen to Twenty One Pilots or Nickelback and drink beer. Forget about life, people, and work."

Except for my mother. My ex-boyfriend, Eli, too.

I want to see him. It's been a while since he walked out on me and never returned.

Dr. Matheson angles his head to the side, deciding whether to ask his next set of questions. I hear him swallow, and it sounds like he has a dry mouth or is uncomfortable asking me a question from the long list on his pad. He is overthinking, I notice. "How is your mother?" When I don't answer immediately, he adds, "How are the nightmares?" My reason for being here.

I sigh. I don't want to talk about what keeps me awake at night, although this past week—year—has been terrifying. "It's been nonstop," I say.

"Have you been to the hospital?"

I nod. "Before I came here."

"Do you want to talk about it?"

"It's scary. Seeing my mother in that hospital bed makes me want to die. I hate watching her wither away slowly."

"Hearing what I'm about to say might not make sense to you now, but in the long run, you'll feel better." He closes his writing pad, leans forward, and folds his hands atop the desk. "Being with your mother in these difficult times is the most important part of this process. You're healing her but also healing yourself."

"How?"

"You're proving to your mother how much she means to you by visiting her daily, holding her hand, and talking. Keep her company. She can trust you. Dealing with hard times toughens you too. As difficult as it is to see her health failing, it is strengthening your mother-son bond."

"I wish I had somebody to call at night and talk to about this," I say, sitting back. "I've got nobody."

"You can always talk to me."

I shake my head. "It's not the same."

"How is it different?"

"We're not close—you're not my boyfriend."

He reaches for his writing pad and sits back in his chair, the nuts and bolts of his seat squawking like a distressed chicken. "Are you thinking about your boyfriend?"

"My ex. And yes."

"Have you been thinking about that time?"

That time.

When my ex-boyfriend, Elijah Ray, left me without a trace last month. He told me he'd be back. "I have a few things to deal with," he'd said. But I never saw him again after he left my apartment that night.

I dig my fingertips into the chair's cushy armrest. Dr. Matheson's prickly question provokes ghastly images of isolation, something I had become familiar with when my mother's cancer spread, and she got sick and was admitted to the hospital. But now, something in my therapist's unexpected analysis directs me back to a frightening, unpredictable past.

"How are you feeling?" he asks, yanking me back to the present, where things are marginally safer.

I look up into his alluring and soft, blue eyes. I am distracted and deviate into the indulgent contours of his kissable lips and smooth, freshly shaved face.

I reach into the pocket of my front pants for my honey-mint lip balm. I apply a little and smack my lips hard, for effect mostly, the taste sweet and delicious. "It's been lonely," I answer. "I don't sleep well. I wake to every small noise. A door opening, the wind in the trees, or the train roaring past the river by my apartment."

Dr. Matheson checks his expensive watch, a gesture I find gratingly unprofessional. He stops writing and sets his elbows on his massive desk, which makes him look small and part of the furniture. "What you're feeling is normal behavior. Loss is not easy. You will be sad for a while. But the pain minimizes over time."

I want to spend another hour with Dr. Hottie. I'm hoping he doesn't tell me our time is up.

He continues. "That's the first time you've shared anything personal about yourself during the two months you've been here."

Interlocking my fingers, I look at the rising anger and resentment I've created in my clenched hands, curling and uncurling. I cough and straighten my stooped posture, the bottoms of my running shoes shuffling over the immaculate floral rug under my chair. "I don't like talking about Elijah—or my mother. But I have to."

"It's a healthy way to help you understand how you're feeling and to lessen the burden and pain you carry every day," he says. "Most people don't know they're feeling overwhelmed until they face it with conversation."

"When Eli walked out on me, he hurt me badly. There was no explanation or recourse for his actions."

Dr. Matheson glances at his watch again—Rolex or Cartier, it's luxurious, that's all I know. He says, "It's traumatic and complicated to deal with alone. I'm glad you were mindful of your circumstances and to carry out a plan to join therapy. It's an age-old tradition that helps open dialogue for greater opportunities." He pauses. "We've got a few minutes left. We can talk about anything you'd like. How would you like to spend your time?"

As I suck in a lungful of air, a sharp pang travels like subliminal messages inside my chest to my brain. Panic attack? Guilt? A broken heart?

I don't want to give my fear a name. I ignore it; fight it. No more lies, I tell myself. My pulse quickens, and my heart strikes like fluttering wings, expanding like a balloon behind my ribcage. I am shaky; I need a fix—anything, a beer or something more substantial, or a one-night stand without strings attached. I flash Dr. Matheson a tight smile; the lilt of his voice, when he opens his mouth to talk, stirs something wicked in me.

When I say anything, it is the end of my session. "The hour goes by too quickly."

"We can schedule a time for next week if you'd like. How's Friday?"

I nod. A buzzing inside my head forces me to close my eyes. Something shudders and skitters across my vision, fuzzy like a thread of film moving from one scene to the next. Through a haze, I see Dr. Matheson pushing away from his desk, standing at a slant, all six foot three of him, mulling and scrutinizing something in the shadows, as he moves toward me.

He towers over me from where I sit. There's a cakey glaze of sweat on my palms. My body is immobile, as if glued to the chair. In an obscure hallucination, I see the outline of Dr. Matheson shifting in front of me, his large hands brushing mine as he lowers himself into a kneeling position on the rug.

Clammy fingertips. Racing heart. Electricity pricks my flesh. Dr. Matheson—James—fumbles in the dark for my belt, his warm, damp fingers sliding under the loop, unclasping it. He is rough; I admire his bravery. He's got guts.

I moan, my erection hardening at his bold touch. My head falls along the back of the chair. He tugs at my leather belt, loosening it for easier access. His hands travel to my tie, untying it, my gift from Elijah.

My thoughts blur as my therapist invades my personal space without permission, and I sit back, allowing it. He manhandles me with the solid and jerky movements of his barbell hands; his labored breathing undresses me as he rips off my pants and jockstrap, rolling my jeans and underwear down to my ankles.

He's a pro on so many levels.

He spreads my legs with his hands and burrows his face into the warmth of my crotch, his mouth finding the slippery tip of my cock. I imagine James worshipping his male clientele after each session. His tongue slides over my boner, and the humming vibration of his mouth sliding up and down my shaft makes me ejaculate a thick, creamy load, my body seizing, trembling, coming to life.

I'm moaning.

But then I startle awake, disoriented, staring around the room to find Dr. Matheson watching me wide-eyed from across the room behind his desk. I wipe saliva from my mouth, look to make sure my pants are buckled around my waist, and stand quickly. I gather my backpack from the couch behind me and hurry out of the room, embarrassed, aroused, and somewhat oddly satisfied.

"See you Friday," Dr. Matheson yells behind me, but I am already out of the office and in the elevator before I can answer him.

Chapter Two

I LOCK MYSELF in my rattletrap car as darkness coils around the parking lot and wait. I feel like a voyeur, sitting in the driver's seat, the fabric of my boxers damp with cum. I watch from behind a thin layer of snow-covered windshield, anticipating Dr. Matheson walking out to his black SUV.

I turn the ignition and flip through stations, landing on a familiar R&B song.

Three tunes later, Dr. Matheson exits the side door of the building with his briefcase and long, dark overcoat, walking quickly through the freshly fallen snow to his vehicle. He is talking on his smartphone and laughing at a joke or something someone says. His boyish smile is infectious. I glimpse myself grinning in the side mirror and am roused by what I see. A brave man, content. Happy and amused, from the looks of it. I imagine my muscular therapist shrink-wrapped in his skin, a bodybuilder with ten percent body fat protected with physical armor underneath his tight suits and ties.

I watch him kicking snow from his patent leather shoes against the bottom of the vehicle. He unlocks the driver's side door and tosses his briefcase into the passenger seat before climbing inside.

Waiting is torturous, but I bear it, blowing out a loud breath, my fingers tapping the steering wheel impatiently as time passes slowly.

The engine of his vehicle rumbles to life, and he waits a few minutes to melt the snow off the front and rear windshields before he drives to the building's main entrance.

I pull out of the lot after him, heading toward my barren apartment, the broken trunk door slamming up and down from the slow, meticulous drive.

I still need to get around to fixing it.

Half an hour later, I pull into the parking lot behind my cracker-box apartment, the metal structure of a small bridge and train track looming like a giant monster rising from the dusk behind it near the edge of the Saranac River. I shut off the ignition and sit behind the wheel, wallowing in the silence, thinking about Dr. Matheson and hearing him talking with that sexy Spanish inflection in the back of my mind.

I close my eyes. My therapist's dark stubble brushes against mine in the dreamy haze behind my eyelids. His sweet peppermint breath, thick and cloying, is heavy in the back of my throat as he slides his tongue in and out of my mouth, panting and whispering dirty words in his dark, drape-drawn office.

I glide my hand down the front of my pants to my erection. The fantasy of Dr. Matheson with me is hallucinatory, our bodies grinding into each other, a consistent rhythm, the sound of damp bare skin slapping against skin, our satisfying moans escaping us. I unbutton my jeans and slide the zipper down to grasp my dick, slippery with pre-cum.

The warm, dank odors of our bodies after sex arouses all my senses, and I arch backward along the headrest, the sound of Dr. Matheson's deep baritone voice urging me to kiss him. "I want to fuck you," he murmurs as he slams against my backside, rough, enjoyable, beautiful. His groans are music to my ears. I can taste his candy-sweet lips, connecting like magnets. His welcoming hands caress me, discovering my pleasurable spots, along my spine, down my back, to the opening of my ass, his wandering, curious fingers guiding me to climax.

I shake awake, my eyes popping open, alert, alarmed, surprised. I suck in a deep breath, my chest heaving, thoughts scrambled. When I notice I am alone, sitting in my car in the deserted parking lot behind my apartment, I look down at my hands, sticky and wet from the friction of my solo hand job.

Leaning back, I close my eyes and breathe unhurriedly, trying to regain composure. I swallow the rush of adrenaline climbing up my throat, and I can't stop imagining Dr. Matheson naked, his muscular body glistening beneath his skintight suits. His arms and chest are ripped from a religious workout, and I envision him lifting weights, running, and swimming.

My mind is hazy, and I must peel myself away from the make-believe dream that is only my imagination. I reach into my glove box for a napkin to clean off the gummy residue from my palms and fingers.

I leave the car and walk to the river's edge, tucking my hands in my pockets, hiding them from the sharp wind. Standing on the embankment in the early dusk, I take a long breath, the air clouding like thick fog.

A car engine rumbles through the night, disrupting my meditations. I turn to a set of blinding headlights slicing across the parking lot. I raise a hand to shield the light from my eyes. Snow dances wildly in front of the headlights. I check my watch: quarter after seven.

My heart sinks.

The ignition turns off, and the headlights dim, submerging me back into sheer darkness, or madness, just me and the sound of a low tide on the Saranac River behind me. The river is not yet completely frozen. Areas closer to the river's edge are solid ice, but the middle of the lake is dangerously thin.

Footsteps approach me, heavy and rushed, snow crunching like Styrofoam chips under his feet. I know it is a man because of the quickening pace of his gait coming toward me and the nasty wheeze of his breathing.

The moment he yells my name, my skin breaks out in goosebumps; somewhere in the trenches of my psyche, my thoughts are drowned out by his familiar, brutal redneck voice.

"I've been tryin' to call ya," my former boyfriend, Elijah, says.

Chapter Three

WE CLIMB THE fire escape to my apartment on the fifth floor and crawl in through an unlocked window.

"Why didn't we use the door?" Elijah asks, out of breath, a deep phlegmy cough brewing in his chest.

I turn on the light built into the stove and look at him. His eyes are buggy, bloodshot, and beseeching. He looks me up and down.

"Because you embarrass me," I tell him, half joshing, half honest.

"That was last month."

"Some of that month we were together, I'd like to forget."

"I've been trying to call you," he says again.

"Something to drink?" I ask.

"Beer if you've got it."

I open the fridge. Eli is in luck. I take two bottles of beer from the door and hand him one. I twist the cap off mine and take a swig before tossing the cap into the sink. He follows, although he has trouble getting his cap off.

"When did you get weak?" I ask.

He ignores me.

I help him, thrusting the bottle back into his hand and throwing the cap over my shoulder into the sink. He removes his leather jacket and hangs it over the back of the kitchenette chair.

"What's crawled up your ass?" he asks, tilting the bottle back and gulping most of the pale brew in one long swallow.

"You," I say, picking up a small pillow off the chair and throwing it on the floor so I can sit down. I moan, satisfied, settling in, lifting my feet on the ottoman and stretching. It feels good to be home. "Where've you been anyway? You leave one day, and I never hear from you. No goodbye. No phone call. Then, out of the fucking blue, you show up like a bad omen."

"Business." He empties his beer and slams the bottle on the coffee table.

"Business?" I almost foam at the mouth with sarcasm.

"A month's changed you."

"You don't know the half of it, Elijah." I pause and sip my drink.

"Calm down."

"Don't tell me to calm down. You don't have the guts to pick up a phone and call me? I was worried. Coming here was a bad idea. You should go." I stand and gesture for him to leave the way he came in, through the window.

"Hold your horses."

"What do you want? Why are you here?" I hope he can hear the annoyance in my gravelly, hurt voice.

"I wanted to see you."

"It's been a fucking month."

"Who's counting?"

"Me. How dare you treat my feelings like a fishing expedition, like it means nothing to you."

He stands and shuffles across the room like he did when we were together; he couldn't be bothered when the going got tough. Something is on his mind. "I care about you, Ralph. Always have."

I notice his worn-out shoes are caked with dirt as he walks around my apartment without a care. My anxiety rises. My shoulders tense and I sit upright. "Can you take your shoes off? You're tracking mud on the carpet."

He saunters to the fridge, swings the door open, reaches inside for a cream soda because the beer is all gone, pulls the tag off, and guzzles it. Foam sprays his face and the tiny, unkempt bristles of his scraggly goatee.

I roar with laughter, throwing my head back.

A deep guttural burp erupts from the bottomless gut.

He wipes his face with the back of his hand, and when he turns, I notice a tattoo in the shape of a triangle on his wrist. Three green eyes are inked in red on every corner of the triangle. I'm sure I never saw that tattoo before today. From the one beer, I imagine those eyes blinking back at me, warning me of Elijah's unexpected presence.

I ask him about the tattoo as he kicks off his shoes in the corner of the kitchen, mud splattering across the vinyl floor tiles. I get off the couch, sighing, spilling my beer on the front of my dress shirt. "You're such an idiot," I say, seething, and I know I shouldn't be so cross with him, but exes are infuriating. I loosen my tie. Eli gave it to me when we first dated. If he notices the tie, he doesn't mention it.

"What the fuck, Elijah?" I say, slamming my bottle on the counter and grabbing a dishtowel to wipe up more of his messes.

Elijah is naïve, oblivious, and just plain ignorant. I don't know what I ever saw in him. I dated him on and off, a year ago, but things went nowhere between us. I started up again when I felt sorry for his living conditions. I'd heard he was sleeping in shelters, at other guys' places, and on the streets, wherever he could find a place to lay his head. But times are different. I'm different too, now.

"You're making a mess." Heat rises up my neck as I crawl on my hands and knees, wiping up the kitchen floor. I want to strangle him.

"Jesus. Sorry. Man, nothing has changed. You're the same old dude." He turns and heads back to the couch.

"What's that supposed to mean?" I yell over my shoulder.

"You don't remember how much I gave to you?"

"The only thing I remember you giving me is an STD."

"You told me it cleared up." He sighs. "Goddamn. You were always an uptight motherfucker."

"I was an asshole," I admit.

"In more ways than one."

"Look, Elijah, why are you here?" I groan, pulling myself up from the floor. "What do you want?"

"Like I said, I miss you."

I roll my eyes. "Always with the drama. By the way, what sort of business has kept you away for a month?"

He tips the soda can back, gulps, and shrugs his shoulders. "Nothing you need to worry your pretty little head about."

"Mr. Ambiguous."

"At least I've changed."

I laugh and toss the dirty rag into the sink. I open the fridge door and grab a ginger ale from the top shelf. One beer is making me feel woozy. I turn back to my ex sitting cross-legged on the couch as if he is moving in permanently. He looks disheveled, exhausted, pale as death. "Are you in trouble? Homeless?"

"What? No. What—why would you ask that?"

I lean against the counter. "Since you're not giving me the complete story, I assume you're not doing well."

"I'm telling you the truth, Ralph. I miss you."

"So, what have you been up to?" I crank the thermostat from 65 to 70.

"Dating. Traveling."

"Really?" I ask, taking my seat in the deep-seated chair beside him. "You trying to make me jealous?"

"I'm seeing a new guy."

I don't tell him about my therapist—or being in therapy. "Do I know him?"

He shakes his head. "He's an out-of-towner. Muscular. Brainy.

Sensitive. Sexy as hell."

"That doesn't sound like your type of guy."

"This dude is. He's got arms like cannons and a big fat dick."

"Such lofty ambitions."

"More than I can say for you."

"What's his name?" I ask, slightly amused and interested.

"Why do you care?"

"Do I have to remind you that you came to me? Spill it. I want to know who's banging my ex."

"Why? So you can steal him from me?"

The urge to laugh overrides my curiosity. I release machine-gun laughter in Eli's face, uncontrollable, ridiculous, cheeky, and I lose my grip on my soda as it slips from my hand. I catch it midway before it hits the carpet, but I'm still laughing, hard.

"You're an asshole," Elijah mutters, a tight smile curling the chapped edges of his mouth, and he chugs down his soda.

"I'm happy for you," I say. "I hope everything works out for the two of you." I toast him with my soda. "I mean it." There is a pause, then I add, "Is he good to you? He better be."

He nods. "We're digging each other."

"Good."

"You made me happy once before, even through the tough times."

"I wasn't as bad as you make me out to be."

"You were rotten sometimes."

"I don't remember you being a saint yourself."

"I never pretended to be anyone I wasn't. You were always

introverted and shit. If you didn't want to talk to me or resolve a fight, you went for a walk or locked yourself in our bedroom."

"I had severe depression. Still do." I sit up, my voice growing angrier.

"You didn't even want to kiss me or hold my fucking hand in public, Ralph. Admit it, you were ashamed of us."

A nerve in my left thumb jerks, and my mouth goes dry. I shift on the chair so hard that the metal feet jump off the floor a few inches. I almost flip backward. I look away from Elijah to a wintry mix of snow and rain falling heavily from a black stone sky where the visibility across the river is low and obscure.

"Maybe you were ashamed of me," Elijah says, pulling me back into the conversation. "But I admire you for your tenacity to keep going."

I bite my tongue and taste blood. I swallow the metallic aftertaste down with soda and turn to him. "I was never ashamed of you. I was just annoyed that you up and left without telling me where you were going and what you were doing."

"I thought we were going to grow old together."

"Stop changing the subject. Did you not hear what I just said?"

"I heard you."

"Then answer me."

"I've had problems."

"What sort of problems?"

"Nothing that I can't handle."

I roll my eyes.

"I've got my life under control. However, it doesn't seem that way to you. Don't worry about me."

"Then why are you here? And don't give me a bullshit response that you've missed me."

"I have missed you. But I came back because you've been on my mind lately."

I am frustrated. "I'm not going to get a straight answer, but it's a typical Elijah response. Sugar coating was your forte."

He chuckles and sits back into the cushioned corner of the couch, which tells me that he's lost interest in this conversation.

"You come back to Grave Point to remind me how much of an asshole I was."

"Among other things. Important things."

"That you have a new boy toy?" I ask.

"No."

"Then what?"

"Nothing. It's not important."

"Your coy act only stretches so far until I lose interest."

"Do you have anything stronger to drink?" he asks, raising his soda and ignoring my comment.

"What do you want? Liquor?"

"Anything to numb the noise. Where is it?"

"You should go, Elijah. I think it'd be best."

He tosses me a grave stare over his emaciated shoulder.

"There's a bottle of vodka in the freezer," I say.

As Eli meanders away from me like a fleeting apparition, I glimpse the hardness in his thirty-six-year-old face. "Do you want a glass?" he offers as if he's the man of the house and this is his domain.

"Nothing for me."

His back is to me as he pours the good stuff. "You sure I can't get you a glass?"

"No, thanks."

"More for me, then." On his way back into the living room, he turns the music on from the stereo system, cranking it a decibel or ten too high for the evening hour, but somehow it fits, drowning the moody silence from the room and my mind.

He joins me in the living room/dining area, raises his drink, and I reciprocate, lifting my ginger ale.

Then I hear a knock on the door. "Shit." I hand Eli my soda can and lumber to the door. I unlock the deadbolt and slide the chain from the lock, easing the door ajar, enough to see my eighty-three-year-old neighbor, Mr. Williams, standing out in the ghostly lit hallway, his eyes milky from cataracts. "Do you mind turning down the loud music? I'm trying to sleep."

He stares at me with his left eye, while the right one is off in space somewhere, looking over my shoulder into my apartment, his eerie presence bordering on skin-crawling creepy.

"You're making a racket," he says.

"I'll try to keep it down." I shut the door and almost slam his weathered old hand in the doorjamb.

"My mother used to tell me, "Don't try. Do it." He steps back into the shadows and points an arthritic finger at me. "You're going to hell. God is coming for people like you."

"Goodbye, Mr. Williams." I shut the door and lock it. "Asshole," I mutter, and wander back into my apartment.

Eli is at my side. "What was that about?"

"My creepy old neighbor with nothing better to do than harass me."

"Call the police."

I turn around. "Mr. Williams is harmless. But he's right. I need to turn the music down."

We gather in the living room, the rap music barely a murmur in the background.

Eli lifts his glass to me. "To friends," he says.

"With benefits," I add.

He smiles into his drink, inhales the aromatic scent, then tips the glass, draining it in one long pull, smacking his lips, content. "I'm gettin' me another."

"Don't get shitfaced," I tell him, and he mocks my warning.

"Don't be a pussy. It'll be just like old times." He is already at the counter, pouring another vodka on the rocks. He is dodgy and unsteady on his feet and I feel I might need to babysit my ex-boyfriend tonight. "You're not driving in these conditions."

He turns, sloshing the liquor over the rim of his glass onto the tiles.

"Are you offering me your couch?" he asks, stumbling back to his chair.

"What other choice do I have?"

He flops on the chair, his head lolling like a marionette doll.

"If I let you drive, I'll feel bad if you get into an accident."

"You've always been the pessimist."

"I've learned from the best," I say.

"Funny, but you do just fine without my help."

"You'll sleep on the couch," I say, standing and emptying my bottle into the sink.

"Where the hell are you goin'?" he asks, his voice garbled.

"To bed. I'm tired. It's been a long day."

"You look sophisticated and cute all dressed up, by the way."

I turn my head to smile, amused.

"I just got here," he says. "Stay with me."

"I haven't slept well this last month. I wonder why."

I think about my nightmares and the therapy sessions. I stare at Elijah in all his glory, stretched out on my couch, making my apartment his home.

"What's wrong?" He sounds genuinely concerned, hooking my stare.

I shake my head, defusing the discussion. "It's nothing."

"Thanks for the couch," he says clear as a whistle, and I freeze in mid-stance, heading to the bedroom.

I turn to him. "Eli, this is strange."

"What's strange?"

I make a sweeping gesture with my hands. "A month has passed. You're in my apartment now, sleeping on my couch. Drunk like old times."

"I'm toasted, not drunk. There's a difference."

"You've always had a smart-ass answer for everything."

"One reason you loved me."

I walk to the edge of the couch where he lies, hunched over a pillow. I hover over him, and he says something that makes me laugh. "You remind me of dark clouds in a stormy sky. Move out of the way and let some sun in."

"There's an extra blanket in the hall closet in case you get cold," I say.

"You seriously goin' to bed?"

"I've got to be at the auto shop early tomorrow."

"Still repairing cars and getting your hands dirty?"

"It's honest work."

"A man who knows how to use his hands turns me on."

I pat him on the shoulder, and he covers my hand with his sandpaper palm. I jerk away from his clammy touch. "Fucking Christ, Eli. You're cold as ice."

"I get that a lot."

"You feeling all right?"

"Fine." He closes his eyes against the embroidered pillow I bought for five bucks at a yard sale.

"Good night, Eli."

"Night, man. Thanks for letting me crash at your place."

He's snoring before I can reply. I wrap his legs and feet with a second blanket from the closet and head to the kitchen for a glass of water.

I run the cold tap for a few seconds, fill the glass, then walk to my bedroom around the corner.

When I turn on the bedside lamp, a ribbon of light stretches across the room to the wood-paneled walls. I peel off my socks before I crawl into bed and pull the blanket up around my waist. I sit against a knot of pillows, reach for a John Sandford novel, and try catching up with Virgil Flower's latest case.

Reading helps silence the voices in my head after a long day. It also relaxes me. It is a more straightforward solution as a sleep aid than a few fingers of scotch or anything more substantial, which comes with a litany of penalties: headaches, vomiting, and brain fog.

My eyes feel like sandbags, heavy and dry, and they start to close after only reading two pages. The paperback slips from my hands, knocking me awake, and I lurch forward. I grumble, wipe my sleepy eyes, and call it quits, bookmarking the page with a dated postcard of Vermont lying face up next to me on the bedside table. My conscious thoughts are of my last visit to the Green Mountain State, a visit and talk with Elijah to try to work out the kinks in our relationship. The trip was partially successful, I recall.

Disheartened, I shut off the light, plunging the room into blackness. Turning and fighting for a comfortable position, I hear Elijah's boorish snores in the other room. Heaving one of the pillows over my head, I crumple and fold it in half to block out the noise.

It reminds me of one of the reasons our relationship failed. I jump out of bed and stumble in the dark to shut the bedroom door. Back in bed, I hide and wait for morning to find me.

Chapter Four

SOMETIME DURING THE night, I jolt awake to Eli talking to someone in the apartment. Groggy and knuckling sleep from my eyes, I toss back and forth, listening, angling an ear to the muffled voices in the dark.

I shudder from a cold draft snaking around the edge of the room and sit up shivering, folding my arms across my body in reaction to being startled awake. I am a light sleeper, awakened quickly by a door opening or closing in the apartment, tree limbs slapping the windowpane, or a car door slamming shut from a neighboring tenant in the lot below.

I sigh and throw the damp sheets off the warmth of my body, heat prickling from beneath the down comforter. An instant chill from the air shocks my cold, bare skin.

I pad across the room to the closed door. I turn the knob and open it. The voices grow louder, more discernible as I walk further into the dark hallway.

Male. Aggressive. Authoritative.

I think I can make out "No," "Not now," and "Don't do this" from beyond the howling wind. But I could be mistaken about the conversation in this early morning as I fight fatigue and the encompassing foreboding.

Looking around the room, I notice the window by the fire stairs is slightly ajar, a cold wind blowing in off the river. I look to where I think Eli is asleep on the couch, the shadowy outline of his body covered by two blankets. As I walk by the sofa, I dodge his sneakers and one of the two blankets crumpled on the floor and save myself from falling headfirst into the coffee table.

I bend to touch Eli's shoulder to wake him from what I imagine is one of his nightmares, but instead, my hand grazes an unoccupied space and the indentation from where a body used to lie.

I blink twice and look up at the open window. I shiver from a chill fingering my spine, like danger is settling in at the edge of my apartment.

My heart banging, I pause and whisper, "Eli? You there?"

There is no response.

I hear movement out on the fire escape, metal clattering under shuffling feet.

Then a shadow crosses my vision along the windowsill, and my ex-boyfriend emerges from the night, crawling out of the gloom into my apartment, backward, feet first. When he closes the window and turns back to the room, heading toward the couch, his temporary bed for the night, I say his name, and he jumps and screams, both hands flying in the air as if startled.

"I thought I heard voices," I tell him.

He shakes his head, waving off my comment. He reaches for the blanket on the floor, jumps back onto the couch, and covers himself.

"Is everything all right?" I ask.

"Yeah. Fine. Why?"

He pulls his feet up to his chest to make room for me on the couch beside him. The acrid smell of cigarettes clings to the inside of my nostrils and mouth. The air is thick with menthols.

"I thought I heard people talking. It woke me up."

He looks at me in the shadows. I see the silhouette of his face, but it is too dark to make eye contact. He rakes a hand through his messy hair and looks away to the window as if someone is waiting for him out on the fire escape. "I have a lot on my mind," he says.

I reach out for his hand, to touch him, calm him. But he is blind, does not see me. "What's wrong?"

He falls silent.

"Is everything all right?" I ask, hearing the heaviness and judgment in my tone.

"I want a cup of tea, please." His voice rises with a sentimentality that I'm not familiar with.

I laugh. "Since when do you drink tea?"

Through shades of darkness, I glimpse his hard, troubled stare. "Tonight. Right now."

"Eli, is something wrong?"

He exhales, and his body language changes as he turns away from me, staring out the window.

I reach for his arm, sliding my hand under the ropey muscle and sinew. His skin is sweaty and cold. He doesn't move or react to my touch but doesn't pull away either. "Were you talking to somebody earlier?" I ask.

"It was the wrong number," is all he says, and adds, changing the subject, "How about that cup of tea?"

"What does that mean? Wrong number?" I don't realize the biting disdain, but Eli reminds me of who I was a year ago. Forlorn. Depressed.

"What's with the sarcasm?" He gets up to microwave the tea himself. As he passes, a heavy cloud of cigarettes and marijuana assails me.

When he turns to me at the kitchen counter, I notice the sadness in his eyes. He'd been crying before I got here; that explains the bloodshot stare and volatile, edgy mood.

"I'm sorry." I stand and walk over to him. Placing my hand on his shoulder, I feel the bumpy groove of his muscle underneath the flannel shirt. "I know when something's wrong."

"I'm tired."

"I know this look. It's more than fatigue."

"I'm fucking serious. I'm just tired." He is defensive and temperamental, even in the way he carries himself, shoulders slumped, his expression inanimate, present but preoccupied. "It's been a few long months."

"Is it work that's keeping you up? This new relationship?" When he doesn't answer at first, I add, "How can I help?"

He sucks down his drink, complaining he didn't nuke it enough.

"It's my job, my number one enemy."

"Can you take time off?"

I don't even know what he does now.

He turns to me. "What do you think I'm doing here, Ralph?"

I shrug; my mind is cloudy. "I've been asking that question and waiting for an answer all night. I honestly don't know, Eli. I'm worried about you."

"That's all you've ever done was worry."

"One of us had to. I had to carry both of us if you remember."

"I'm not doing this. Not now. Not at this hour."

What time is it?

He brushes past me, the corners of our shoulders touching. Eli has been territorial ever since I've known him.

He falls back into the deep sofa, leaning his heavy head back, his eyes closing. He exhales, his ragged breath cagey and exasperated.

I crawl up next to him, curling my legs beneath me and sliding a hand behind his sweaty neck, twirling the stringy threads of his uncut hair between my fingers.

He is relaxed, sprawling down the sofa's length, his clasp on his teacup firm. He turns to me. "I don't know what I'm doing."

I am speechless, staring into his hypnotic hazel eyes. I grip the back of his neck and pull him into me, kissing him hard, our loose lips moist and slippery, like two awkward adolescents making out for the first time. His breath tastes stale, boozy, and skunky with pot.

He pushes me back with a light shove. "I'm not looking for sympathy."

"This isn't pity."

He sighs. "What would you call it?"

"Would you rather I kick you out of my apartment and tell you I don't want to see you anymore? I'd be happier knowing that you were out of my life forever. Maybe it would be best if you had stayed away. You complicate everything."

"Wouldn't be the first time."

I pull myself up and am ready to hit anything—the wall, the chair, myself, Elijah—square in the jaw. Anything to release the built-up resentment inside me.

"You're still angry," he says.

"Are you going to psychoanalyze me now?"

"That's somebody else's job. Not mine."

Dr. James Matheson materializes in the murky depths of my mind.

"Why am I so angry?" I ask, as if Dr. Matheson is in the room. "Huh? Tell me."

"You're hurt," Elijah answers instead.

"Hurt! Hurt?" I force a laugh, saliva spraying his face. I unlock my legs from under me. They're numb and prickly.

Eli wipes my spit from his cheek. "I don't want to fight."

I take a welcome breath, wipe tears from my face, and stare into the chilly night. "I'm sorry. I don't know how to deal with this—us—anymore."

His small hand falls across my leg. "I'm tired of fighting, screaming, and acting like the old us."

I nod and nuzzle up next to him, tucking my face in the warmth of his neck.

"I'd like a hot bath and forget about everything right now." He burrows his nose in his armpit. "I stink."

I pull back and kiss his cheek. "I'll draw you some warm water."

His bitter breath is stinging. He kisses the top of my head. "I appreciate it." He starts to undress. I grab his empty cup and head to the sink.

I go to the window and lean out to inhale the crisp November night. From the corner of my eye, I catch sight of movement from across the river. My gaze falls to the miles of trees surrounding the area and the burning orange light of a cigarette sparking in the blackness. The shadowy figure tries to camouflage himself in the forest across the river, but I feel I am being watched.

Chapter Five

MY BATHTUB IS the size of a coffin and only fits one adult body. The two of us in it together are a tight squeeze. We sit upright, cross-legged, and I feed Eli day-old grapes.

I've added bubbles, his favorite pomegranate scent, and the moment feels like sexual magic. "This brings back exciting memories for me," I say.

Physically, Eli has the look of someone who lifts weights. He is bad boy pretty, and I am falling in love with him all over again like I did the first day I met him. "Do you remember the nights you'd come home from work, and I'd have a hot bath waiting for you?"

"It feels good." He sounds lonely and depressed.

"Do you remember our first date?" I toss a red grape into his mouth.

"We went to an Eli Roth movie."

"Carnage and candy go hand-in-hand. I smuggled in a pound of peanut M&Ms."

"We made out in the back row."

"We missed most of the gore."

"Not my fault," he says. "You were a horn dog that night." Eli reaches over the tub's edge for his black tea.

"Me?" I feign innocence. "I think you're mistaken."

He smiles and takes a sip. He swallows and sets the cup on the bath mat. "I remember you on your knees, begging."

I bark with laughter. "Begging? That's far-fetched. You were good but not Oscar-winning, if I recall."

He pumps his arms in the air as if he's celebrating a victory, and the cords of veins and muscles bulge as he flexes. His unworried, gratified look is priceless, and I grin at his brief moment of happiness.

We settle silently for a few seconds, and his hands brush my leg under the water. I look up at him and notice he is deep in thought. As relaxed as I remember him, the last time we were together, a month ago.

The air is sweet with the smell of pomegranate-scented bubbles and his heady musk.

"Eli?" I say, stirring him from his musings.

He mumbles back to me, staring into my eyes, but I sense his mind is elsewhere.

"Are you feeling all right?" I ask.

"I'm fine. Just tired. It's been a long week."

I lean against the back wall with my glass of red wine.

"I needed a bath," he says. "I was filthy."

"When was the last time you showered?"

"A few days. Work's been busy."

"What are you doing these days?"

"Anything. Everything." He is evasive.

"It doesn't sound stable."

"I get by."

"Where do you live?" I ask.

"Vermont. South Hero."

"Are you still at 15 Bear Road?"

He smiles. "In the apartment above Mac's Bar."

A torrent of memories resurfaces; I think I am getting to know this man all over again. One particular night a year ago materializes in my mind. In those days, we were dating and fucking, and I'd sleep over at his place. Those momentary sensations disperse like a whisper in the wind, gone forever. "What brought you across the lake to Grave Point?" I ask.

"I've been thinking about a lot of things."

"What kind of things?"

His boozy, unstable stare catches me. "You." The tough guy bravado he sported during his arrival disappears and is replaced with a vulnerability that carries many questions.

"Why am I on your mind these days?" I ask, emptying my glass and setting it beside his nearly empty teacup.

He closes his eyes, and I think he hasn't heard me. But then he says, "I wanted to come and see you before I left town."

"Where are you going?"

"Home."

"You sound elusive again, and it makes me nervous."

"That's the last thing I want you to feel."

"Stop dodging the issue, Eli. Where are you going?"

"Back home."

"South Hero?"

He nods but doesn't seem sure of himself.

"What does that mean?" I ask, mimicking his movements, shimmying in the candlelit room.

"Let's talk about something else."

"Are you in danger?" I ask, my tone weighty with concern.

"What? No."

"You sound scared."

"Me, scared?" He laughs, but it is forced and controlled. Unspontaneous, not serious like someone who is in immediate danger.

"Does this have anything to do with that phone call you received earlier?"

A beat. "I've already told you. That was the wrong number." He catches me staring at him. "Why are you looking at me like that?"

"I'm curious, concerned, and scared shitless. You come back into my life without warning, without calling in advance. You're gone for a month, almost two. And out of the blue, you appear, but then you have to leave again. I find that fucking bizarre and disrespectful."

"What reasons do you have to feel that way?"

"You're acting odd. You drive back into my life after weeks of being MIA, and you beg for a place to crash. You look like you haven't slept in days, and now you're dodging my questions left and right."

"Nothing is going on. I promise. Just work. Loose ends that I need to tie up."

I reach for one of the two white bath towels hanging on the shower rod. I pat my hair and body dry and step out of the tub, the cold air tickling my skin. I shudder.

But not only the chill in the air drives me to the edge.

Chapter Six

I DON'T REMEMBER how beautiful Eli is until he enters my bedroom. He is bare-chested, his skin glistening, still damp from the bath. I peek over the top of the mystery novel I am reading and ogle his muscles, chest firm like a linebacker's, his upper body toned and hard as stone as he saunters over to me.

His hair is wet and stringy at the edges, and I can't take my eyes off his piercing stare, drifting over to me, hard and hungry, unblinking. He is a different kind of man than I knew him last month. Tonight, he seems wild and distracted.

I close the book and set it on the nightstand. I miss the edge, and the paperback novel falls to the floor. The racket doesn't deter or unhinge me. I keep my watch on Eli, my gaze unbroken.

"Can't sleep?" I ask, pulling the thin sheet up around my waist, covering my rebellious erection.

His smile is genuine, flattering, and determined. He stands at the foot of the bed as if waiting for permission to crawl between the sheets.

He doesn't have to ask more than once.

"Get in," I say, smirking, patting the untouched spot beside me in bed.

My hand glides down his smooth back, rutted with muscle. I stop, my fingers brushing a deep line of ridged bumps along his lower back, close to his thin, wiry waist. "What happened here?" I ask, tapping a finger on the rough, scarred skin.

"Accident." He is breathy in my ear, sharing a secret.

"I didn't notice it earlier in the bath."

"It's not important."

I know when Eli wants me to end my ten-question examination of him.

Kissing is a distraction, and he bows his head into my neck, caressing, his tongue grazing the length of my torso.

"I guess this means you're staying the entire night," I say, shivering from his mysterious touch, tongue and mouth marking his territory. I reach to turn off the lamp, plunging the room into silvery moonlight.

After a long make-out session, our tongues tangled like stretched taffy, and moaning amid the palpable sexual tension, Eli asks me to fuck him. I tell him I don't have condoms. He says, "We're not kids anymore."

He smells woodsy, sweaty, and desirable, and I don't want to disappoint him. Even if he's come all this way for a one-night stand, I still love the man I knew before.

"I want to make things right," he says.

"What do you mean?"

"Between us."

"It's been a year, and you coming in and out of my life whenever you feel like it hasn't helped," I say. My gut clenches, and I close my eyes, cringing. I pull away from him, drowning in disappointment. I taste and smell his warm cinnamon breath from the tea. His left hand finds mine, reassuring me everything will be all right, and the tips of his damp fingers graze my knuckles.

"I'm here now," he says.

I nod, but it is quick, knowing he cannot see my reaction in the dark. "I'm confused about why you're here, that's all."

"You've been on my mind lately."

"I'm in therapy," I say as if it is an answer to all my problems.

"Because of me?"

"For us, but yes. When you left—" I think about the morning we said goodbye and went our own way. Eli moved from the small upstate New York town of Grave Point to South Hero, Vermont. I relocated closer to Saranac Lake, sold our one-story fixer-upper in the boondocks, and rented an affordable tiny place here at River Brook Heights.

Our separation was amicable, but to this day, spending a life without Eli is like living with a terminal illness. I can't bear a future without him. The day Eli and I packed our bags and moved on with our lives was when I lost my identity.

Seeing Elijah in the flesh after a month apart is both a cause for rejoicing and uncanny. I have too many questions that will never get answers, but I'm afraid of what he will say. Honesty is not always the best policy.

I slip my hand out from beneath his and hold his face. Scrambling for him in the semi-darkness, I almost poke him in the eye with my index finger and apologize profusely. He silences my rants with a moist kiss, and my mind is woolly and lightheaded from his mint toothpaste/cinnamon breath.

"Shut up and kiss me," he says, and I obey.

*

LATER, MY BODY limp with exhaustion, Eli holds me in his arms.

"How do you feel?" I ask.

"Reborn."

"Don't get religious on me," I tease him, twirling his chest hair between my curious fingers.

"Sometimes faith is all we've got."

"You've never struck me as a religious type."

"People change."

I nuzzle my chin in the warmth of his damp, sweaty, musky underarm and stare across the room toward the bright moonlight spilling through frosted glass.

"Don't go silent on me," he says, and I shudder at the sound of his voice. His stubble is rough against mine, and I gaze at him, his eyes glistening like gems in the pale light.

"Can you stay a few days?" I muster enough courage to ask.

He sighs and shifts, lifting his arm gently from behind my head and folding his arms across his hairy chest.

The room is suddenly chilly, or maybe it is me, and I start shaking on my side of the bed, alone, out of Eli's grasp. "Now it's you who's gone quiet."

"I'm thinking." I hear a scared little boy in Eli cowering in his salvo of snaps.

I reach for him and rub the knot of muscle up and down his arm. "Sorry."

"No. Don't be."

"I just want to know where we are right now."

"Somewhere. Anywhere."

Elusive Eli.

*

LATER, AFTER WE'VE come hard and wiped away the evidence with bedside tissues, silence swallows us. We lie side by side, not touching, drifting in and out of sleep, the oncoming sounds of a train barreling in the dark woods by the apartment, along the tracks of the river, its horn screeching like a braying donkey in the night.

Eli starts panting, almost hyperventilating, and shadows swirl in the ether of my mind: wounded scars I never dressed, cleaned, and worked through. I think of my mother, and my eyes fill with tears.

I push myself up on an elbow. Shaking, I reach out a hand to Eli as if he is one of those old scars; I am hovering over him. "Eli? Eli?"

He shudders awake, writhing as if in pain. His body heaves forward, gasping for breath; it sounds like he's dying.

Startled, I jerk away, trembling, my heart beating in my ears, muffling my senses. I am too scared to talk. I close my eyes against the foreboding presence of the oncoming train, the clank of the wheels. My senses are crossed up and interlaced like a recent memory. I hear my mom calling me, asking politely to help her with her pain.

No words are forthcoming.

The vibrating tremors of the train passing by the bedroom rattle the windowpanes and our wineglasses on the nightstands, and it sounds like the horrors of a new world war.

Eli shudders and cries out for help, and his animalistic noises cut me to the core. I am on the edge of the bed, my hands at my mouth, stifling my screams. I'm panic-stricken as the night swallows me whole, like the opening jaws of a Great White or a double-barrel shotgun.

Waiting anxiously for the train to pass, I clutch the edge of the comforter in both my fists, squeezing, squeezing, squeezing, until my hands hurt, and a blinding pain shoots up and down my arms.

My eyes clamp shut, and I clench my teeth, nauseous and light-headed from the metallic merging of flavors in the back of my throat. Eli is screaming harder, louder, leaving him reeling. I am crying, listening to his haunting sounds.

Then, all goes quiet.

Eli stops screaming—my heart hammers.

Kneeling on the floor by the bed, I peer over the edge at him. Tinnitus sets in both of my ears, and I lay my head across the twisted sheets, my eyes closed. I mumble and begin to pray, an unusual method of defense.

I feel Elijah's calloused hand in my hair, abrasive but familiar, yet not, as he tells me he is okay. "How are you?"

"What the hell just happened?" I ask.

He draws back, and I hear him shuffling beside me, reaching for the sheets and throwing them off him. He moves across the room, the shadowy outline of his naked body strolling toward the window, staring out at the dead of night. He is breathing hard. He moons me with a perfect, pale, firm ass.

"Eli?"

Hands at his side, he drops his head in front of him as if he's lost in thought, thinking or praying silently, I can see in the bright moonlight his stiff posture slumping, shoulders trembling. The sounds of a wounded man fill the silence. It's unnerving.

I approach him, treading lightly, the loose floorboards creaking in the same place by the foot of the bed.

As I place a hand on his shoulder, he shudders beneath my embrace. "Eli?"

He raises his head and stares out the window. "Life does us no favors," he says.

"What do you mean?"

Crossing his arms over his chest, he pulls himself back into a composed, straight pose, legs splayed, assertive. He shakes his head. "I've lived hard, broken many rules. I've sinned."

"So have I."

Another head shake. "I hate myself."

"I wish you wouldn't talk that way."

He sucks in a deep breath. "I've got nothing more to offer any-body."

His words scrape the edges of my mind with scalpel-sharp preci-sion. "Come to bed."

The pressure and heat of his grip on mine reassures me he is still with me in the present.

"Come with me," I say, guiding him to the king-size bed. I help him slip beneath the covers and reach for the lamp. A soft light infuses the room, and I offer tea.

He asks for a glass of water, and I head to the kitchen, telling him to stay there. "I'll be right back."

Ten minutes later, I return with a glass of water and a hot mug of tea and set them on top of an old issue of *Popular Mechanics*.

Eli holds out a hand to me, gesturing me into his arms. I crawl across the bed and into the heat of his body, tucking my head under his chin and closing my eyes, pining for peace.

"I took a chance coming back, hoping you'd be here tonight," he says.

"Things happen for a reason."

His body moves as he leans forward. "Don't get philosophical."

After a few minutes, I ask, "Is everything all right?"

He is hesitant as he reaches for his water. Ice clinks as he lifts the glass to his mouth and drinks.

"Eli?"

His chest heaves as he stirs and sets his glass back on the nightstand. "I don't want to go back into the closet. Those days are too painful. The hate, the fear."

I stare at him, confused. Is he talking in riddles?

He is acting stranger than usual, and I am not confident everything's fine.

I allow Eli his space, and I recall our past when I was too intrusive, to the point that it drove us apart. We'd fight for hours or flee to separate corners of our apartment.

Some nights, Eli would go for long drives when our fights got too heated or one-sided. I locked myself in my bedroom, and when he'd come home, he'd sleep on the living room couch, far away from me.

I hug him now, hoping the demons he is still fighting all this time later are at bay.

"I'm tired," he says, and it is my cue to climb to my side of the bed and find whatever sleep I can.

Leaning over, I kiss him hard and taste the bitter beer notes on his breath: denial, anger, and jealousy after these last years.

"Goodnight," I whisper, punching my pillow into shape under my head.

"Night." His voice is barely audible. The springs in the mattress whine and ping under Eli as he reaches to shut the light off.

Chapter Seven

I WAKE TO an empty bed and a new terrifying truth.

Eli is gone.

The unfeeling dead zone inhabits the rubble of my brain as I scramble out of bed, unraveling my legs from the sweat-stained sheets, and dash to the window.

A new layer of fresh snow blankets the parking lot behind my apartment as I stare down at the empty spot where Eli had parked his pewter-grey truck.

There's a shiny silver key on the windowsill and a torn piece of paper wedged under it. I pick up the crinkled paper and read three words scribbled across it in an almost illegible hand:

My apartment key.

I shudder and question why Eli would leave me his key. An

unsettling chill invades my room and needles my bare skin, and I wonder whether Eli is just a figment of my imagination. I pocket the key and head to the bathroom to get ready for work.

After leaving a frantic voicemail on Elijah's cellphone, the second in the last twenty minutes, I head to work in a hurry, exceeding the speed limit by thirty miles per hour, the broken trunk door slamming up and down in protest, reminding me I need a new car. Adrenaline and rage drive me through the early morning streets, as deserted as a ghost town at this hour. I ignore the blaring police sirens and flashing red-and-blue lights behind me as I speed through mountains and along a strip of highway, passing closed antique and convenience stores along the way.

It is not until I come to a complete stop at a four-way intersection on the outskirts of town that the light turns green, and I pull over to the shoulder, my tires sliding across a patch of black ice.

In the rearview mirror, I watch as a female officer reaches for her two-way radio in the driver's seat and lifts it to her mouth, her lips moving unusually fast. She will undoubtedly scan my license plate number in the database.

My hands tremble at the sound of the driver's side door of the police cruiser slamming shut, and a skinny uniformed brunette ambles cautiously to my side of the car.

Fingers drumming unsteadily against the steering wheel, I am preoccupied with another dismissal from my ex-boyfriend, but the intimidating presence of the female officer outside my window rattles me further.

A French manicured finger raps on the closed window and jars me out of my skin. I look up at the wayward gaze of the firm-eyed officer staring at me through the rain-speckled window. It must have rained in the night. Up close, the police officer's face is long like a horse, and her green, steely eyes bore into me like a medium reading my thoughts.

She signals me to open the window. I power down the window and blow out a heavy breath.

"I was speeding," I say before she speaks and writes me a ticket.

I don't make eye contact with her. I am staring straight ahead at an oncoming brown Jeep, going fast, then slowing down once he sees the cop's presence. The vehicle is caked with salt and mud from the winter roads, and I imagine Eli behind the wheel, singing along to his favorite loud R&B songs.

The heavy weight of the officer's stare hovers over me as my gaze falls across her unlined, youthful face. I place her in her late twenties or early thirties.

The Jeep crawls by, and over the buzzing tick of its engine grinding the air, I hear Officer Tate, according to her nameplate pinned to her left breast pocket, say, "Where're you headed, sir?"

"Work," I tell her, and apologize for speeding, even though it's probably too late.

"Where do you work?"

"Sherman's Auto Body Shop on Kittery Road."

"Is the door to your trunk broken?"

"Among other things. I need a new set of wheels too."

"You need to get the trunk fixed, sir."

"I'll repair it when I get to work."

She stares ahead at the empty stretch of narrow road in front of us as if she could see my business premises in the distance.

She turns back to me and says, "The roads are slick. Be careful."

I nod, not sure how to respond.

She hasn't asked for my license or registration, which is puzzling.

"Why were you speeding?" she asks.

"I'm late to work."

She nods, and a crack in her smile reveals she is more human and likable than she leads on.

The moment goes from strange to madcap. "This is a warning," she says. "I'm going to let you off without a ticket. I'm in a generous mood today." It feels like friendly fire. Then she adds a barrage of uncertainties. "If I have to pull you over again for speeding and your trunk door isn't fixed, I won't be so generous next time."

"I appreciate it. Thanks, officer."

"Slow down. Drive safely. Get your trunk door fixed."

I nod. "Will do."

"Would you like an escort?" Her breath clouds in a thick mist.

I grip the steering wheel, thinking about Eli. Where is he? "That won't be necessary."

She pats the door to reassure me. "Drive safe."

I turn the key in the ignition and nod, looking at her, then the highway ahead to the next ten miles on Kittery Road.

*

TWENTY MINUTES AFTER arriving at work, I check my voicemail for messages from Eli.

Nothing.

My boss, Pete Mulligan, a pumpkin-shaped man with toothpick sticks for legs, is on the wrong side of fifty and cantankerous. He hates it when I walk through the front doors at an unbearable hour. He looks at me as if he will slay me and broil me for lunch. "Where've you been?" he asks, seething. He wipes beads of sweat from his bald head with a grease-stained rag.

"I got pulled over for speeding," I tell him, shedding my heavy winter coat and hanging it inside my locker in the employees' room adjacent to the front desk.

I can feel Pete's stern gaze as I walk past him to the back room, where a two-door red sedan waits for my service. He tells me I have three appointments today, keeping me busy until late afternoon.

Work clears my mind, and I am relieved to be changing engine oil, turning brake rotors, and working under the hood of classic cars. But today, I'm anxious, my mind in overdrive, thinking about Eli.

What happened to him last night?

Why did he leave?

With no note, cell phone, or Facebook message, I am a nervous wreck, imagining the worst, my thoughts a jumble. I fumble around the inner guts of a 1989 red V8 muscle car, fidgeting around the cylinders and engine to focus on other things I can control.

Pete asks me why I am so quiet as he stands beside me, blowing his nose with the same rag he used to wipe the top of his head. I am nauseous at the smell of his sour body odor.

"I'm under the weather," I say.

"The flu?"

"Something like that."

He grumbles. "I need your head in the game, Ralph. We've got a lot of appointments today."

I push off the front of the car and stand inches from his greasy, bulbous face. His breath is warm and rank, and I detect a faint whiff of booze. "I've got a shit ton on my mind," I hiss.

He punctures my space, stepping closer to me, his worn boots scuffing the floor between us, his Green Giant presence testing me. I back up, giving us both room, and a sharp pain in my head sends me reeling. I wince.

"You all right?" he asks.

I close my eyes. "Yeah. Yeah. I'm fine."

He pats me on the shoulder, and the heaviness of his grip knocks me backward. "Can I get you a Tylenol?"

I shake my head.

"If you need anything, you know where to find me." He turns and plods off toward his storage-room-sized office at the front of the shop.

I work through the morning break, checking for messages from Eli on my cell phone every ten minutes. I grab a soda from the vending machine and slip out of the shop by the side door into a blinding cold sun. I type Eli a text:

Where are you? I'm worried. Call me.

When I don't immediately hear from him, I head back inside, back to the greasy underbelly of my next appointment.

Changing a car engine is a dirty job, but somebody has to do it. My hand slips a few times, and my knuckles get scraped in the process, blood oozing from my fingers like oil. I step away from the work and bang my right hand, and by mid-afternoon, Pete tells me to take a break. "Go get a burger or something." His tone is demanding, deliberate, and domineering.

Shrugging him off only elicits a barrage of criticism. He is standing in my face again, even when I ask him to back away, and I want to deck him. Asshole.

As he turns and stomps off toward his cubicle, I ignore his fuck-you under his breath. I reach into my back pocket for my cell and stare down at the screen—no new messages. I start typing furiously, my fingers flying across the tiny keypad, trying to string together coherent sentences as fast as possible.

Where the hell are you, Eli? I let out a painstaking sigh, my heart beating erratically. Then I hear Pete yelling at me from across the drafty, sun-speckled room.

Eli's smile flashes across my vision, a drifting mirage. Tears prick my eyes.

"It's lunch break. Clock out!" Pete screams.

Snatches of sadness seize me. I wipe my face with a knuckle and am overcome with panic and concern. The last time I saw or heard from Eli was last night, eight hours ago. I rush out into the cold afternoon without my jacket or other belongings, my lungs burning from the exertion.

"Ralph!" Pete's grating voice scrapes the edge of my nerves.

I wave a hand at him without looking back. "I've gotta go."

"You need to clock out!"

Everything is hazy. "I need to take the day off," I say, heading to where I carelessly parked my car by the chain-link fence.

"What the fuck, man? We're booked solid today if you haven't noticed."

"I gotta go!"

"Ralph!"

I get in my car, turn the key in the ignition, and peel out of the lot, the back tires spinning up slivers of ice and snow in my haste, my eyes glassy and stinging from crying.

Hearing Pete yelling my name in the rundown doorway of the auto shop sends chills through me. "What the fuck!" he says.

In the rearview mirror, I glance at his thick outline. His bulk fills the doorway, his arms tossed back in an angry alarm, and his expression is manic and befuddled, mostly pissed off. He runs a fat hand over the egg-shaped dome of his Humpty Dumpty head.

Chapter Eight

I PULL OVER to the side of the road along the highway and turn on my hazard lights. I inhale a deep breath and close my eyes.

I'm unsure what to do, but I scroll through a list of telephone numbers on my cell. I think about calling my therapist's office, my fingers hovering over the button.

I could call the police and report a missing person. I'm overreacting, I tell myself.

Vehicles whizz past me at racing speed, horns blaring at me sitting in a no parking zone, and a driver yells at me to get off the shoulder.

Shaken, disgruntled, winded, as if punched in the stomach, I dial my therapist's office to see if he can see me.

Fifteen minutes later, I am sitting across from the birdlike Phyllis, my therapist's secretary, as she chatters about Dr. Matheson's punctuality. "He'll be here in a few minutes," she says in a North County drawl. "He's running late."

She looks at me as if I'm bothered, irrational, or neurotic. I stand and pace the room, up and down the Oriental carpet runner, and stop at the window overlooking the deserted parking lot below, to the barren snowy landscape of the Adirondack Mountains miles beyond.

"Would you like something to drink?" Phyllis asks, her voice soft and muted against the easy-listening music through the office speakers. "Water? Tea? A soda?"

I turn to her. "Thanks, but no. I'm good."

Almost twenty minutes later, Dr. Matheson walks through the lobby doors to the waiting room, his expression half smiling, his hair slightly disheveled, damp, and uncombed as if he's just stepped out of the shower or finished a quickie in the parking lot.

His perfunctory gaze falls on me, and I draw a ragged breath, hoping I don't look like a complete idiot. Seeing his dashing good looks makes me dizzy and weak-kneed. I can smell his cologne from across the room. It is piercing, heavy, and manly. I want to drink him like a tall iced tea.

Raising a manicured hand, he motions me into his office, opening the door and stepping aside, letting me enter first. Passing him, I inhale his warm, masculine scent, and for a moment, I forget about Eli and my reason for being here.

Dr. Matheson flips on a switch along the back wall, and the room ignites with dazzling white light. At his request, I sit in a chair across from his desk.

He organizes himself, setting his briefcase on the floor by his chair, removing his coat, and hanging it on a peg behind the door. I take off my winter coat and drape it on a small brass hook next to Dr. Matheson's.

I watch him comb the scruffy sprigs of hair on his head with a supple hand, and he clears his throat, pulling out the leather chair and settling in it. "Good afternoon, Ralph." He is a two-finger bourbon drink; I'd like to take my time sipping him. His jagged, hardy voice transfixes me.

"Thanks for seeing me on such short notice," I say, noticing my hands stained with grease and blood.

"Tell me what's going on."

I fidget with my fingers. "May I use your bathroom first?"

"Of course."

I stand. "I didn't realize—" I hold out my stained hands. "I'm coming from work."

He nods, tightening his Rolex on his left wrist.

"I'll be right back."

In the restroom, I slather my hands with liquid soap from the dispenser and wash vigorously under warm water, the raw open wound on my hand stinging. I remove most of the grime from under my nails and wrap my knuckles in paper, splashing cold water on my face to help wake me up. I stare at my puzzled expression in the mirror, the dark circles under my eyes, and the deep wrinkles lining my forehead. I grip the edges of the sink, the tremors in my hands undoubtedly genuine.

What am I doing?

I splash more water on my face, turn off the faucet, and dry my face with a paper towel. I check my cell phone for messages—none from

Eli. I head back down the hall to Dr. Matheson's office.

"What brings you here today?" Dr. Matheson asks the moment I take a seat.

I lean forward and scratch my head. "I'm worried."

"About what?" He opens a drawer and gathers his trusty yellow legal pad and fountain pen.

"My ex-boyfriend."

"He's back?"

"He arrived last night."

"What happened?"

"I don't know."

"You don't know?"

"Eli's disappeared again."

"When did he go missing?"

"He left sometime in the night."

I sit back, legs splayed, hands bunched in my lap, squeezing. I turn and glance out the window. It is raining; sleet taps the glass.

"What happened?" Dr. Matheson asks, heartfelt, supportive.

I cough and shift, and I am nervous and reluctant to talk about someone who can't defend his side of the story. "I woke up this morning for work, and he wasn't there."

"Where did this happen?"

I swallow hard and fiddle with my sweaty hands, folding and unlocking them, one of my myriad nervous habits. "My apartment."

"He stayed the night?" He sounds curious, his voice piqued by my answer.

I stare down at the floor at my foot tapping the floor. "Yes."

"And this morning he's gone?"

Another nod.

"Did you try calling him?" he asks.

"Many times."

"Does he live locally?"

I shake my head. "Vermont."

"Did he call you?"

"No."

Silence stretches out between us.

"I'm worried," I say, repeating myself, detesting the drone of my voice.

"It's understandable." He changes tack, looking into a different angle of the story. "Do you think he's in trouble?"

"I don't—" I sigh, slouch in my chair, and stare at Dr. Matheson's movie star looks. His alluring eyes seduce me: his ageless handsomeness, dimples the size of keyholes, and a smooth, tight smile.

"What is it, Ralph?"

I shake my head and say, "Maybe he drove home and didn't tell me."

"Would he leave without telling you?"

"Yes and no. Eli would have woken me if he were going to leave. I think. And no, there was no note in my apartment." I don't mention the apartment key. I stand and meander to the plate-glass window. "I don't know whether or not I should call the police."

"How long has he been gone?"

I shrug. "Eight hours."

"You know, Ralph, if you're concerned about Eli's safety and whereabouts, you don't have to wait twenty-four hours to inform the police."

I dig out my cell phone from my front pocket and enter my password to access my email.

Nothing.

"Ralph?"

I shake my head. "He hasn't responded. Not a word."

"Why do you think Eli would leave without telling you? Did the two of you fight?"

Looking up from the white screen, I feel like throwing up. I don't want to rehash last night's quarrel. I ignore the doctor's question and am frozen with fear, and I start to tremble. My mind rewinds to a communal time between Eli and me. An assortment of images from last night's unexpected visit plays over and over. I see Eli smiling back at me, his smoky breath on mine, his body strong like an ox, pressing into me, the firmness of our bodies rocking in rhythm.

Unable to control my intense feelings for him, I jerk forward in my chair as if propelled by puppeteer strings, my shoulders quivering, and the first wave of grief rocks me. I yell out Eli's name as if that will bring him back.

I hear Dr. Matheson pushing away from his desk, the springs of his chair groaning beneath his swift movements. He is at my side in a flash, handing me a box of tissues, leaning close enough to my face that I can smell his rugged, earthy masculinity.

I wipe my face with my hand, and as I lean forward enough to pluck two tissues from the outstretched box, I brush Dr. Matheson's hand with mine.

Unfamiliar energy surges through me. The doc's skin is warm and gentle, his knuckles bristling with a forest of soft hair.

"Thanks," I say as he stands over me, giving me time. I blow hard into the tissue, and he hands me another before taking his professional position behind his desk.

I sniff and wipe my nose, my eyes sore from crying.

Dr. Matheson folds his arms across his athlete's chest, staring at me with a face that exudes friendliness and warmth. "Would you like a glass of water?"

"No, thanks."

"Do you want to keep talking?"

I cough up a wad of phlegm. Tossing the balled-up tissue in the trash by Dr. Matheson's desk, I nod and grope around in my thoughts for answers, a reasonable explanation for Eli's strange disappearance.

I sit across from him. "Eli and I dated a year ago. Went our separate ways, reconciled and tidied up a few household jobs, and got back together a month ago."

"How would you describe your relationship?" he asks.

"Complicated."

"Did you love each other?"

"On and off."

"Why did he come back?"

I shrug. "I don't know."

"Was he trying to make you angry?"

"I—I don't know." I stare into the gloomy November landscape outside the large plate-glass window to skeletal trees bending from the ripping cold wind.

Dr. Matheson stops talking and moves, his arms falling to his side. He studies me. I feel the weight of his stare.

I don't turn away. I raise my gaze to his and hold it.

I want to walk the few short paces it will take me to get to the other side of his desk, crouch, kiss him hard on the mouth, and hold his face in my hands. I want to do things to him that only two men could do to each other behind closed doors.

"What are you thinking about?" he asks, and how he emphasizes *you* hints at the intimacy of the moment between us, making the session personal.

Hesitantly, I hold back, unable to tell him the truth, how I feel about him, his approachable tolerance, good looks, and the dewy sweet smell of him that penetrates and stretches me like a big fat cock. "It's not like Eli to get up and leave without a word," I finally say. "But he's been gone for a year, returns a month ago, and pretends we're the same people. I don't know who he is anymore."

"Do you want to call the local police from here?" he asks, and his hand on the phone unsettles me, making the moment feel real, permanent.

I get up and reach across his long desk for a tissue. He slides the box closer to me, and I pick out a few sheets, grinning at him—a nerve in my jaw trembles. I tear my gaze away from his so he doesn't see the curiosity in my eyes.

"Coming here may have cost me my job," I say, striding over to the window, a furious blizzard kicking up a whirlwind of ice and snow. "I don't know what to do."

I hear him forcing a hurried breath of air out through his nostrils. "Remind me where you work?"

"Sherman's Auto Body Shop."

He acknowledges with a quick nod.

"I couldn't stay at work," I say. "I wasn't thinking clearly."

"Understandable. Did you explain the situation to your boss?"

I blow out air through the gap in my teeth. "The narcissistic prick wouldn't understand." I wipe my runny nose and stare at a mass of blinding whiteness. "I couldn't stop thinking about Eli."

I hear Dr. Matheson sigh, the chair under him creaking. "Did Eli give you any indication where he'd go?"

Last night's incident evokes strong memories. I see us naked in bed, our bodies twisted into one. I remember him asking me to enter him, the moment heated and perpetual and memorable, etched in my psyche like the remnants of a kiss.

We're not kids anymore. I hear his composed, laid-back voice as if he is standing in the room with me.

I mindread the note he left me on the windowsill and finger my apartment key.

"Home." I tear off pieces of tissue.

"Where's home?"

"Vermont."

"Would he lie to you about that?"

The question shakes me. I turn around. Dr. Matheson is staring my way, his head angled to the side, his hair in disarray. "Why would he lie to me?" I ask.

He shrugs. "I don't know Eli. You do."

I take a deep breath and turn back to the window, to a fierce wind whipping about, conjuring unhappy thoughts inside me. Eli wouldn't lie, I tell myself. Not to me. I stand and head to the window. My knees are wobbly as I stagger backward, rocking slightly on the balls of my heels.

Dr. Matheson is in front of me, holding out a hand for support.

He gestures me back to my chair; his outstretched hand is merely there as a prop, guidance, beckoning me forward, which I try to do but am left empty-handed, reaching into dead space.

I fall back into the leather cushions of the couch, my palms damp with sweat, my heart knocking hard like a battering ram, my pulse quickening. "Would you like a glass of water?" Dr. Matheson asks.

Nodding weakly, I lean back.

He pours ice water into a stubby thick glass and hands it to me, an ice cube clinking. Leaning forward, I sip it as if it is the best, most expensive drink in the doctor's collection.

Occupying his chair behind his desk, Dr. Matheson asks, "Are you all right to drive home?" His question indicates our time together is over.

My hand shakes as I set the water glass on a granite-topped coffee table next to me and look over at him, feeling fuzzy, like my head is packed with wool. My eyes are tired and heavy. I inhale and knuckle a hand over my flushed face.

"I'm imagining the worst," I tell him.

He nods, sitting poised, professional, with a cool-headed manner about him. "I understand."

"Given the circumstance, I don't want to think about it."

"What scares you the most, Ralph?"

"That's a loaded question."

He sits patiently, waiting for a response.

"Do I need to answer the obvious?" I ask.

"Please."

The sound of leather crunches under my grasp as my fingers dig into the armrests. "Eli." My mouth is dry. It is hard to swallow; my eyes mist over. Catching my breath, I add, "That something horrible has happened to him." The words sound alien and cold on my tongue, coming out of me as if I'm speaking a foreign language and learning to talk for the first time.

"Does he have any other number besides his cell phone?" he asks.

I have to think. "If Eli does, I don't know. We've—"

He never told me. I was never privy to Eli's private life or much of anything from the last year, living our separate lives. I recall Eli's elusive behavior the previous night, which begs the question, could Dr. Matheson be right? Is there some conspiracy going on? Have I been played again?

I shake off the foreboding presence pressing against my chest, the unbearable weight as suffocating and lethal as approaching death.

"What were you going to say?" he asks.

I look up at him, numbed by his inquiry. "Hmm?"

"You were about to start a new thought. What was it?"

My face burns hot and I reach for my water glass. "I don't remember."

The moment I answer, Eli's face glints across my mind in a freeze-frame shot of our fleeting time together: lovemaking late into the night, grunting, pleading, crying out each other's names, talking in the dark, whispering.

I see him coiled in the corner of the bed as the train roared past the apartment.

I drain my glass and set it on the table, creating a thin, damp ring on the corner of it. Sitting up straighter, pulling myself into a healthier posture, I stare across the dimly lit room, trying to lure Dr. Matheson's direct gaze my way.

I can tell he is bored from the way he sits sideways in his chair, stealing a glimpse at his wristwatch, then over at me, to the overcast day outside, as if he can't wait to leave.

I imagine he may have an appointment and somewhere else to go, but he's being polite and keeping me here.

His eyes tell a different story. They're hungry, keen, and ruminating. "It must be exhausting," he says.

"What do you mean?"

"To be on guard at all times, to build a wall around you."

"I don't understand—"

"I think you do, Ralph."

"Are you going to psychoanalyze me now?" I am sarcastic, short, and rabid with my response.

"I get a sense you're holding something back." After a beat, he pauses and adds, "Are you uncomfortable discussing your personal life with me?"

"No. I, um, I don't know how to feel."

"About what?"

"Everything. Anything. My life is a train wreck at the moment. I'm scared. Anxious. I don't know what to do, or how to translate my feelings without sounding like a bad cliché."

"Just talk. Tell me what you're feeling."

"That's just it. I'm feeling mixed emotions; I don't know how to describe them." I bend forward, holding my head in my hands. "There's so much to process; I can't think clearly."

"Relax," he says, and it feels like he is sitting next to me, his soft voice calming. "Whatever happens, it'll be fine."

"I was recalling an intimate moment with Eli," I tell him, evoking my train of thought from earlier.

"What were you thinking?"

"Do you want to know?"

He nods slowly, leaning forward, delighted that I am talking.

I am aroused by Dr. Matheson's interest in my sexual proclivities. "Before Eli disappeared between the hours of last night and this morning, I can't stop thinking about the way he made me feel during sex."

Dr. Matheson stares at me deadpan, unfazed.

"He wanted me to fuck him last night." I disclose a private moment between my ex-boyfriend and me as though Dr. James Matheson is one of my buddies, someone I can confide in, to indulge all my darkest secrets. "After our time apart though, the sex was different from other guys."

"How so?"

"It was an out-of-body experience as if it was our first time. It was magic, real, even beautiful." I run my tongue over the bumpy patch of dry, cracked skin on my bottom lip where Eli bit me during foreplay. "The sex was limitless after being away from Eli for so long. But it also felt like it was the first time for both of us, two strangers passing in the night."

My direct response prompts Dr. Matheson to shove away from his desk and cross one leg over the other, sitting self-consciously as though I've managed to make him uncomfortable.

"Did you see or date anyone after you and Eli separated last year?" he asks.

"No."

"Why not?"

"I don't want to share my life with anyone but Eli."

"What if somebody else comes along?"

I stretch my legs. "I think I should hit the road."

"Ralph." He uncrosses his long legs and stands, pushing back his chair, his voice pressing and specific. He comes around to the front of the desk and sits on it. I wait for him to say something. "If you need to talk, call me."

I nod hesitantly, wondering if he's even talking to me. "All right. Sure. Thanks."

"Will you be all right to drive? Can I call you a taxi?"

I am disappointed that he doesn't offer to drive me home himself.

"I'll be fine," I answer.

"Drive safely." The earnestness in his tone is pleading, parental. He stands and hands me a small white card.

I look down at his name, vocation, and phone number.

"If you need to talk, call me—day or night. I don't usually give out my private number, but if you leave a message, I'll return it as soon as possible."

He is giving me access to his private line. I feel privileged. Hopeful. Eager. I hide my enthusiasm behind a thin smile. "Thanks," I say, grabbing my coat from behind the door. As I crawl into it, I drop the card into my coat pocket. My hand brushes Eli's apartment key.

"I'll see you soon," he says, returning to his desk. I wave a hand at him dismissively, thanking him without turning back. I fling the door outward to an empty waiting room, passing Phyllis at the front desk, her long, manicured press-ons clicking across the keyboard. I dash to the bank of elevators, breathless and sweaty.

No worse for wear.

Chapter Nine

THE CAR ENGINE clicks and sputters in the below-zero parking lot as I attempt to turn the key in the ignition.

From when I arrived at Dr. Matheson's office until now, the temperature has dipped close to freezing. Swearing under my breath, I wonder how I will get home.

When I try to start the engine a third time, luck is on my side, and my car rattles to life.

I wait a few minutes before I feel languid puffs of heat blowing from the vents across my face and warming my hands.

Still parked, I step harder on the accelerator, revving the engine and resurrecting the ancient jalopy.

The roads have not been plowed or salted, and the long, curvy stretch of highway is like an ice rink under my tires.

I am the only car on the road, I notice, navigating the brutal winter landscape, using both hands to steer. My car jerks and slides across the slick pavement.

In my mind's eye, Eli flashes me his smile, his shadowy face marking a permanent memory. Sharing beers at a local bar the night we met, I knew I wanted to spend the rest of my life with him. The way he made me laugh and cry, pushed all my buttons, and burrowed under my skin with all his annoying bad habits, I didn't want to spend another day with anybody else.

I exhale forcefully, shuddering and pushing the memories of the last year aside, praying and hoping that Eli is safe and unharmed.

The hiss of my car tires on wet pavement feels like I am dancing with danger, skirting toward a dangerous end, miles of woods on either side as I pull out from the long, wintry road.

I drive along barren roads to my apartment. Before I turn into the lengthy gravel driveway, I am greeted with red and blue police lights slicing through the dense mist that settles along the embankment, a ghostly swirl of chaotic colors.

I exhale a breathy whisper, my body rigid and rusty from the cold.

I shut off the car, yank out the keys, and push open the driver's side door. I step out into an arctic chill.

My breath catches. My heart knocks hard. As I slam the door shut, snatches of panic seize me, and I rush toward my apartment to a knot of police officers circling beneath the stairs leading to the fire escape, their voices stifled against the cutting wind.

Voices crackle over the police scanners. I start shaking from the unnerving buzz of activity humming around me. Snow and ice crunch under me as I crisscross the frozen ground to a group of male and female police officers murmuring at the far end of the property, near the edge of the slushy river.

Halfway to the stairs, I hear a booming male voice behind me, or maybe it's coming from inside the hallowed halls of my head, warning me to stop.

My heart strikes like a match—my face warms and pricks with panic. My hands are sweaty, shoved deep into my coat pockets.

Looking around, I can't locate where the voice is coming from. As the cold wind batters my face and skims my open coat collar, I turn to see a tall, agile, middle-aged man approaching me, hobbling a little. Despite the weak gait of his left leg, he is swift for a man his age. I figure him to be fifty, maybe older. He looks tough, military fit, with a buzz cut. His eyes, shiny beads of dark marble, penetrate me in the enclosing darkness. "Mr. Ashton?" he calls out.

The informal use of my name unnerves me, a hook twisting in my stomach.

When I don't answer, the tall man asks, "Are you Mr. Ashton?"

I nod weakly, my hands trembling inside the leather lining of my coat, my fingernails cutting like shards of glass into my palms. I feel dampness. Blood? Sweat?

He stands too close to me, and I feel and taste his warm coffee breath. I nod again, my mind clouded with too many unpleasant thoughts.

"Is that a yes?" he asks, his breath fogging the intimate space between us. He is fidgety, his stern gaze fixed on me like my mother's.

I nod.

"My name is Officer Steven Edwards."

"What's going on?" I ask.

He holds up a picture, the edges damp and torn from weather and wear. I lean in to get a better look. Alarmed and shaken from a sudden memory, I stare back at the dim image of Eli and me taken sometime last year. During one of our regular weekend road trips, we were standing and posing on a line of boulders at a rest stop on our way to Lake Placid. We had pulled over, I remember, because Eli had to take a pee and stretch his legs. "Where did you get that?" I ask the cop.

"My team and I got a phone call earlier from a dog walker who identified a body lying along the water's edge." He hooks a thumb over his shoulder to gesture to the choke of naked shrubbery near the Saranac River, fifty feet behind the apartment. "According to the victim's driver's license, his name is Elijah Ray. Did you know him?"

"Wait. What?" The sounds of the choppy river and the officer's brusque voice fade. "Is Eli…is he all right?"

His eyes dart to his fellow officers off to the side. He turns to me and flashes me a deadpan stare, his gaze glassy from the cold wind. Maybe he's been drinking. "I'm sorry."

I glare at him but don't speak. My lips seem to have been glued together, and I can't open my mouth. I shudder; a dull ache burns behind my eyes.

"We've been questioning other tenants in the building about the victim. I'm waiting on a search warrant to enter your apartment."

"You need to search my apartment?" I ask, incredulous. "Why?"

"We're dealing with a death, sir. It's routine."

I stare over the officer's hulking shoulders at a beehive of commotion behind him, people entering and exiting the apartment's main entrance.

Holding my stare, Officer Edwards shifts from one leg to the other, the weak one, the hurt one. "Mr. Ashton, is this a picture of you?"

I stare at Eli and me acting like fools on our way to Lake Placid—good times, old times—our arms exaggerated in pose and outstretched in the air, comically droll smiles plastered on our goofy faces. "Yeah. It's me—us. Eli and me." I sound defensive.

"Did you know Elijah Ray?"

I want to tell him we're in the pic together. But I keep myself in check.

My throat tightens. I stare down at the ground, the tips of my boots snow-covered. I kick the snow and ice off and look into Officer Edwards's chocolate-brown eyes. His stare is unflinching, hard as stone, unbreakable.

Frantic and anxious, I pull my hands out of my pockets and ball them into tight fists. The brisk air stings my clammy skin.

"Please answer the question." The officer's voice is impatient, growing louder, almost growling.

"Yeah. I knew Eli." My brows furrow. My mouth tastes sour. I shiver, not from the cold but from all the energetic bustle of activity.

"What was your relationship with him?" he asks.

I freeze and think about how to answer. Boyfriend? Friend? Lover?

"We were together."

"Boyfriends?" The word flies from his mouth in a comfortable re-tort as if rehearsed. As if he knows Eli and me and sees through the pain, guilt, and fear on my face and in the way I stand, fidgeting with my hands, my foot tapping like a piston in the crunchy snow.

Puzzled, I look at the murky outline of the Saranac River, search-ing for answers.

"Mr. Ashton." Stern. Foreboding. Officer Edwards doesn't take his eyes off me. "Answer my question."

I nod. "I can't believe this is happening." I wipe tears from my eyes. "Where's Eli now?"

"At the city morgue."

"I'd like to see him, make an identification." I feel shaky and un-stable, drowning in quicksand. I am at a loss for words. I don't hear the officer standing before me, talking, gesturing with a quick jerk of his head, or his glare glowering and burrowing into me.

His mouth moves, but I don't hear him. "Mr. Ashton, can you come to the police station with us?" He waves his younger partner over to me. "Officer Taylor and I would like to ask you more questions."

"Wait a minute. Are you arresting me?"

"No. It's just procedure." He holds up the photograph of us. "I've got some questions for you."

I turn to him, my lips burning raw against the cold night. "First, I'd like to see Eli."

Another police cruiser drives into the parking lot, snow and gravel popping under the tires. A large man on the wrong side of sixty ambles down the stretch of driveway to Officer Edwards and me and hands him a piece of paper. "Sir." He is breathless and smells of pastrami.

Officer Edwards thanks him and looks at me. "This is a search warrant, Mr. Ashton."

I nod affirmatively.

The young deputy opens the back door of the police car and ushers me inside, covering my head with his hand, so I don't smack it against the roof of the cruiser.

Officer Edwards gets behind the wheel, keys the ignition, and pulls away. We ride along the pebbled driveway, out to the interstate, to a new cruel nightmare.

Chapter Ten

A FINE RAIN needles the windshield of the police car as Officer Edwards drives along Interstate 11, heading to the city morgue, ten miles from my apartment. Officer Deputy Taylor occupies the passenger seat, drinking something hot from a paper cup, tendrils of steam drifting from the half-cracked lid.

Static from police scanners crackles, and the voices on the other end sound otherworldly.

I sit in the backseat, staring out into a windy night as the bleak, wintery Adirondack landscape flies by in a quick blur.

Officer Edwards pulls to the main entrance of the morgue as nausea and hesitation anchor me in fear.

I want to vomit, anticipating the carnage awaiting me in the basement of the morgue. Edwards parks the cruiser at a side door, and his younger partner gets out to open the rear door.

A blast of arctic wind assaults me. I am having second thoughts, picturing images of dead bodies with missing limbs. I manifest hellish snapshots of Eli's fate and what happened to him.

"Mr. Ashton." It is Officer Taylor crouching in front of me. "You don't have to ID the body today. You can take a few days."

I shake my head. "I need to see him."

"This way, then," he says, and he watches me, standing under an orb of stark white light emitting from a nearby lamppost. Taylor's stare is weighty and holds shady secrets.

I crawl across the leather seat and get out of the police car. I lean against the cruiser's side and brace myself from the chill in the air and what awaits me inside the bowels of the building.

Officer Taylor asks me how I'm feeling.

"I just want to get this over with."

"Follow me." He shuts the door, and we stand in the chilly air for a few seconds until I feel strong enough to enter through the metal doors.

Officer Taylor checks in with a fair-haired female receptionist staring at a computer screen at the front desk, her eyes tired from lack of sleep.

I look behind me. Officer Edwards is close, buying coffee from the vending machine.

After a few awkward pleasantries and obligatory procedures, I follow both officers down the quiet corridor to a set of elevators at the end of the hall. We ride down to the morgue and are greeted by a fat, fleshy bald man waiting for us on the other side of the doors when we step off.

The glare from the fluorescent lights bounces off the mortician's big-framed glasses, and he looks eyeless momentarily.

We step out into a starkly lit corridor. Dr. Barry Ackman introduces himself with a stiff handshake. His grip is dry, cleaver-heavy, and forceful, a professional bodybuilder from another life.

Officer Edwards introduces him and his partner, then me, gesturing in my direction. I am shaking, too anxious to speak.

"Come this way." Dr. Ackman continues down the long hallway at a brisk pace.

The air is stagnant and smells of sage and pine-scented candles. I wrap my arms around myself.

At the end of the hall, the mortician opens a door, and we follow him into a ten-by-twenty room, drapes drawn against a rectangular window on the far wall.

Reaching for the doorknob to an adjacent door near us, Dr. Ackman stops and says, "When you're ready, knock on the glass." He disappears through the door, and Officer Edwards and Deputy Taylor motion me to the closed window, taking positions on either side of me.

I feel like I've taken this trip before, staring death in the face. It's curious, I think, recalling my life with Eli, those brief happy moments, and the inevitable end that comes to all of us, sooner or later. For Eli, is it sudden?

Everything dies.

Officer Edwards's guttural voice sounds to my left. "Whenever you're ready, Mr. Ashton."

Blocking out the voices in the room and the whispers in my head,

I say a prayer that the body on the other side of the window is somebody else, that this is all a mix-up, and Eli is home or somewhere safe, worrying about me as I am about him.

Boots shuffle and Officer Taylor sips his coffee loudly and annoyingly as if I'm wasting his time.

I close my eyes. My shoulders stiffen. "I can't do this." Panic sets in as if I am buckled in on a roller coaster for the first time and am sweating to get off the ride, my heart about to burst.

Officer Edwards says, "Take your time."

I take a deep breath. Tears come hard and fast and spill down my face. I lose all sense of self and bring a trembling hand to my mouth. Without thinking, I knock on the glass.

My breath snags in my throat as he draws the curtain, and I stare out into the white light of a tiny, broom-size closet beyond, my gaze fixated on the face of my former boyfriend. White as snow, he lies on a metal table, looking as if he's sound asleep, twenty feet of space and glass separating us.

His face looks like ground meat, beaten badly, barely recognizable. A deep, sharp cut in his carotid looks like the work of a professional.

I can't stop shaking. I cry out Eli's name and heave forward, smacking the glass hard with my right hand. It takes both officers to pry me away from the window. Officer Taylor spills hot coffee all over the front of his uniform and cusses under his breath. Officer Edwards grips me in his lumberjack arms to keep me from falling to the floor and making a fool of myself.

Chapter Eleven

I RIDE TO the police station for questioning and sit in an interrogation room with forest-green walls and a bad smell. I've been sitting alone for half an hour, listening to muffled voices in the hallway, talking, laughing, and telling jokes as if I'm here for the hell of it, just passing the time. Nowhere else to be.

A faint whiff of mold burns my sinuses, my eyes itch and sting, and the metal chair feels like a hard, cold brick under my ass.

When the heavy metal door opens, I am about to rest my head across the unsanitary tabletop. Officer Mighty Green Giant strolls in, a territorial gait in his long legs, fatigue masking his face. He is accompanied by his brooding partner, Deputy Taylor, twenty years his junior. Red hair, bushy mustache, hazel eyes; his uniform is skin-tight against his flagpole physique. He puts on a tough bravado that I've seen in many of the guys I have bedded.

Both officers pull out chairs and sit across from me. The deputy appears young enough to be my nephew. Nineteen. Twenty. He looks his age under the fluorescent lights, but I am sure he is older by a few years, though not much. He sips water from a paper cup.

Officer Edwards bends down to read through pages of paperwork spread across the table. He adjusts his wide-framed glasses, which I had not seen him in earlier, and straightens his slumped posture. He coughs into his hand.

Deputy Taylor stirs in his seat, arms crossed over his skinny chest, face molded into a tight grimace, agitated, exhausted. He looks as if he'd like to be anywhere but here.

"What's happened to Eli?" I ask. "Who did this to him?" My voice shakes and cracks. Knobs of sweat break out along my neckline and armpits. Moved by an impulse, my breath quickens, and my blood pressure spikes.

"We're looking into it," Officer Edwards says, trying to keep eye contact with me steady. "You've been brought in for further questioning because earlier this evening, we got a call from a witness outside your apartment. The witness discovered Mr. Ray's body along the embankment of the Saranac River."

Blood rushes in my ears like Niagara Falls.

"We found this picture inside the inner lining of Mr. Ray's coat pocket." Officer Edwards slides the photo of Eli across the table.

My head buzzes, and I sit back, trembling, fraught with fear. I grow faint at the memory of Eli lying dead on a cold table in the morgue. I clench and unclench my hands. "This isn't happening."

"When was the last time you and the victim were together?" Officer Edwards asks.

I tense. My breath accelerates; I sound like an asthmatic bulldog. Anxious, I grit my teeth. "I feel like I'm being charged."

"It's routine, Mr. Ashton. We're trying to form a record of events."

"Last night," I tell him. "Eli was with me in my apartment."

"What time was that?"

I have to think hard. I see nothing but darkness curling around the corners of my thoughts. "I'm not sure. Early. Six. Seven." I don't mention coming home from my therapy session with Dr. Matheson. "I had run an errand."

"Between six and seven?" Officer Edwards repeats. "Was Mr. Ray staying at your place?"

"Yes." I nod, but I know the officer can see the uncertainty in my baffled expression. I did not understand Eli's motivation for arriving unannounced at my apartment after being away for the last month.

Edwards writes in his weathered old notebook, scribbling fast, pressing too hard on the pencil, and the tip snaps like a broken twig. He swears under his breath, tosses the pencil aside, and recovers quickly by holding his hand to his partner. Deputy Taylor passes him the remains of his stubby pencil with the end chewed off.

Dazed, I fall back into the chair and stare skyward, my vision drifting off from exhaustion. I fight off fatigue, lurch forward, and gasp. "May I have some water?"

Officer Edwards jerks his head at his partner to fetch me a drink.

Officer Taylor stands, goes to the water cooler in the corner, and fills a Styrofoam cup.

With trembling hands, I reach for it. Sip it. My throat is parched, and it's hard to swallow.

"How long were you and Mr. Ray together last night?" Officer Edwards asks.

"All night."

He looks at me, and I feel his white-hot judgment branding me.

"When did you notice that he was gone?"

"Some time in the night. I woke up. He wasn't there."

"So, you didn't see him leave your apartment?"

I shake my head. "He must have slipped out while I was sleeping."

I can hear Eli's satisfying moans in my ear, and the lost rekindling of our shared, secret moments together, a peaceful reminiscence of our past.

Officer Edwards looks through his notes and scrubs a hand over his well-tended beard. "We've interviewed other tenants in the building to see if they heard or saw anything unusual. Not many witnesses were forthcoming." He looks up at me. "We spoke to another tenant named Joe Williams, who lives down the hall from you. Do you know him?"

I shake my head. "Not personally."

"He told us he knocked on your apartment door."

I wait for Officer Edwards to continue. When he doesn't, I say, "He wanted me to turn down my music because it was loud."

"What else?"

I shrug. "What do you mean?"

"Did the two of you talk about anything else?"

I am being baited. I shake my head. Then, a thought seizes me. Edwards waits for me to continue.

"He told me that my kind of people were going to hell," I say.

"What did he mean by your kind of people?"

I roll my eyes, shuffle the prickling numbness in my feet, and swear under my breath, my suspicions of this dog-and-pony show intensifying. "What does this have to do with Eli?" Tears sting my eyes. I see my ex-boyfriend lying on the slab in the cold, dark morgue, pale as death.

"What does your neighbor mean, Mr. Ashton?"

"Mr. Williams is a homophobic asshole! He hates gay people."

"Did you and Eli fight last night?" The curve in the conversation and his tone catch me off guard.

I scrunch up my face. "What? No."

"We've got statements from other witnesses in the building that they heard you and Mr. Ray yelling at each other."

I am agitated, favoring my right hand as it trembles. "Yeah. We were loud, but I wouldn't call it fighting."

Officer Edwards's calculating stare makes me jittery. "What was the discussion between you and Mr. Ray about?" he asks.

I fold my arms over my chest and kick out my feet; my body angles in an uncommunicative, unresponsive, self-protective pose. I am ready for a scuffle, my voice argumentative. "Eli and me. Our future together."

"What happened to your hand?" he asks, nodding at the eggplant-dark bruise on my knuckles.

The tone in his question sounds squirrely. A knee-jerk reaction erupts, and I pull my hand away from the table. I hide it in my lap, away from Officer Edwards's questioning gaze. I look at his worn face, pitted with acne scars below his facial hair.

"I hurt it at work," I answer.

"Where do you work?" Officer Edwards asks.

"Sherman's Auto Body Shop on—"

He holds up a weathered hand and scribbles in his pad with the other as if he knows where the auto shop is located and I am wasting his time. He removes his glasses and sets them next to his coffee cup.

"Was there any physical altercation between you and Mr. Ray?" he asks.

I bite down hard, ruined by the relentless round of twenty questions. "No."

"Mr. Ray's body obviously took a bad beating," the officer says. "He sustained a few knife wounds to the chest and neck."

My stomach lurches. I stand, towering over the two cops, weak and sickened by the latest discovery. "I didn't kill him!"

"Mr. Ashton, can you please take a seat?" Edwards asks.

"I didn't kill my boyfriend. I wouldn't hurt him."

"Please, take a seat. Let's talk."

Taking deep breaths, I follow the officer's composed voice and sit, wiping my sweaty face with the back of my injured hand.

"Tell us what happened." It is Officer Edwards, his tone discerning, pitchy, definite.

Nervous, I rub my hands together, leaning back and staring at the white ceiling lights. "Eli stopped by my apartment unexpectedly. It's been a month since we've seen each other."

"So, you aren't in a relationship?"

I sigh, frustrated. "We were. We've had problems like every couple. Eli walked out on me for the last time a month ago, and I never heard from him until last night. We're still friends."

Officer Edwards writes in his notepad. "Where was Mr. Ray coming from?"

I shake my head. "I don't know. Home, I think he said."

"Where's that?"

"Vermont. South Hero."

"Had the two of you been in contact since your separation?"

"No." I look up at him. I want to scream and cry at the thought of Eli leaving me again.

"Did Mr. Ray say anything about why he was coming to see you?"

I shrug. "Eli told me he was in the neighborhood and wanted to see if I was home."

"He came from Vermont just to visit?" I can hear the skepticism in his question.

"I—I don't know. I guess. Why's that so strange?"

Silence, and he writes in his notebook again. "I'm just trying to piece the parts together. How did Mr. Ray seem to you?"

"What do you mean?"

"How was he acting? How would you describe his behavior?"

I think back to last night. "His usual self," I answer and am assailed with tentative emotions.

"Which was?"

"He looked and seemed genuinely happy. He wanted to know what I've been up to."

Officer Edwards glances at me momentarily, then turns to his partner, Deputy Taylor, sitting quietly, catching a curious look from his superior. He turns back to me.

"What did the two of you talk about?" Officer Edwards asks.

"Our lives. What Eli's been up to."

Officer Edwards leans into me. I can smell a trace of stale cigarettes. "What has Mr. Ray been up to?"

I picture Eli lying alone, cold, and lifeless in the county morgue. My eyes are hazy with tears. "I don't know—"

"Mr. Ashton, I know this is hard to talk about. But your testimony will help us find Mr. Ray's killer."

Finally, I say, "Eli told me he missed me. But then he left again. Poof. Gone."

"Where was he going?"

"He didn't say."

"Did he mention anything about living in Vermont?"

I shake my head. "I don't remember him talking much about his life away from me other than wanting to get back together."

"So, the two of you just sat and talked all night? Listened to music?"

"We had a few drinks."

He nods. "Go on."

"It's private," I say and recall Eli's mysterious behavior, distracted from our lovemaking. Something was wrong, but I didn't share that puzzle piece with Officer Edwards.

"Nothing is private," Officer Edwards says. "This is a murder investigation."

I run my hand over the opening of my shirt, through the small bristles of hair poking out of my collar, arousing memories of Eli and me in bed, our bodies rocking back and forth, Eli pumping himself so far up inside me, his wet breath as he whispered in my ear, "You like it rough, baby, doncha?" I recall arching my body back far enough so Eli could shoot his thick load of cum into my gut like a turkey baster.

I shift to conceal my blossoming erection at the dreamy image of last night's sex, the manly musk of sweat saturating our skin. In my mind's eye, I glimpse the faded triangular tattoo on his arm, inked with a prism of rainbow colors, remembering our mysterious life.

I let out a rushed breath. "Eli and I were intimate last night. It felt like old times. But—"

"But what?"

"He was acting strangely."

"Strange how?" Officer Edwards holds his pencil at the ready, annoyed that I have forgotten to provide a larger piece of the puzzle.

"He was distracted," I answer. "Something was on his mind."

Edwards asks, "Did he say anything that might have alluded to your theory?"

"No," I whisper, knowing there is more to Eli than I am letting on. My head falls to my chest.

Officer Edwards again: "Mr. Ashton."

I lift my head, and we lock stares. "I don't recall. Eli didn't say much. But I had a feeling that something was on his mind."

"Like what?"

Like he was in danger, I want to say. But instead, I answer, "I'm not sure."

Silence.

Officer Edwards sits back, sighs deeply, and gathers his papers. He nods to his partner and says to me, "Stay close, Mr. Ashton. We might need to speak with you again."

Chapter Twelve

I DECLINE OFFICER Edwards's offer to drive me back to my apartment. I call a taxi on my cell phone while waiting on the front walk, hunched against a wintry mix of snow and rain blasting in my face.

Edwards hands me the photo of Eli and me that he found at the scene and turns and heads back into the hospital. "Thanks," I say, barely functional now.

I hear the officer's heavy, determined footsteps fading behind me as I stare at the glossy image of Eli and me in a familiar embrace. Tears stream down my face in a hot, hurried mess.

Twenty minutes later, a middle-aged taxi driver with a mullet and a sagging beer gut picks me up in the hospital parking lot. He drives through heavy snowsqualls and delivers me to my apartment. I open the door and get out, handing him my ten-dollar fare through the driver's side window. I turn and dash into a bitingly frozen night, dodging any small talk the driver wants to share, and head in the direction of my apartment.

I remember always leaving the top window of my apartment unlocked and climbing the wooden stairs to my fire escape on the side of the building. I stop mid-way up the creaky metal steps and glimpse the marble-dark blackness of the river, weaving through the vast stretch of naked woods and train tracks at the edge of the complex.

I pull the photo of Eli and me that Officer Edwards gave me out of my pocket and hold it up to the pale lamplight, wavering in the wind. How did Eli end up near the river in the dead of night? Where did he go when he slipped out of my arms last night? A bigger question: Who killed him? And why?

I climb the rest of the way up the fire escape and yank open the window leading into my living room. It is caked with ice and snow, and I struggle with it for a few seconds until it cracks open. I climb through it like someone familiar with jimmying locks and doors. Inside, I pull off my coat and hang it over the arm of the kitchen chair.

I make chamomile tea and add honey, but the weak brew is too bitter. My stomach churns. Nothing tastes good.

I head back to the living room window in my pajamas—a white T-shirt and red plaid boxers—and gaze out onto the empty backlot, searching in the dark for the inevitable answers to Eli's murder. I glance at the yellow crime scene tape flapping in the harsh night, a ferocious wind screeching beyond the barrier like bagpipes. A magnetic restlessness pulls my gaze to the snowy patch of frozen land beyond the river's edge, to a landscape of trees, their knobby, skeletal limbs outstretched as if a clue in the night is trying to tell me something.

A rash of unanswered questions floats across my consciousness in a haze, a puzzle I vow to Eli in silent prayer to solve. I will find out what happened to him for his sake and mine.

For a moment, I am taken off guard, pulled away from the crime scene, as the salty sage scent of Eli implodes inside me, his voice urging me to investigate his death.

My loss is heavy, and I drown in sadness. Lightheaded, I collapse to the floor. I lie motionless, staring at the ceiling, listening to the uncanny silence in the apartment.

I sit up a few minutes later, head to the kitchen, and pour three fingers of Jack Daniel's into a drinking glass. I grab a box of salted crackers to absorb the alcohol.

I am numbing my pain to forget about the unwelcome news of losing Eli. Again—permanently, this time.

The insatiable smooth taste of whiskey helps me unwind, and my thoughts blur, and the nuts and bolts of my skull loosen, like uncorking a bottle of wine.

I fall into a chair at the kitchen table and finish my whiskey in a long gulp. Dazed and bone tired, I am unable to stand. I try to get to my feet but stumble backward into the chair.

An hour later, I wake in the dark on the kitchen floor.

Chapter Thirteen

IT IS SOMETIME in the night that I jolt awake, screaming, my skin drenched in cold sweat. My face stings like someone hit me with a baseball bat.

I know it is dark because a ring of moonlight slices through the living room curtains on the far end of the room. How I got from the kitchen floor to the couch in the middle of the night is a haze.

Trying to sit up only makes me want to vomit. Illness, mortality, and the realization that I am alone and Eli is dead provoke unexplainable explorations from the darkest depths of my dreams.

Silence feels inexorably loud and foreign and explosive in my head. My apartment is lifeless as if I am waking to the last days of a zombie apocalypse, and everyone is dead but me. The air smells like the morgue where Eli lies alone. I knuckle my eyes and suck in a big breath.

My lungs feel heavy; it is hard to breathe.

My mouth is stiff and dry from alcohol, my throat thick like leather hide. It is too painful to swallow. I try to move my legs, but my feet are heavy as cement blocks, anchoring me in place. I cannot adjust and stretch or kick off my sneakers from earlier.

I hear the faint whisper of a door squeaking closed somewhere in the apartment below me. Rapid, muffled voices of people talking, but the sound is indecipherable in the adjacent tenements, under floorboards, ceilings, and through walls. I might be hearing things though, I tell myself, the beginning stages of hallucination.

The weight of restlessness forces me to clamp my eyes shut, and the stabbing tension behind my eyes intensifies, a burning feeling like a raging fire bursting inside my head.

When the nightmares arrive, the ragged pain of Eli's death galvanizes my grief. I sit up, gasping. My heart drills and splits through my ribs like a chainsaw—my damp skin stings in the frozen air.

A cloying surge of adrenaline aggravates every sense, and I climb out of bed and stagger to the bathroom to take a long, hot shower. The steam hits my face, and I breathe in the gingery spice of Eli lingering on the shower walls and the bottom of the tub, his masculine, grungy scent sticking to me like a memory, long gone but close.

I drown my thoughts and fears under the rush of hot water blasting my face. As I turn off the nozzle and reach for the bath towel hanging over the rod, I hear a voice—an older male, brusque, a cigarette smoker—whispering, asking, no, demanding me to stay calm. *Don't listen to anyone*, he says. *Figure it out for yourself.*

"Eli, is that you?" I whisper to the empty bathroom.

A car horn blares somewhere outside, in the parking lot below, too close to my window that I feel the bathroom walls shaking. The vibrations, like those of an annoying motorcycle revving, unnerve me, and I lose my grip on the bath towel, the far-off sounds quick-fire and piercing.

Figure it out for yourself.

Eli's face flickers across my vision. I see him chugging a bottle of beer on my couch, a sentimental smile on his face when I tell him I miss him, and the delicate friction of our bodies as he slides in and out of me, moaning. I pump and grunt and collapse under the pressure of his gunfire release. The heat between my legs grows warm and heavy, and the surge of emotions rushes from me like a burst of ecstasy, our bodies rocking and pulsing and fumbling in the dark, our skin slippery with sweat and jizz.

When the sex is over, I bend down and kiss his soft, pierced earlobe. He whimpers my name in a measured manner.

He asks me to go again, but I am exhausted, my body spent as if it has swum its last lap, stumbling languidly to the finish line, dog-tired and dispirited.

A car horn blares outside the bathroom window—a bark in the night—yanking me from the imaginary embrace of Eli's arms. I swing around and wipe filmy steam from the glass panes, flipping off the ceiling light to get a better look into the parking lot below.

It is nearly empty, except for the fuzzy outline of a vehicle—truck or car?—idling under a line of trees along the river's edge.

Who is the driver waiting in the dark? I wonder as I pull on a fresh

T-shirt and pair of boxers and wander to the kitchen for a bag of frozen peas for my sore, stinging face.

*

SOMETIME IN THE night, I startle awake, screaming and swatting the air, my chest heaving. My skin is soaked in sweat, trickling down my neck and back and collecting in my chest hair. The pillowcases and bed-sheets are clammy, like sleeping on damp ground.

Out of breath, I pull myself upright and rearrange pillows behind my head. I clutch my chest at the familiar pain roosting like an old friend. It takes a few minutes for my eyes to adjust to the darkness in my bed-room.

My head feels thick and sticky with cobwebs.

Across the room, rain and sleet smack the windowpanes. A wind howls beyond the tree line and riverbank, a giant animal awakening from hibernation.

I reach for my glass on the nightstand and take slow sips of stale, tepid water. Moistening my mouth makes me feel half-human.

Lying back on the damp pillows, I close my eyes and start to doze. I rub sweat from my face with the back of my hand.

I can't sleep.

Bloody and bruised images of Eli lying dead in the county morgue rattle me awake from a nightmare and keep me awake until dawn breaks through scudding clouds and an armor-gray light reaches me in my de-teriorating landscape of broken dreams.

Chapter Fourteen

I SHOULD SAY a prayer for Eli.

Unable to sleep, I toss and turn and flash back to the remains of my ex-boyfriend covered in a sheet on the morgue table. At 5:46, I drag myself out of bed, my thoughts muzzy and unclear at this unreasonable hour.

I shit, shower, and shave, leaning over the sink and staring at the exhausted face looking back at me: a powder-pale complexion and skin that hasn't seen a lick of sun in weeks. My right eye is swollen, and I question whether it is infected.

I wipe shaving cream from my cheek, and the pain is excruciating.

Yawning and moaning against a few hours of sleep, I head to the bedroom dressed in sweatpants, boxers, a T-shirt, and a sweater. I grab my heavy coat from the arm of the chair where I left it last night and pull on a pair of shoes while brewing coffee for a to-go thermos.

I leave a light on in the living room to establish life and occupancy in the apartment and snatch the photo of Eli and me from the wine crate coffee table on my way out. I grab my car keys from a green plastic bowl on the hallway desk and lock the door behind me.

*

I DRIVE FOR miles until I reach the ferry docks on the south side of town.

The sun is high in the morning sky, and the air is cold as I creep along a near-empty parking lot at the lake's edge, pay an exorbitant fare for a roundtrip pass for one passenger, and board the ferry to Vermont.

There are more travelers than I expected at this early morning hour, and the crossing on Lake Champlain could be smoother.

I am the second to last vehicle to pull onto the ferry, the boat's jerky movements nauseating me. I squeeze in next to a rusted, mud-smudged truck with Vermont license plates. An empty gun rack hangs from a taxidermy pair of deer antlers on the back window. A hulking man behind the wheel and his scrawny male passenger chug soda or beer cans.

A sage-green late model Fiat pulls in behind me, its driver lighting up a cigarette, singing off-key, and bopping like a teenager to a tune on the radio.

The aggravating sound of a motorcycle engine punctures the peaceful morning and idles somewhere on the boat.

I close my eyes and lay my head back, listening to the lake churning and rolling around me as if something is stirring beneath the surface, gusts of water spilling over the metal railings and spraying the car's windshield. A fierce wind blows the mast.

Falling back into a light sleep, I glimpse a snapshot of Eli in my mind's eye. His mysterious presence in my apartment a few days ago brings up questions about his unusual behavior, which is shady and suspicious.

Who or what was he running from?

Heaviness stirs in my groin as I recall his firm body pressed up against mine in the shower, telling me how much he missed me. "I love you more than all of my mistakes," I hear him say. He slides his cock into me, slowly and gently, after asking for permission to enter me, slamming me up against the shower wall, knocking over bottles of shampoo and body wash. We fumble, our feet sliding along the slippery bottom of the tub, fighting to find the proper traction to keep us from falling. Arranging my left leg on the edge of the tub, I feel Eli's strong arm under me, navigating me into a more compromising position, inserting himself further inside me, up, up, up. For a moment, a minor pain shoots through me as if I've been stung. My eyes clamp shut, and I growl in protest. Eli senses my discomfort, but I tell him not to stop. I combat a few minor annoyances, biting my bottom lip and working through the rising doubt of our lovemaking.

I smile at the thought of our spur-of-the-moment tête-à-tête, the sudden rush of pain in the beginning, and hearing Eli's conciliatory sounds reverberating off the shower walls and filling all my senses, taking pleasure and pride in his gracious charity.

I shake awake from that far-off dream and open my eyes, staring out onto the horizon and the ghostly outline of lake houses and trees dotting the rocky embankment. Through the early dusk and windswept morning, the endless lake looks foreboding, my destination unreachable. I move to rearrange the stiffness between my legs after dreaming about Eli. Thinking of my ex, I want to retreat to the warmth of my apartment, slide into the coolness of the bedsheets, and flee into the safety of his arms.

I'd give back the time I lost in those selfish years when I said stupid things to rile and aggravate and push him away. For no good reason. All the wrongs I made to better myself, to get through those trying times. "Fake it until you make it," I say as if Eli can hear me.

What I know for sure now is that Eli came back into my life for a reason. But why? I remind myself why I have come this far. I need answers. Eli deserves them. So do I.

A flash of anger sparks in my brain, and I wipe my moist eyes. I whisper, "Fuck, fuck," and smack the steering wheel with a closed hand. Up ahead, I see the dock materializing through a light fog and rain, the wooden beams of the boat slip coming into focus. The water slams hard over the edge of the ferry onto the platform, the impact of the ride rocking the boat back and forth.

Switching on a reading light overhead, I reach for the photo of Eli and me sticking out from inside the visor. I stare at his ambiguous smile. Tears spill from the corners of my eyes and fall across the laminated picture. I wipe my thumb over Eli's face, blotting it dry. I turn the picture over and read Eli's current physical address inscribed in barely legible handwriting.

My next stop is 15 Bear Head Road, South Hero.

Chapter Fifteen

I FOLLOW THE rusted white truck off the ferry and wave at a female employee bundled in layers of shirts and coats, hunched against a raging wind.

Around the bend, I drive through a murky landscape of rolling waves crashing across the lake's surface and a growing line of vehicles waiting to board the next ferry. I pass one of the two ticket booths and stop at the yield sign up ahead, breaking behind the white truck. The red fleece-sheathed driver signals right, as do I, and we drive along a snow-swept road, past lakeview mansions that belong to doctors, lawyers, and dentists.

When Eli and I lived together, we'd cross on the ferry from Vermont to Grave Point for a spontaneous road trip. He promised me, "I'll buy you a dream house one day." I took it as a joke. But taking care of me was always Eli's top priority.

Up ahead, the truck driver signals left and sharply turns down a dirt road paved with a dusting of fresh snow. I notice the Fiat two vehicles behind me, trying to pass the motorcycle, which rides close to my bumper, almost tailing me. The driver of the motorcycle peels by, passing at dangerous speeds and surprising me with its loud, violent behavior.

I grip the steering wheel and watch in terror as the leather-clad motorist barrels through the line of traffic, its grating mufflers roaring in the distance as he disappears around the bend.

I take a deep breath and continue along Grand Isle and into the town of South Hero, with acres of farmland and residential housing dotting either side of the road. I pull up to a four-way intersection, the light blinking cautionary yellow. A gas station and pizzeria stand on my right.

I signal and wait for oncoming cars to pass before I turn, driving at ten miles an hour past an antique barn, a convenience store, local restaurants, and a credit union.

I take a right on Bear Head Road and drive down an unpaved dead-end lined with apartments, a flower shop, and an ice cream parlor. Both closed for the season. At the end of the road, a pink neon sign burns against a foggy light mist, revealing a massive stone building on the riverbank named Mac's Bar.

As I pull into a snug parking spot under a bare elm tree and a bank of rocks dusted with snow and ice, a wave of sadness guts me. My shoulders sag beneath a weight of sorrow, and I start crying. I lean too far forward, and my forehead smacks the steering wheel, eliciting the loud horn that startles a flock of blackbirds nesting in a nearby tree.

As I leave the car and stand against a battering cold wind blowing off the frozen lake, I imagine this trip is one of Eli's bad jokes, and he will greet me when the door opens. I take a deep breath and climb the stairs to the big oak door waiting for me.

Staring up at the three-story slate-stone building, I am flooded with memories of years past, wishing I were here for other reasons besides murder.

Caught up in my thoughts, I hear a rowdy crowd of middle-aged men leaving the bar out of a side door, stumbling toward a rock wall separating the parking lot from the lake, and landing a few yards from the bar's wraparound porch. Football-player-sized men stumble in a rebellious manner as if they've been drinking before dawn and climb over a snow-covered fence to the water's edge, their rambling, slurred voices echoing across the mile stretch of the icy lake to a band of houses lining the snowy mountainside.

I shake off a tickle of panic and dig into my pocket for the photo of Eli and me tucked into the thin lining of my winter coat. I look to where six men huddle around one another in lurid, animated conversation by the rocky shoreline, their backs to me, smoking cigarettes and staring out at the endless picturesque vistas of Lake Champlain.

I turn and ascend the wooden stairs to the front door. Eli and I frequented Mac's Bar occasionally on weekends to unwind from busy workdays, so today feels different and somewhat strange without Eli at my side.

As I grab the cold, rustic doorknob in the shape of an oar, an old-time country duo sings about a recent breakup, their crystal-clear lyrics blaring inside from the same jukebox Eli and I requested our favorite Dolly Parton song to slow-dance to.

Mac's Bar is a popular hangout for the college-aged circle-jerk demographics, so it is a Twilight Zone moment for me when I walk through the door. A dozen pine tables furnish the main room. The tops are scarred and ringed with beer bottles, and leather booths and stools timeworn from years of use.

Nothing much has changed, I notice, in the last year, except for the male clientele, thirty-somethings and older sitting at the bar, shooting the shit and chugging beers.

I notice Eli's favorite hangout spot in the bar: the pool table in the back of the room awakens fond memories from our lighthearted excursions, just the two of us laughing and clowning around, our frustrations sloughing off from the long work week.

The air smells of beer and body odor, the patrons' voices boisterous, loose, and unfiltered from the early-hour drinks as if they've been pulling all-nighters.

I walk over to a bald, bearded bartender at the counter who is mixing a woman a dry martini. His nameplate reads Trent. I order a beer from him and take the swiveling leather chair next to the female patron. She turns sideways and winks at me; her eyes are widely spaced, and when she hooks my gaze, I am unsure whether she is looking at me or over my shoulder. I am drawn to her heavily penciled lavender-purple lips, a full tight line of amusement tugging into a smile. Her lipstick and eye shadow are the pale color of crocuses or larkspur. No deep laugh lines, I notice, and her forehead is unmoving from an overdose of Botox.

She stirs a sizeable green olive in her glass before she raises the toothpick to her mouth and bites down on the salty fruit, cleaning the toothpick with one long draw between her lilac-colored lips.

Her appearance is striking, almost hypnotic, with a gaunt face, narrow, hawk-like nose, sharp jawline, and a touch of blush hiding the incision marks near the earlobe from a recent facelift. The way she sits is unladylike, though; her legs spread apart, the tips of her combat boots poking out from below the gray hem of her dress, military-masculine.

Pink, satiny gloves cover her arms, and her bony shoulders protrude under the flimsy fabric of her floral spaghetti strap dress. She is in shape, a brawny beauty, and must work out three times a week. Her arms are the size of cantaloupes.

I turn to the bartender, who slides a plastic coaster before me and sets my beer on top. "Can I get you anything else?" A hint of a Canadian accent hidden beneath an upstate redneck twang.

"Burger and fries," I say, scanning the menu. "Extra cheddar."

He is tall and hairy; his face is friendly. I like a man with facial hair. Eli comes to mind as I drown my woes in my beer.

I feel the female stranger's eye on me as I down the rest of the beer and gesture to Trent for another. This time, I sample whatever is on tap and sip the dark Guinness as the burly man resumes his bartender duties. He turns his back to me and wipes the counter clean of spilled beer and pretzel dust.

"I don't reckon I've seen you in this neck of the woods before," the voice beside me says.

I look to my left, where the low, throaty voice draws me out of my hazy state. The alcohol is already setting in, making me tired. I grip the glass Trent set in front of me and take a generous gulp.

"Don't look so scared, sweetie," she says again. "I won't bite." The patron's hand settles on my arm. "You're a good sport. Welcome to Mac's. I'm Janssen." She removes one of the gloves to shake my head.

My gaze falls to the large mitt gripping mine—a thistle of flaxen hair bristling around knobby, arthritic knuckles.

"What happened to your eye?" Janssen lifts her hand to my face and touches my cheek.

"An accident."

"Looks more like you connected with the end of someone's fist."

She extends her fleshy hand, marked with liver spots. I take it firmly, and she holds on longer than I'd like, two passing strangers meeting for the first time.

"When did this place become a gay bar?" I ask, shifting the conversation.

"Last year, sugar. Early April," Janssen says. "Just in time for the blossoming of a new spring and its hungry ducklings." She gestures to the knot of young and middle-aged men circling the pool table with their long, pointy sticks and determined stares.

I tip my glass to my mouth.

"Have you been here before?" she asks, leaning so close I can smell her delicate perfume, the aromatic scent of irises.

"In a different life," I answer.

"That sounds ominous." She stares, smiles, and twirls her rainbow-colored nails through the strawberry curls of her Dolly Parton wig.

I nod, leaning back and polishing off my Guinness.

"We've all got a past, sweetie," she says, invading my personal space, looping her arms around my shoulder, and squeezing me into her idea of an intimate embrace.

Our mouths are inches away from a kiss or close enough to whisper secrets to Trent, the bartender. "How long are you planning on staying—?" she starts to ask.

I turn to her. "Ralph."

"That's a strong name. Ralph. I like it." Janssen flirts with me, teasing and running a finger through my short hair, along my neckline, up to my earlobe. I shiver and ask Trent for a third beer, another Guinness. "So, how long are you in town for?"

When Trent delivers the cold draft in a tall new glass, Janssen pipes up and, in a singsong voice, says, "Long enough to watch my performance, I hope."

"Performance?" I look to her, then to Trent, who seems amused with our animated banter. He continues to wipe glasses, taking orders from other patrons, and listening to Janssen and me chitchat about the change of scenery to Mac's Bar.

"I'm a singer," Janssen says.

"I, um—I'm just passing through."

"You didn't answer my question." She sounds dejected. "I have a big number to perform later today around noon. I wish you'd stay."

I look out the corner window to my right where the men from earlier stand in front of the lake, now engaged in one another's company, laughing and lighting cigarettes and cigars.

Staring back into Janssen's optimistic, fresh face, I nod, slugging back my drink. A longing to be around people sounds like the perfect therapy I am looking for to occupy the current state of my busy, broken thoughts. "Why not," I say. "Sure."

She slaps me on the back, and I sit up straighter. She screams out, "Amen!" and suddenly, I feel like I'm back in church with my parents, sitting in the last pew by the main doors, my father, a devout Christian, always ready to cart me out by the neck when I fell asleep, snoring loudly, embarrassing him.

"Wonderful!" Janssen leans in and plants a kiss on my left cheek. She leaves traces of her lilac lipstick that I'll have to wash off later. She spins around on her bar stool and winks at me as she dashes across the room, stomping in her laced leather boots, sashaying by tables and the rowdy, raucous group of drunk men at the pool table. She exits through a rear door in the back of the room.

A popular boy band song comes over the jukebox.

"You've made Miss Janssen a happy woman." Trent is at my side, observing me like a hound dog, his massive forearms resting on the bar. His aftershave smells similar to Eli's, commanding and spicy.

"I've got a question for you," I say.

"Shoot, bro."

"I'm in South Hero for a reason."

He keeps eye contact, waiting for me to continue.

I reach inside my coat pocket and pull out the folded photo of Eli and me from last year. Sliding it across the counter to Trent, I ask, "Do you know him?"

Trent pushes himself off the counter's edge and grabs the photo between his meaty forefinger and thumb. He holds the picture up to me at an angle, under an arc of florescent bar lights, comparing to what I looked like two years ago, grizzly and bearded, a baseball cap pulled over my eyes. "Is that you?" he asks, somewhat amused but curious.

I nod. "Funny-looking, I know. But yes."

"How did you know Elijah Ray?" he asks.

I clear my throat. "We dated a year ago."

"No shit?" He grunts. "Too bad. Eli was a nice guy." He leans in and whispers, "The police were here a few hours ago, searching his apartment."

I reach for the beer. "The police were already here?"

Trent grips me with his Keanu Reeves stare. "Two hard-faced bulldogs from across the lake, asking questions."

I need help to stay civil. I take a deep breath, trying to convince myself I am here for a good reason. "I need to use your restroom."

"Let me get you the key." Trent returns a few minutes later and hands me a silver key.

I drop a twenty-dollar bill next to my empty beer bottle, but Trent slides it back at me. "On the house. Sorry about Eli."

"Thanks." I slide off the stool and head to the staircase at the back of the room near the doors where Janssen made her dramatic exit a few minutes ago.

Lightheaded, I reach out for the tops of bar stools to help me navigate through a crowd of other patrons. A few pro-wrestler-type guys bump into me, unapologetic, sloshing their beers and glasses of scotch across my path.

I walk past the restrooms and look behind me to see if Trent or anyone else is watching me.

The coast is clear.

I reach out for the railing and ascend the stairs. The early morning sun cuts through the stained-glass window on the top floor, temporarily blinding me.

Halfway up the stairs, I am eager to hide inside the quiet quarters of Eli's room. I yank out his apartment key from my pocket, which he left on my windowsill before disappearing.

I climb the stairs to the first floor and reach the top of the second, out of breath and lightheaded from the beers, the last of the floorboards moaning in protest under me. The heat of the sun on my back feels like a warm kiss. I stare across the railing to the closed door across the hall.

Yellow crime tape in the shape of an X closes off the doorway to Eli's apartment.

My heart strikes hard. I start to sweat. My hands tremble, and I flush, warm and tingling—the left side of my face itches.

Standing at the door, I feel like an intruder entering a stranger's home. I reach for the knob. It is locked. I slide the key into the slot. I swing the door open and pocket the key.

I think somebody is watching me from behind the other keyholes in the hall.

Turning back to the room, I notice Eli's apartment has that lived-in look. I crouch under the crime scene tape and enter, shutting the door quietly behind me.

I am assaulted with the stale tang of sweat and cigarettes as if the room has been closed up for months.

My breath catches. I am frozen in fear, muddled in sadness. Tears do not come, not now, but I feel like an outsider rummaging through another person's life.

You don't know what you've got until it's gone.

I shake off the strange feeling that Eli is talking to me.

I shouldn't be here, I tell myself. Yet I have to know what happened to him.

The jarring music from downstairs is muted by the floor-to-ceiling carpeting and the location of the apartment, two floors from the main room.

I notice Eli's bed is made, the duvet and bedsheets perfectly folded in hospital corners, as if he hasn't slept in it for days. Earbuds and a white iPod lie across the top of the pillow. I step further into the room to a corner table where a mystery novel and a bottle of cologne are propped up against a clock radio.

A novel? Eli didn't strike me as a reader. I never saw him reading when we were together.

Am I in the right room?

I open the nightstand drawer and rummage through unused note-paper and envelopes, a green plastic rosary, an everyday watch, and a glossy gay magazine with a beefy, naked jock leering back at me from the cover.

Closing the drawer, I turn to the only window in the room and look out onto a row of trees dividing the lot and a scant view of Lake

Champlain. The weathervane on top of the red antique farmhouse next door shifts from the changing wind.

Behind me, I hear humming. I turn to the sound of a mini refrigerator rattling in the far corner of the room, adjacent to a closed door belonging to a closet or bathroom.

I walk over to the fridge, crouch to open the door, and peek inside at a shelf lined with half a dozen unopened bottles of cheap beer, a paper plate stained with greasy fries, and a half-eaten cheeseburger.

I close the door, stand, and open the thin redwood door next to it. I step into a full-size bathroom. The fresh, pungent smell of cologne saturates the air. A green toothbrush—Eli's favorite color—and a tube of toothpaste lie on the counter in a pool of water. A supply of the usual amenities—mouthwash, soap, lotion, shampoo, and conditioner—occupy the sink and shower stall.

It is a sparse apartment, nothing out of the ordinary. Comfy for a single person.

Walking into the bedroom, I look around the tight quarters. What happened? Turning back to the bed, I stumble to the made mattress and box spring by the window, my body feeling old and used for the first time, my brain soupy and riddled with fog.

A wave of exhaustion smacks me like a hand pushing me from behind, and I collapse face-first onto the comforter-drawn bed, wrinkling the perfectly made linen.

I cringe and close my eyes at the watery light spilling into the room from the oval-shaped window above my head.

Though the day is still young, the weight of my recent dilemma wallops me firmly in the head like a boxing match of banging blows.

Wiggling on my back, I pull myself up to the headboard and prop myself against the pillows, pondering my next move.

I twist my neck to catch the sun's rays high in the open sky. I see Eli smiling at me in the shadows of the light, and I am crying on cue, broken and lost and reeling with horror.

Too many questions occupy my thoughts. I have no answers, nothing to improve the clockwork of my eight-hour circadian rhythms.

I wipe my face with my sleeve to dry the tears and yank the drawer open, remembering the rosary inside. I wrap my fingers around the plastic beads and hold them to the light.

I am not the religious type. I recall my childhood, sitting between my mother and father in church, listening to other people's voices, praying aloud to the mimicked lines of God's words. As a kid, I found church-going and praying in public strange, a pastime only to celebrate privately.

I set the rosary back beside the skin magazine and close the drawer. I squeeze my eyes shut and lie back on Eli's bed. When I open them again, something across the room stirs and provokes my attention. I stare at the closed door twenty feet across the room.

Grunting, I sit up from among the flat pillows. I walk to the door, grip the knob with clammy hands, and open it.

A new mystery begins.

Chapter Sixteen

I AM OUT of Eli's apartment in a marathon runner's record. I close the door and lock it.

I grasp Eli's journal, my sweaty handprints blotting the worn, leather edges. A door rasps open somewhere in the hallway and yanks me away from my thoughts. I lift my coat and hide the journal under my shirt.

Poking my head around the corner, I notice a woman in her seventies or eighties, with white hair and a piercing stare, watching me from beyond the gaping blackness of her apartment.

"Hello." I walk toward her.

The woman is silent. Deaf? Frightened?

I smile. "My name's Ralph."

Her eyes are owl-big and curious behind thick bifocals. As I step closer to her, she recoils. I get a feeling she might slam the door in my face. She retreats into the shadows, and I hear the sandpapery sounds of her bare feet scuffling across the linoleum floor. She watches me with a firm resolve as if I am a danger to her. As suspected, the chain lock slides back into place and the old woman retreats into her apartment.

"Ma'am, I'm sorry if I startled you. I didn't mean to. I was just—"

"What do you want?" Her sharp, abrupt tone pricks the hairs on my neck.

"I was looking for somebody." I jerk a thumb over my shoulder at Eli's closed door. "Have you seen anybody coming and going from the apartment across the hall?"

The chain link unclasps under the woman's hand, and her prune-wrinkled face emerges from the coiling gray matter. Shadows mask the silhouette of her silvery-pale face.

"Have you seen anybody in apartment 2C?" I ask.

"What do you think I am, a busybody or something?" Her bite is slow and ragged from age.

I want to nod yes but refrain, keeping a modest expression. I'm not particularly eager to discourage the woman from talking. "There's nothing wrong with keeping an eye out."

Her meddling eyes grow inquisitive, opening as big as a half-dollar. She pulls the door open more comprehensively, the old hinges squawking.

My gaze falls to her cleavage, an unaccustomed gesture I would have not generally acted on with the opposite sex—but her half-dressed appearance is shocking. The tree-bark texture of her decolletage skin is a mummified nightmare from the mind of Stephen King. Her breasts are as saggy as melting wax, cupped in a Princess Leia-like metal brassiere.

What the fuck is my initial mental response. But as the woman wanders out into the sun-kissed corridor, I take a few generous steps backward, making an excuse to make a phone call.

"The bar has been buzzing with policemen," she says, hoarse and phlegmy.

I cock my head in her direction.

"The young man who rented it—is he in trouble?" She trails off as if she's had a momentary lapse in memory.

"Worse," I say.

A hand flies to her small, cracked lips.

I wait for a response or answer, which feels like hours, but when she sticks out a reproachful, pencil-thin finger at me, it feels accusatory. "That young man," she says, adding, "I remember seeing him the night before last. He looked troubled."

"How do you mean?" I ask.

She scratches the top of her rack of thinning white hair. "The way he looked." She chooses her words carefully and thinks about what to say next. "He was filthy, as if he'd been in a scuffle." She brushes a fragile hand across her lined forehead. "He was bleeding. The top of his forehead."

I remember the jagged scar above his eye when I saw him in the morgue.

The woman continues: "I remember because I opened my apartment door to see what all the commotion was about. Poor young man."

Of course, you did—busybody.

"What was going on here?" I ask.

She fingers a faux string of pearls hiding her shriveled neckline. Cheap theater jewelry jangles around her skeletal wrist. "Look here, young man, are you with the police? Maybe I shouldn't be telling you any of this."

"We were friends, the victim and I." I pull out the photo of Eli and me and raise it close to her face, stepping closer for her to get a better look. The filmy gaze of her cataracts raises suspicions that she is certifiably blind.

Then she proves me wrong. "Handsome. Both of you."

I smile.

"There were loud voices," she adds, passing me back the picture, her hand trembling. "I heard people arguing. It woke me up."

"Did you see anybody?"

"The young man who was renting the room and two other gentlemen. I use that word loosely. They were scumbags, the visitors." Her body language and voice change. She is feisty and enthusiastic, angling to divulge all of the dark, dirty secrets surrounding Elijah's death.

"Did you hear what they were fighting about?" I ask.

"I heard one of the rent boy's visitors talking about going to the lake." She leans into me, whispering, looking up and down the hall for any eavesdroppers. "If you ask me, something fishy is going on."

"Did you see what the two guys looked like?" I ask.

We stay silent until she finally says, "One of the scary-looking guys was tall and had a beard, dark eyes, the devil's eyes. He was bad-tempered and used the F word a lot."

I listen to the music from downstairs, switching from early sixties Bob Dylan to an oldie by Fleetwood Mac.

"Do you know what time all this happened?" I ask.

She thinks, shaking her head, then nodding. "Wait a minute. Six, maybe seven. I don't know exactly. I was in bed early, watching TV—a crime show."

Sounds accurate. I recall Eli arrived at my place around eight o'clock, brooding, mysterious, and lugging a tote bag overflowing with a year full of bullshit and lies. His cagey behavior when I woke to voices in the living room awakens old wounds. Who was he talking to?

"The other man was shorter—so high." The woman uses her yard-stick-thin arms to estimate the height of one of Elijah's night visitors. "Red hair, short, buzzed. Cruel eyes." She shivers, wrapping her arms across her bony frame. "He stood face to face with your friend like a soldier. I thought he was going to kill Rent Boy right in front of me."

Calling Eli Rent Boy makes him sound irrelevant, like the lowest denominator. I thank her and turn to walk away. The woman without a name stops me midstride, roping me back into another shocking revelation. "He was scared. Agitated."

"Who?"

"Rent Boy."

I take a deep breath. "Why?"

"I heard them arguing about a business deal. Drugs, I guess." She pauses, then adds, "If someone threatened me like the mean men threatened him, I'd be scared for my life too."

"How did they threaten him?"

"One of the ugly guys socked him in the eye."

"They beat him up?"

"He looked like you. But a bigger shiner." A mischievous smile crept across her face. "They pushed him around. Bullied him," she says with enough contempt to keep me grounded.

Heat crawls along my neckline. "Have you seen the two men since it happened?"

"Nothing. Just the cops."

I thank her and turn to leave.

"Will you be at the pride concert at noon?" she asks.

"I've got to get back home," I answer. Then I think of Janssen, who invited me to her one-woman concert. I guess we'll both be disappointed.

The white-haired woman and I slip into an uncomfortable stillness.

She says, "I'm sorry about your friend. I wish I could be more helpful."

I nod. "You've been more than helpful." I hand her the restroom key Trent gave me and ask if she could return it for me.

I wait until she enters her apartment to take the emergency stairs and slip out the side door.

*

IT IS LIKE opening a channel to a different dimension. I sit in the driver's seat of my car, holding Eli's journal, the contents overflowing with letters and notes written in Eli's scraggy handwriting. I reel at the unexplainable mention of suicide, revenge, and murder packaged in Eli's suspicious, hate-fueled conspiracies. I am fuming, white-knuckling the brown leather journal.

Suicide? Eli would have never killed himself, not in a hundred years. My gut clenches as I read Eli's shocking, end-of-the-world scenarios to kill himself.

When we were together, Eli never talked about death or suicide.

I unwind rubber bands from around rolls of notes folded between pages of the journal. I read with disgust about marginalization and feeling "frightened" and "worthless."

Frightened? Of what? Fury simmers in the pit of my stomach. Reading the letters, I am stunned, unspooling another thick entry of thoughts, one of last week's journals, titled "Revenge."

The word is underlined in dark, thick lines three times to emphasize his anger. The handwriting is barely legible, a messy, hurried hand pressing hard across the white paper. An indentation of Eli's nearly illegible scribbles is visible on the backside of the paper when I turn it over and brush my fingers across the rough, bumpy grooves of the words, like reading braille for the first time.

"Men are scum," Eli writes. "These men. I want to kill them slowly. I want them to feel the pain that I feel. My eye feels swollen from them hitting me. I want this nightmare to end. I want my old life back. I am tired of running and hiding and lying."

My eyes sting and blur with tears as I continue reading. The mounting suspense of Eli's thoughts reads like a mystery novel. But the pain is real. On another page, Eli recounts his life as "a dangerous, violent nightmare that never ends."

I replay what Eli's neighbor—Miss Marple—said to me. According to her, Eli and two tall men were in a heated discussion about a business deal gone south; Eli verbally threatened during an exchange of angry words.

I recall Eli's physical appearance two nights ago when he arrived at my apartment. The bruises around his eye and his visually shaken state of mind make sense, according to the old woman's story.

Peeling my eyes off the daggers of Eli's words, I look out the driver's window, diverting my thoughts to anything other than Eli's death. But I can't. A shitstorm of questions rises, and my internal clock ticks fast and loud as the stakes grow higher and more dangerous by the second in finding Eli's killers.

An idea grabs me as I stuff the letters back into the journal. I remember the urgency in Eli's warning me: "I don't want to go back into the closet. The hate, the fear, and the violent words."

Hate, fear, and violent words. Eli directed me here, I believe—to his apartment, the journal, and the painful secrets of his past.

I curl up in a fetal position, pulling my knees to my chest. I exhale an excruciating breath.

Then my cell vibrates in my pocket and shakes me awake. A familiar name flashes across the screen. I clutch the phone in a bloodless grip and scream.

Lee Ashton, my so-called father.

Chapter Seventeen

I NEED HELP deciphering what Lee is saying. He sounds drunk, or maybe it is a bad connection.

I hear the words "your mother" and "hospital," but every other syllable and sentence sounds stilted. "Get here, son. As soon as you can."

Son. Like the tines of a rake scraping the length of my spine.

"What's happened?" I stare out onto the peaceful vista of the vast choppy lake, resembling Thomas Kinkade's painting in its delicate brushstrokes and soothing harmony.

Lee rambles on, and I want to hang up because the man and I were never close. Booze and an affair with an airline stewardess half a continent away set our family back three steps. After discovering his unforgivable, blasphemous secret, I don't know how Mom put up with him.

Hearing Lee's familiar drill sergeant voice after a year of not speaking to him regurgitates unpleasant recollections of the man I had called Dad.

I roll my eyes when he tells me, "It's urgent. Get here fast, Ralphie." My childhood nickname. "I don't know how long she's got to live."

I know my mother, Doris, has been in and out of the hospital with breast cancer. A double mastectomy last year proved successful in its early stage of detection. But things went downhill—fast—soon after: the cancer had metastasized to her lungs. She was in remission for months. Now, the dreaded c-word revisits like an incurable virus that won't die, making itself at home inside the vessel of my mother's frail body. A bag of bones, my mother doesn't look like the woman who raised me—painstaking decisions from the family landed Mom in the hospital for four months. Then six. Then eight. Now this, returning to assiduous memories of broken promises I won't be able to mend.

The devastating disease seems prevalent in a small paper mill town with its relentless daily emission of toxic pollution.

Call me selfish, stupid, or immature, but I refuse to see the vibrant, hardworking woman I once knew start to deteriorate and wither like a bed of soggy leaves in front of me. I want to remember her the way she was, not the way she is now, a soulless, desiccated corpse.

County Hospital. I close my eyes at the thought of returning to that house of horror. Back to the place where death welcomes you with open arms: a place where people go to die.

My father mutters and laments, and his voice cracks and sputters, not from a loss of words but from the raw emotions that are his responsibility now. Step up to the plate, Old Wise One, and take charge. Swing, don't miss. But I have no sympathy or confidence for a calculated man so full of hate and wrongdoing.

I lean my head onto the closed driver's window and close my eyes. I let the sun's warm rays heat the side of my face. My thoughts of Eli dim slowly like a fading sunset. Hearing about my mother's current condition triggers unhappy thoughts and a jumble of unconditional feelings, wants, and needs. The idea of seeing her lying in a hospital bed stirs unpleasant thoughts. Unlike Lee, the tenacious bully I can't yet acknowledge as Dad. I teem with rage at the memory of his bulbous features, abused and ruined by years of drinking and wrong choices.

Trying to get a word in over his complaints, I want to scream at him or hang up. Forget he called. I slam my fist against the steering wheel, frustrated and furious. Then I think *my mother needs me* as I fight the urge to drown out his petulant diatribe.

I want to say: "You should have thought about Mom and me when you cheated on her while flying the friendly skies." I stay calm and passive, although my curled-up fist tells a different story. I feel unwell and lightheaded.

"What time can you come?" he asks in my ear.

I answer, "Over an hour. I'm out of town."

When he questions my whereabouts, I tell him I'll be at County Hospital when I get there and hang up, slamming my cell phone against the glass window. "Fuck you, Lee!"

Calling him by his first name jumpstarts my heart and leaves a lingering bad taste in my mouth.

Chapter Eighteen

THE FERRY RIDE back to Grave Point is an accordion-slow slog, the lake choppy, whitecaps churning like science experiments gone haywire, waves beating the side of the boat, splashing over the railings, and misting the windshields of other vehicles in line.

My father's phone call unsettles me like an abscessed tooth. I drown out his manipulative paternal voice by turning the radio station to rock 'n' roll and dousing my unhappy memories with an LSD-acid trip.

A seagull swoops and glides in the pristine sky, and I wish I could be free-spirited and carefree too. The jerky waters below boil like a witch's cauldron.

The hull slices through a channel of broken ice as the endless white expanse of the lake rages in stomach-churning motions. Cars and trucks and a brave young man on a motorcycle swarm the small interior of the ferry's cabin. I am crammed between a pea-green Volkswagen Beetle and the leather-clad motorcycle biker I met on my way into Vermont.

My thoughts are broken by my trunk door bouncing up and down, open and closed, from the erratic shifts in the wind. I take the opportunity to close the trunk by tying it with a ten-inch bungee cord, hooking the end to a loop inside the truck.

A bitingly cold north wind cuts across my face as I tie the knot and dash back into the heated car, rubbing my hands in front of the hot air blowing out from the vents.

I stare out at the roiling lake and the motorcyclist before me.

Eli used to ride a motorcycle. I recall our trips through South Hero to South Burlington and Middlebury. I was—still am—petrified of riding without a seatbelt, my arms interlocked around his waist, always afraid I'd fall off. Eli never exceeded the speed limit or showed off, I remember. He was always in control.

As I stare out at the short, twentysomething young man in front of me, removing his white bike helmet and shaking his shoulder-length blond hair against a gust of wind blasting off the water, he reminds me a lot of my younger self. Adventurous. Innocent. Reckless. Immortal. His face is peppered with a scraggly, half-grown beard. A tattoo in the shape of barbed wire coils the length of his thick neck, and down the back of his flannel shirt. The wind tugs the corners of his white muscle T-shirt. His stare is curious as he observes other travelers and the vast open waters of Lake Champlain.

An atmospheric fog glides over the lake's surface. It is serene and beautiful, a pristine afternoon.

I turn down the music, leaving the singer whispering to a tune about love and loss and how he isn't getting back his lover.

Eli is a ghost from the past.

My thoughts turn to Eli. Like a memorable painting, I fight like hell to keep his image alive. I do not want to lose the image of us or our time together. A perfect smile was on his face as he waxed philosophical on living. "Live like there's no tomorrow." A lingering chill scuttles across my neck as if looking back on Eli's words. "You're here today, then gone forever."

What did he mean? Was he trying to tell me something? Recalling his journal entries, I wonder how long he's been struggling.

Lost in thought, I am unaware of the ferry pulling up to the docks fifteen minutes later. I open my eyes after drifting off, and the bumper-to-bumper vehicles ahead of me are moving at a meandering pace. Rear lights glare red on the now overcast day.

The motorcyclist adjusts his helmet over his windswept hair and donkey ears. I turn the ignition and watch him teetering on the bike, fighting to find a balance against the stiff wind slamming against him. Finding his footing, knocking the kickstand out of stationary position with the back of his boot, he revs the gears, inching forward slowly, waiting for a light-blue Camry and a pickup truck to drive off the ferry first.

He reminds me of Eli, cautious, methodical, and responsible from behind. I shift into drive and follow him, nodding at the paunchy college-aged guy working the ferry line and waving at me as I pull off the swaying stern of the boat.

The man on the motorcycle is gone when I reach the top of the hill.

I turn right and follow twenty miles of forest and lake homes to a campground and a gas station on my left. I stop at a light, wait for it to turn green, and continue driving along Route 3 to Grave Point.

I pick up a hot coffee and drive along roads slippery with rain. An hour later, I arrive at County Memorial and park in the visitors' lot. I drive in circles, debating whether I want to stay. My body stiffens and strains at the thought of seeing Lee again.

I sip my hot coffee and pull into a space twenty feet from the main entrance. I shut off the ignition and sit in stony silence, thinking about what I will say to Lee when I see him. Nausea stabs me at the thought of talking to the man who abandoned my mother and me on Christmas Day a few years ago.

I open the car door, slam it shut, and hunker against a chilly late afternoon as I meander toward the front doors to the hospital. My heart races; my palms glisten with sweat. Inside the foyer, past the automatic sliding doors, I pull out my cell phone and make a call.

Chapter Nineteen

MY STOMACH LURCHES at the sight of Lee, the man I called Dad.

He looks the same: punch-drunk, bald, bug-eyed behind thick bi-focals. He is pigeon-toed and strides toward me down the hall, using a cane to help guide him. He is out of breath and wheezy when we stand arm's length from each other. His face is as red as beets. Hypertension has not killed him yet.

I can't look him in the eye. Before he opens his mouth, I say, "No small talk. Where is she?"

"Shit, son, are you feeling all right? What the hell happened to your face?" He brings a hand to my face, but I jerk away, stepping back.

"Where's Mom?" I ask.

"Third floor. Room twelve. You should get that eye checked while you're here."

Disgusted, I shoulder past him in the direction of the elevators.

I stop by the flower and gift shop and shell out sixty-five dollars for a stuffed purple monkey and a vase filled with lilies, carnations, and a single sunflower.

The elevator doors open, and an electronic female voice from somewhere in the ceiling speakers reminds me that I am on the first floor. I get on with a young, cheerful female intern who boards the car next to me. I nod, she says hi, and the doors close between us.

When the doors open on the third floor, the smell of disinfectant and chicken masala permeates the air, and a pang of nausea assaults me. TVs blare on the highest volume as I pass rooms to get to my mother's. Patients break out in fits of coughing. I walk by the nurses' station and feel different sets of eyes on me as I hurry along, holding the vase of flowers and purple monkey tightly.

Room 12 is at the end of the hall, tucked around the corner, hidden from view. Illness invades me as I step closer to the open door. I can smell death: a decaying unpleasantness stings my nostrils. But it could be worse: at least my mother is still with us.

I walk into a shadowy, gray room. The drapes are drawn, the only illumination drifts from the flicker of a mounted flat screen. My mother is sitting up in bed watching a soap opera.

She smiles when she sees me standing at the side of her bed, holding the stuffed monkey and colorful bouquet of her favorite flowers.

"Ralph!" She claps her hands like a child. "Oh, son. Come over here." She reaches for the remote control to mute lovers in a quarrel. "Jesus! What happened to your face? Have you been in a fight? Did someone hit you?"

I must calm her, or she will change the subject and make it all about herself.

"It looks worse than it feels," I say.

"What happened?"

"I fell."

"On what?"

I reach for her hand.

"You should have a nurse look at it," she says.

"I'm fine, Mom. Don't worry."

"That's what mothers do. We worry. It's in the cloth of motherhood. I'm so happy to see you, though." She holds out her arms for a hug, her embrace as thin as spaghetti noodles.

I carefully set the vase and toy monkey by her purse on the nightstand and wrap my arms over her scarecrow frame. She is terrifyingly fragile.

"How've you been?" she asks.

I smell pain relief cream in the air, sharp and biting. My mother's hair is reasonably combed, and her face has a blush of makeup to liven up her appearance, eyes, and lips.

Her energy is heartening. She's always been the fighter of the family.

"Pull that chair over here and sit next to me," she says.

I don't believe what Lee told me on the phone. Mom may look sick, but she's got the energy of a firecracker.

I drag one of the hardback chairs from under the muted TV and pull it close to my mother's bedside.

"Where have you been? What have you been up to?" she asks.

"I work a lot."

"You look exhausted."

"I've heard."

"Are you feeling well?"

I nod. "Life is busy these days, Mom."

"You seem jumpy. Are you sure everything is all right?"

"I'm okay." I sit hunched over in the chair, the adrenaline of the past few days' events hammering me hard.

I notice my mother's IV cords running through her right hand, and her skin is colorless and veiny from age, dehydration, and chemotherapy. Even in her decline, her attitude is still spirited and hopeful.

"Have the doctors been in lately?" I ask.

"Every day. To say hi, mostly, and see how I'm feeling." As she turns to reach for the cup of water on her tray, her smile wanes, and panic and sadness fills her gauzy stare, the heartbreaking reality of awful things to come. I notice she does not want to hear the news. Nor do I, for that matter, both of us struggling with the approaching reality of death.

We're all on borrowed time. If lucky, my mother's time is close, maybe in the next few weeks or months. I don't want to see her grow any frailer or atrophy and lie in bed, weaken, and disintegrate. She will fight for her life because she is my mother. She is strong. I feel the strength in her hand, though brittle, and her battle with this incurable disease makes her a warrior mother in my eyes.

I know she knows that the end is near. Dying is like dreaming, I once heard somebody say. Maybe it was her. It could be the groggy patient speaking through the hazy dose of morphine. I heard friends tell me that their loved ones knew when it was time to die; they could feel it in their bodies. The way that the universe's energies ask us to take it slowly, accept death, and welcome it.

I manage a convincing smile when I glimpse my mother watching me. I can't help but struggle to sustain my expression as it turns into grief for both of us.

She looks different: bald, emaciated, and bony, the punishment of cancer. She tries to talk, and the words come out distorted as if she's drunk, dizzy, or sleepy. I tell her not to waste her energy. "Stay calm and relaxed." She is restless, blinking back tears. I pluck a tissue from the box on the nightstand behind her purse and hand it to her. My hand is shaking.

She sniffs and wants to cry but is obstinate and keeps an air of resilience. She doesn't like to upset me.

"Where do you work?" she asks, wiping the end of her red, raw nose.

"An auto repair shop."

She already knows what I do for a living. My eyes prick with tears at the downward-slope trajectory of her forgetfulness.

"Do you like it?"

"It pays the bills."

"That's not what I asked."

I shrug. "Yeah. I guess. Cars are my passion."

"Always have been." She smiles, revealing missing teeth on the top and bottom rows.

If you don't have health, you've got nothing—from my mother's lips.

I look at her now and wonder what happened: aging and time and death come to all of us, sooner or later.

"I'm sorry—" I begin.

My mother shakes her head, and a fat tear wells in the corner of her eyes. "Don't blame yourself, son."

"I should've been a bigger part of your life."

"You're here now."

"It's too late."

"It's never late."

"For me, it is." I want to cry, but I don't. I have to stay strong.

She falls into a deep silence and turns to the TV, staring vacantly at the actors' faces. "Don't talk like it's the end," she says.

"It sounds like denial, then," I say.

She clutches the edge of the bedsheets, simmering with hate and regret in her tight-fisted grip. It is written on her face as she bites down hard, and a muscle in her jaw jerks and crunches. She taps her wrinkled foot beneath the white blanket.

"Mom."

She nods, and tears spill like a broken water main. Her shoulders start to shake. I stand and place my hand on her arm. "I didn't mean to hurt you."

"I'm not mad at you, Ralph."

"Or discourage you," I add.

"I worry what will happen to you when I'm gone."

"Don't worry about me."

"I'm your mother. It's my job to worry."

"I'll be fine."

"No, you won't."

She's right. I lean in to hug her, comforting her as much as possible now while we're still together.

She smells unclean. Showers are rare these days. She is bedridden. I offer to sponge-bathe her. Wipe her down with lotion like I did when she got home. She refuses, adding, "That's the nurse's job."

The skin on her face is as tight as a drum, the outline of her skull is much more conspicuous; the skin around her eyes is vacuum-sealed, her Sinatra blues wide and bulging from the sockets, frightening to anyone who has never seen death staring back at them before. Her nose and mouth jut like an exclamation point, bony and prominent.

"Do you want me to open the curtains so you can see the sky?" I ask her.

"The light," she says. "It's too bright. It hurts my eyes."

"Do you want anything to read? Newspapers? A paperback novel?"

She shakes her head. "I can't see my hand in front of my face," she answers, and the thought dissipates as if time is stealing memories from her dementia-seized thoughts.

I sit back down. "Mom?"

She tilts her head to the side to look at me, but it is too much of an effort, and she winces, shifting back and staring up at the silent tele-vision.

My stomach lurches with anxiety. My left leg trembles and I have to lean back in the chair, cross it, and stop it from shaking.

She closes her eyes; the paper-mâché skin around her mouth hangs on her face like torn wallpaper.

Silence gives me time to think about Eli in his new home downstairs in the cold, dark, uninviting morgue.

I have to find out what happened to him. Who killed him? Who were the men who visited and beat him at his secret apartment in Vermont?

Footsteps out in the hall break my concentration. Two nurses race by my mother's room and down the hall to a patient screaming for help. I turn to my mother, who is unfazed by the sudden confusion; she is engrossed in a scene with two actresses. I watch my mom breathing, the small cavity of her beehive chest rising slowly, then sinking, barely moving.

I wonder if I have upset her. She isn't talking or making eye contact with me. It's as if she has collapsed into a cocoon of silence.

The chair squeaks under me as I stand and reach for her arm, touching the cold, paper-thin skin with my warm fingertips. She stirs. I lean over the bedrail and kiss the parchment patch of fleshy skin on her forehead.

"Are you leaving?" she asks, looking at my worried face.

I whisper, "No. I'm going to the cafeteria for a coffee. Would you like anything?"

"I can't eat. I'm nauseous."

"How about a cup of chamomile tea?"

She inhales briefly, and it looks like she is going into cardiac arrest, her chest heaving, her face folded in pain and agony.

"Mom?"

"I'm fine. Fine. The bed's uncomfortable. I've got bedsores on my ass because I can't move."

"Are the nurses turning you every hour?"

She mumbles and starts to pull herself up by the handrail.

"Can I help?" I ask. "What do you want me to do?"

"I want to sit up. My back is stiff and sore."

"Let me go get a nurse."

"Ask for Claire."

She falls back against a mound of pillows, her face overthrown with defeat. Her gnarled face etched into deep sadness. Losing her independence is tough to accept. It would be for anybody.

"I'll be right back," I say.

She grips my wrist. "Thanks, son. I love you."

I nod, turn, and race out of the room.

The nurses' station is empty, so I walk to the main desk near the elevators and restrooms. I talk to a middle-aged receptionist folding and stapling papers into a tall, thick pile on the counter. She adjusts her glasses, fingering them back on the bridge of her bent nose, and looks up at me, her thick French accent drifting out from between the gap in her teeth. "Can I help you?"

I see her staring at my black, bruised eye.

I look at her nametag: Brenda.

I tell Brenda about my mother's request for Nurse Claire. "Claire is with another patient, but I can page her immediately."

"Can you have her stop by my mother's room when she can?" I ask.

Brenda nods and goes back to her paperwork.

I thank her, head around the corner, and push open the door to the stairwell.

Chapter Twenty

I TAKE THE stairs, two at a time, down to the hospital cafeteria.

I am lightheaded when I reach the bottom. My blood sugar is low. I remember that I have to eat today.

Nothing looks appetizing. The egg salad includes onions, and my stomach drops at the sight of employees without hairnets.

At the registers, I pay for my large coffee with sugar and cream and a small chamomile tea for Mom.

I head to the vending machines and fold and unfold a five-dollar bill until it is straight enough to fit into the sensitive slot. I need a shot of something sweet, so I push the buttons for a candy bar and another button for a ham and cheese sandwich on a whole wheat bagel and find a quiet corner by the main doors to devour my lunch.

I notice my hands tremble again as I take a hearty bite of the dry sandwich. Doctors, nurses, and resident assistants travel in packs, chatting about weekend plans as they sit among their peers.

The room is buzzing with chit-chat and laughter and sounds like an overstimulated echo chamber. I wolf down the entire sandwich with a gulp of coffee and stand to leave. I set the tray on the conveyor belt and eat my chocolate bar on the way to the stairs, climbing to the third floor.

When I reach my mother's room, a nurse hovers at my mother's side. The tall Black woman does not introduce herself to me, but as I pass the bed, I read the name Claire on the white nametag pinned to the right side of her uniform. She adjusts my mother's IV lines, too preoccupied to mind me.

My father is nowhere in sight, I notice. Thank God. He is probably smoking a cigarette outside, making new friends with a female employee, buying her a drink over idle conversation, or already on his way home with her.

My boots squeak across the polished parquet tiles. The nurse turns and acknowledges me; her ear-to-ear smile is over-the-top but warm and encouraging. My mother seems to like her. She talks kindly to her and returns the smile.

I place the paper cup of tea on the tray beside my mother's bed, and she looks at it strangely as if she asked for something else. She stares up at the nurse, blank-faced and spooked.

There is something different about how my mother looks at me; it is as if I'm a stranger who has walked into the wrong room. Her expression is a slate of confusion: emotionless, an unblinking, ghostly gaze. The same thing happened the last time I was here. I sit by the window and watch my mother struggle to speak, glancing at me then over to Claire, who looks just as befuddled as my mother.

The gentleness in Claire's smile and behavior—a woman's generosity—and how she touches my mother's arm seems to bring order to my mother's escalating anxiety. Mom closes her eyes and falls back against the rearranged pillows behind her. The bedsheets are clean. My mother must have requested new linen, or she stained the sheets with an unexpected piss while I was out of the room.

The nurse moves slowly around the bed, tucking my mother's legs under the thin white sheet. But she stops, at the request of my mother, leaning forward, her face screwed in disdain and pain. My mother points to the bottom of the bed, and I notice that her fingernails must be cut. She cries out, and Claire asks, "What's the matter?"

My forehead furrows as I stand, shoving off the window seat too quickly. I sense a muscle in my back pull. I sit on the edge of the soft cushion and wait, watching Claire struggle to understand what my mother is trying to tell her. My mother is crying, screaming, and jamming a finger at the foot of the bed. "My foot, goddamn it!"

Claire hurries to the bottom of the hospital bed, unwrapping my mother's feet from the sheets, asking her what's wrong. "Where's the pain, Doris?"

"Charley horse," my mother says. "Left foot!"

Claire slowly and carefully reaches beneath my mother's left foot with her hand and massages in clockwork gestures. My mother's left foot jerks and spasms but soon falls limp back into a comfortable position in Claire's palm.

Claire is quiet but effective. I like her a lot. She is compassionate and patient with my mother, who needs a strong hand, someone to guide her.

I don't know if I am the right person to help her. I feel hopeless sitting on the chair watching, holding my coffee like an idiot, my mind foggy, and my heart banging so hard I am afraid I'll need to visit Dr. Matheson's office.

After Claire calms her, she returns my mother to a peaceful position in bed. My mother asked the nurse if she would mind rubbing lotion on her dry feet. Like I used to do. But I don't think my mother knows I am in the room.

I sit back and wonder what my role is here. My mother is in good, professional hands now. Am I making things worse by being here? Does she even know who I am? I'll have to leave again, I understand. I've got my life to live, a dilemma of my own: Eli's murder.

My mother sinks back into the hospital bed, dissolving into the sheets, shifting into the curves and folds of the mattress and pillows. Her mouth curves and twitches as she eyes me. She looks scared, her gaze weak. I get up and stand at her side. She reaches out for my hand. I take it in mine.

I thank Claire, and she gestures with a limp, "Yeah, I know." Her face tightens with a sleepless gaze from years of working with the ill. "We'll take care of her." A glimmer of hope in her eyes forms a lump in my throat.

She taps my hand with her red, stubby nails. "I've got to check on other patients."

I nod in affirmation, but when I turn to my mother, she looks up at me as if to say, "Don't leave me alone."

"I'll check on you in an hour, Doris," Claire says before leaving the room.

My mother forces a weak smile as if she's the only patient on the floor, but I know she doesn't want to be alone.

I whisper, "I'll be right back." She holds my hand with enough strength to give me hope that she still has some fight left in her. "I won't be gone long," I add.

Her hand slips from mine, and I turn and leave. I find Claire at the nurses' station talking with her colleagues.

I stand off to the side until she finishes. She sees me leaning against the wall and walks over to me.

"I'd like to talk to you about my mother," I say.

"Give me two shakes, and I'll meet you in the family lounge down the hall. I must do my rounds and check in with my other patients. I won't be long, sweetie."

I am still called sweetie in my thirties.

I pass my mother's room. She is either asleep or watching TV and doesn't notice me. I wait in the lounge around the corner and watch a hard steady rain hitting the window. I am alone in the near-dark room, just my thoughts and me.

Sitting in one of the unoccupied plastic chairs, I lean back, close my eyes and inhale deeply. My coffee is too cold to finish. I toss it in a nearby trash can and reach for a *Rolling Stone* magazine, but my mind is too preoccupied with other things to read or skim it.

Half an hour later, I hear footsteps approaching from down the hall and an elongated shadow falling across the floor. Nurse Claire joins me, pulling a chair out from beneath the card and puzzle table in the corner.

Rain beats the glass, and voices from patients and nurses stir and echo down the hall like ghostly whispers.

Claire asks me, "How are you doing, Mr. Ashton?"

She remembers my name in a sea of many faces.

I tell her, "Uptight," "nervous," and "not sure what I'm going to do."

"Is there anything I can do to make this transition easier? Do you want an ice pack for that nasty bruise?" She points at the Picasso work of art taking shape on my left eye.

I shake my head. "I'll be fine, thanks."

She looks honest, compassionate, and unbiased.

I speak freely and without a filter. "I don't know if I have enough time to say what I want to my mother."

"Then go talk to her." She is not sarcastic, judgmental, or pretentious. I've seen some nurses speak honestly with the patients' families: blunt and intense. Claire is a generous soul, an angel. I notice the tender look in her eyes.

"I'll never receive an award for the best son of the year," I say as if it matters.

"Sometimes it's hard to see a loved one in their final days."

I am startled when she estimates my mother's life: days, weeks, tomorrow, five hours from now.

"How long do you think she'll be around?" I ask.

She shrugs. "Cancer is unpredictable."

"Surely you've been around this kind of thing to know when the end is near."

"With cancer patients, it's difficult to pinpoint."

"But you said days."

"Your mother's cancer is advanced. She's in stage four."

"Will she die today?"

"No. Or tomorrow or the next day."

Neither of us speaks.

Thunder cracks like a whip, and it sounds like the end of the world outside, rain and wind battering the building.

Claire says, "Your mother isn't quite there yet. She's tough and won't take no for an answer. But eventually, we'll have to talk about palliative care."

"What's that?"

"It's a relief stage for patients with serious illness such as your mother's. The goal is to provide comfort and quality of life for the patient and their family."

"How will I know when my mother will need it?"

"You and your mother will be able to talk to the doctor about which course of action is best for your mother."

"Besides palliative care, what is the other option?"

"Hospice."

"What's the difference?"

"Palliative medicine relieves suffering and is used to help the patient improve their quality of life. Hospice focuses more on quality of life rather than cure, to live each day to the fullest."

I close my eyes.

Claire reaches across the table and touches my arm. "Maybe you can talk with your mother about which route to take. If you'd like, I can notify your mother's doctor about our talk today so you can sit down with him and discuss what you think is best for your mother as we move forward with her treatment."

"This is so sudden and confusing."

"That's why we have people on staff who can help answer your questions and help you through this difficult period."

I nod.

"Have you spoken to your father about how you should proceed?" she asks.

"We're not close."

She waits for me to continue.

"It's devastating," I say, standing and walking over to the window. I jam my hands in my pockets and stare at the hard rain hammering the tops of roofs and trees. "We're here today, gone tomorrow."

I glimpse Claire sitting at the table, staring back at me from the glass.

"I blame myself for not staying in touch with my mother better," I say. "My father has made life unbearable for both of us. He and I didn't get along and never saw eye to eye. There was always animosity between us." I rock back and forth on my heels. My chest is tight. My head hurts.

I hear shuffling behind me, a chair scraping across the floor. There's a presence at my back, and a hand grazes my shoulder. Claire says, "You shouldn't blame yourself. It's not your fault your mother's sick."

"Dying," I correct her. "She's beyond sick. She looks—" I can't finish the sentence because the following words scare me. I close my eyes and say a silent prayer.

I think of Eli, the end of his life, without me.

I turn to Claire, who waits for me in the lingering, cold darkness.

"What can I do for you?" she asks again, a firm smile tugging the corners of her mouth.

"Thank you for helping my mother," I say.

"You don't have to thank me. It's my job. I enjoy doing it."

I am quiet and hesitant to talk.

Then Claire says, "Talk to your mother, Mr. Ashton. Tell her how you feel. Tell her what you've always wanted to talk to her about."

I stare at the floor, at my mismatched socks: one white, one gray.

"You'll get through this," she says.

"I don't know what to say to her."

"Tell her you love her. Start there."

I see the sight of my pale mother lying in the hospital bed, and I start to cry. Claire pulls out a chair and asks me to sit down. I accept it and sit down as she shuffles to the other end of the room and stands in the shadowy corner of the doorway near the gender-neutral restrooms. She takes the tissue box from the table and hands it to me. I pull out two tissues and blow my nose hard. Grieving ignites like a needling ache from head to toe.

Claire asks, "What's wrong?"

I close my eyes. "Everything." Apprehension stirs like electricity in my veins.

"Can I get you a soda? Tea? Coffee?" she asks, and the thought of anything carbonated or acidic provokes an explosion in my stomach.

I shake my head.

"Are you afraid of talking to your mother?" she asks.

I taste bile in my throat. I wince and stand to get a bottle of water from the vending machine.

"Sit," she says. "I'll get you a bottle from the employees' office." She leaves and returns shortly later. "Can I get you anything else?"

I uncap the bottle and drink. "No, thanks."

"Take it one day at a time," she says. "That'll make things easier for you." Her pager vibrates on her waist. She pulls it off and stares down at the screen. "Duty calls. I've got to go." At the door, she turns and adds confidently," You may not see it now, but everything will be all right. It gets better. Trust me."

I am at a loss for words.

"Let me know if you need anything," she says. "I'll be here until ten." She smiles and sets off in a brisk run around the corner, her determined, fast footfalls fading out of earshot.

*

I CHECK IN on my mother, but she is sleeping. I take the stairs down to the second-floor chapel and meditation room. The chapel sits across from a bank of elevators and an out-of-order water fountain. As I enter the silent chapel, I notice I am alone. I sit in a hardback chair at the front of the shoebox-size room.

I take a deep breath and stare at the earth-tone wallpaper—a ten by twenty watercolor of blue skies, lush foliage, and a meditative forest of flowers and small birds.

Soft fluorescent lighting illumines tranquility in the room. Silence calms me, centers me, and helps me quiet my thoughts.

I am overcome with deep sadness. Remaining memories and sudden disappearances ransack my catalog of moods. I stand, but my legs are too heavy to move or walk. I barrel through the subsequent slow, tortuous seconds, removed from the current setting, my breath labored, pulse-quickening; it is difficult to think or see clearly, and I drown in uncertainty.

I fall into the chair as if a hand grips me from behind and holds me in place. A moment with my mother three weeks ago resurfaces like a far-off dream; before her transfer into the hospital, reality set in, and the landscape of our lives changed forever.

*

MY MOTHER LIVES in a dilapidated one-story house on the Saranac River.

It was fifteen miles between my house and hers. I pulled onto the narrow shoulder of the road and parked under a sagging birch tree because she was so close to the river that there was no available parking space.

I sat in my car for ten minutes, staring out onto a gloomy mist burning off the lake near where I grew up, a precursor of bad memories.

The past was a murky playground, challenging to avoid.

I yanked out my keys from the ignition and opened the driver's side door as a soft rain spit at me.

I stood by the side of the road, staring at my childhood home, waiting to enter.

Pains set up sharp in my stomach. I knew what I was walking into, past the broken slates of the derelict front gate and an unplowed postage-sized patch of lawn.

Lights burned orange and yellow in all four bottom-floor windows—chimney smoke clouded the gunmetal-grey sky.

I walked toward a Christmas wreath hanging on the faded blue front door, my mother's touch all year round.

The door was unlocked. I did not need to knock, as if my mother expected me.

As I gripped the cold glass doorknob and invited myself into the hearth and home of my mother's lonely existence, I yelled, "Hello," but silence answered me.

My mother loathed surprises, especially birthdays, since her big day fell on Christmas Eve. She didn't like uninvited guests, including friends and family, especially Lee. I'd hoped I would be the exception. But I wasn't aware of the framework of my mother's mood swings on days like these.

I wandered farther into the house, stepping into a bedraggled maze reflecting my mother's current state of mind, circumventing and dodging unopened boxes stacked ceiling-high on the back wall and in the middle of the unlit hallway that hadn't been dusted or vacuumed in some time.

I wondered if Mom had canceled the cleaner who I paid $150 a week to clean her house.

Again, I yelled my mother's name as I passed large windows overlooking the naked stalks of pine and maple trees and the lazy views of the Saranac River cutting through the backyard. My mood reflected the desolate landscape of winter visible through the dusty windowpanes.

As I approached the archway leading into the dining room and kitchen, I heard the faint sounds of my mother humming. Was she singing?

I'd never heard her sing. Not out loud or to me, even growing up.

"Mom?"

She stood at the counter, her back to me, staring out the kitchen window, stirring ingredients into a mixing bowl. One of Lionel Richie's old songs played on an outdated radio they didn't make anymore. I was right: she was singing along to her music.

"Mom?"

She lost her grip on a spatula, turned to me, and gasped.

"Sorry to surprise you," I said.

"Ralph?"

"It's me, Mom. How are you?"

"Jesus H. Christ. I've missed you. Where've you been?"

"Mom. We saw each other last week, but I'm good."

Good? I've been shitty since Mom got sick with cancer.

I could have been a better liar. If anybody could see through my fakery, it was Mom. "You look peaked," she said. "Are you feeling all right?"

"I'm fine. And I'm sorry for dropping in unannounced."

Tears swam in her aging eyes. "I've missed you, Ralph."

I was at a loss for words. But then I said, "I've missed you too."

She continued staring at me with startled eyes, almost spooked. She turned and pointed through the dirty glass into the backyard, bleak in winter for upstate New York standards. "I wish I could go for a walk," she said. "But this old body refuses."

"What are you baking?" I asked, changing the subject.

"Bread. Cookies."

"It smells heavenly."

"I've missed you, son."

"Maybe we should get together more often."

"I don't like company."

I reminded her, "But we're family."

"I hate your father," she said, animosity filling the high-pitched tone of her voice. It felt like she was sucking air out of the room.

"He's been gone for ten years, Mom."

The motions of her bowl-stirring quickened.

"I came to check on you," I said, still standing in the doorway, trying hard not to invade her space.

She sighed and stopped stirring. I knew she cared that I was there to check on her.

Communication was not the glue that bonded our relationship.

"Do you need anything?" I asked.

She seemed occupied, lifting her tired gaze to the milky-white light of the pale day. She stared at something along the riverbank, something or somebody passing in the undressed cover of trees.

When she didn't answer, I took another step into the room. I gripped the back of a chair and stood ten feet behind her at the table where we ate breakfast and dinner as a family for many years. Until everything went to shit, and cancer became a permanent fixture in our lives, separating and changing us.

"Can you grab the cinnamon shaker from the top shelf?" she said.

Anxiety engulfed me like a tidal wave. My sneakers squawked, walking across the sticky, unwashed kitchen tiles. My fingers became waxy as I reached for the metal handles on the top cupboard doors. I clamped my eyes shut at the rising fever of guilt and anger of my childhood. Days and weeks of dirty laundry piling up in the hall closet. The house smelled dirty and dead, an unpleasant return to reality, as if the entire building required refurbishment.

"Has Elenora been here?" I asked, referring to my mother's house cleaner.

"I don't care about small talk, Ralph. Can you pass me the cinnamon? Please?"

Please.

Sounds like an apology, not a command.

The hinges screeched open, and I stared into a hidey-hole of my mother's hidden hysteria—disordered shelves, canisters of spices, salts, and sugars arranged randomly.

Fear settled in the deep marrow of my bones as I stood glaring at her threadbare housecoat, hanging like a lifeless second skin on the wasted form of what used to be my mother, Doris Ashton.

She was a paper-thin image of a stranger. Even in remission, she looked different, alien, and unflinchingly scary. Not my mother.

I didn't realize she was standing behind me when I turned to inquire about the clusterfuck of her new life.

"Mom?"

She pointed a trembling hand at the opened cupboard behind me. "Top shelf. Right side. It's near the basil." She strolled around me and gripped the countertop with one hand, raising a frail, thin arm. The results of chemo were cruel. Her veins looked like thick blue worms under the skin.

I turned to help her, sighing. I clambered through a mix of herbs and spices until I found the cinnamon and handed it to her.

She grunted a weak "thanks" and shuffled across the room back to her baking bowl, a pride-and-joy pastime she relished. She was the happiest person cooking in her kitchen. Especially when she had the house to herself, when Dad abandoned us, left one morning for work, and never returned.

It was a blessing and a curse when he walked out of our lives.

I loathed that wretched man.

I stared at the back of my mother's head, a bowl-shaped bald dome wrapped and disguised beneath a red-white-and-blue bandana. She was humming softly; she didn't need the sound of the radio. She seemed as happy as she'd been before cancer transformed her life, stole her dignity, and spoiled her spirit.

I reached my hand out to touch her bony shoulder. But I left it hovering inches from her body. I was shaking, I noticed, too scared to accept the god-fearing reality that she'd be gone one day. As I retracted my hand and covered it into a ball with the other one, tears stung my eyes.

I strolled around to the other side of her, near the window, staring out onto the sluggish river, flowing like a tired snake past the bare bones of the house.

I watched my mother's hands move in circular confusion across the sugar-speckled faux-marble countertop. Dialing back anger at my mother's withered appearance, her hands crinkly like parchment paper, sadness clouded my thoughts. I felt tears on my face and the salty taste of failure.

"If you want to help, grab some dough and start kneading. No tears. Not in my house." A mushroom cloud of flour misted before us as she knuckled a palm-sized amount of dough against the counter.

I sneezed against a tickle in my nose and blew out some of the grainy residue from my mouth. My mother's short bark of a laugh surprised me.

I turned to her, a grave determination in her eyes. There was still a fight in her. She looked happy, strangely content in the most severe circumstances. "Knead, boy. Knead."

"How've you been?" I asked, knuckling my dough before stretching it out with a rolling pin.

"Is that why you're here? To check up on me?"

I stopped rolling and turned halfway to meet her ghostly gaze. "Like I always do, Mom."

She laughed, but it was more mocking than accommodating. "I've missed you," she repeated.

My face colored from the heat of embarrassment. Was it resentment? "I know."

She pressed hard on her small mound of dough, stood up as straight as possible with the strength she could tolerate, and said, a trace of hurt and concern in her voice, "You're acting like your father."

My fingers curled into my palms, and I squeezed. Hard. "I'm sorry?"

"You should be." She was winded, gasping like a broken radiator, as she turned and hobbled over to a chair at the kitchen table, wiping her floured hands on her apron.

I uncoiled the rigid posture of my palms and sat next to her, drawing my chair closer until our shoulders touched. "Has the nurse been in today?" I asked.

"Every day this fucking week." The audacity of her unrestrained response stunned me. "Damn it, Ralph. Where have you been? We always made a pact that we'd talk on the phone every night when you moved out of the house, no questions. No excuses." She jabbed a sharp finger at me. "You broke that promise, son," she added, her voice cracking, choking into deep sobs. She looked away to the grimy window. I glimpsed the sadness in her eyes.

I gently touched the bulky fabric of the housecoat covering her skeletal legs. "I'm sorry we haven't been in touch every day. I've been—"

"Busy," she answered. She waved a fragile hand, dismissing me. "Boyfriend problems?"

We hooked each other's stare. I caught a fleeting glimpse of joy in her tear-stained eyes.

I nodded. "It's been rocky."

"What's his name? Edgar? Eddie?"

"Eli."

"I didn't like him when I met him the first time," Doris said. "He reminded me of your father. Distant. Vain. Preoccupied."

"We're trying to work things out," I said. "But I didn't come here to talk about Eli."

My dad's hideous face flashed across my thoughts, his insufferable presence.

"I'm right here." I brushed her hand with mine, a gentle reminder of how fragile and fleeting life was.

We sat in comfortable silence for the rest of the afternoon, soaking up the last daylight hours.

*

I STARTLE AWAKE as if dreaming. A door in the rear of the hospital chapel room yawns, and I turn. I am still sitting in the hardback chair, hearing a murmuring of ghostly voices echoing in the corridor outside. I turn halfway and am revisited by a childhood nightmare. My face warms and pricks at the unsettling image of the devil himself standing in the doorway.

The outline of Lee Ashton fills the big oak doorframe, watching me.

Chapter Twenty-One

"I THOUGHT I'D find you here," he says.

I stand to leave, but he blocks my path to the door. He's holding his cane in his left hand, waving it as if saluting or motioning me to stop.

I ought to kick him in his bad leg and run. But for some reason, I freeze as if I'm six years old again and being reprimanded by a father I never had.

"Where are you going in such a hurry?" he asks.

"To see Mom."

"She's sleeping. I was just in her room."

"I'd rather be anywhere but here right now."

"You've been in the chapel—"

I look up at him, my heart banging, my temper simmering on the cusp of frenzy. My face is a hard stare, and the heat returns to my cheeks—a muscle beneath my right eye quivers. I turn my knuckles into fists inside my pockets. The room is reeling. I feel unsteady.

"You! I don't want to be in the same room with you," I yell, shuddering, my voice bouncing off the walls. I want to hit him with his cane and break him open like a piñata.

I hear people whispering and shuffling out in the corridor.

"You need to control your temper right now," Lee rasps, hobbling toward me.

I stand in place. "Or what? You'll hit me?" I breathe, trying to control my nerves, and meet his dogged stare. "You'll never change, Lee. It's like it was growing up in that horrible house with you."

"What are you talking about?" He is edgy and restless, nervously tapping his cane on the floor and shifting from side to side.

"I don't need to tell you how terrible you were to Mom and me. Always yelling and controlling us like we were your puppets."

"You're not making any sense."

"You don't remember hitting me in the face and pushing me downstairs when you came home drunk, looking for a fight at two o'clock in the morning?"

"That's the past, son."

I seethe at him calling me son. I clench and unclench the tightness in my jaw. "You were never a father. You left us on Christmas Eve. You walked out, and we never saw you again until Mom's diagnosis last year."

"Marriages don't always work out, son."

"Bullshit. You never made it work. You had that little side show with a blonde flight attendant everybody in the family knew about. And don't call me your son. You're not my father. You gave up being a father, husband, and provider when you left us. A father provides emotionally, spiritually, physically, and financially to his family. You're a poor excuse for a human being."

His laugh is nervy. He is agitated, shaking, fidgeting, looking around the room. I've awakened a dormant animal. Lee looks unnerved, gripping his cane like he might hit me.

"I don't find any of this amusing." I fold my arms across my chest, hiding my trembling hands, suppressing the urge to strike him. I want to hit something; I am livid.

"You've always been a melodramatic child," he says. "I can see why you majored in theater. It fits your type to a tee."

"My type? What's that supposed to mean?"

He grins, and the crimp in his cruel smile riles me. "You know—" He waggles his limp wrist in my face.

In a flare of panic, I grab his open collar and yank him forward, my right hand fisted in a ball of retaliation, grasping and wrinkling the fabric of his shirt.

"Who's angry now?" he mocks. "Get it out. Hit me, Ralphie. Come on. Do it."

My mind fills with horrible images of Lee mocking me as a child, taunting me to hit him back during one of our many verbal contests. My mouth is dry, pasty, and in need of water as I glare at him with enough hate to kill an entire country.

"The difference between us is that I've never hit you in public," he says, hissing the words, inflaming the fire. "Give it a try," he urges me. "Hit me. It'll make you feel better."

Mom's face turns on in my mind like a light switch. She is smiling, her face ivory-white and comforting. But soon, she is gone too, fading out of view.

I shove Lee back a few inches, and he loses the grip on his cane and wobbles on his arthritic bowed legs. He falls off to the side into a chair, reaching for the wooden arm to keep him in place.

"You're a piece of shit," I yell in his crumpled, embarrassed face. The surging anger swims inside my veins like hot lava. I can't bear to look at Lee, so I turn and head down the aisle to the rear doors.

I hear him rearranging himself in the thickening shadows, straightening his rumpled shirt collar and coat, and sighing. "I thought we could talk about some things, Ralphie," he says.

I grip the doorknob and stop. I feel lightheaded and queasy from the sight and sounds of Lee shifting behind me, wheezing and coughing up chunks of phlegm into his checkered handkerchief.

I turn around. "You never knew how to talk to me or Mom," I say.

"I'm here now."

"It's too late."

He looks from across the room. "Don't preach to me how late it is, Ralphie!"

I rush toward him at the speed of a hungry gazelle. "You've been nothing but a cancer to all of us." I lean over him in the chair, reversing the roles of father and son. I am immediately shaken at my own choice of words.

Cancer.

"Do you want to talk about how much time we've all lost?" Lee hisses, white-knuckling his cane at his side. He struggles to stand, and I don't help him. I step back to give him space as he wobbles in front of me, pointing the end of his trusty wooden cane in my face. "Where the fuck have you been?" he asks. "Your mother needed you these last two months."

"I've been there. I've called. I've visited. You haven't. You just recently came into the picture when you learned Mom was sick. She called you."

"She called me because you weren't there."

I shake my head. "Always making excuses and blaming others for your guilt. You were the deadbeat, not me. I love Mom. Your definition of love is cheating on her with a fucking stranger. Somebody you met on a plane after you walked out of our lives. So, don't preach to me about where I was when Mom got sick. I've been in her life more than you ever were."

We both slip into a staticky silence, breathing hard.

In the soundless seconds that tick by, I see Eli in my mind and am quiet because I know Lee wouldn't understand what I am going through. "You mock me and call me a faggot for most of my childhood, and you want me to explain where I've been?"

I take an inch forward in front of Lee, nose to nose. I can smell his cheap cigarettes and Johnnie Walker breath. I want to knock the smug judgmental smile from his pock-marked face. "You've put Mom and me through enough hell. You've got no right to question my life or behaviors."

"If not for me, then do it for your mother," Lee says, shifting the stormy sails of the conversation.

"That's why I'm here. That's why I've always been here."

"Remember this, son. When your mother dies, you will have no one. You'll be orphaned and alone." He pushes past me and barrels through the door, leaving me to ponder and brood about a motherless future.

Chapter Twenty-Two

IN MY MOTHER'S room, all is quiet except for the EKG machine in the corner, expelling soft, frustrating beeps, more like burps. I sit in a hard-backed, uncomfortable chair by her bed, watching her sleep, wondering if she's dreaming, her chest rising and deflating like a water balloon in slow but steadily failing repetitions.

After returning from my quarrel with Lee in the downstairs chapel, I am frazzled, my frayed nerves thrumming among an unnerving tic of jerky spasms in my hands and arms. My fingers rise and fall at the same tempo as my mother's erratic breathing.

As I leave the room to grab a soda from the vending machine in the family lounge, I turn to glimpse my mother, earmarking her face to memory as though it will be the last time I see her, gone before I return. I shudder at the fragile leftovers of her frame, hidden beneath the sheets, her bony right foot jerking sideways, tapping to an imaginary tune. I notice she is wearing the rainbow wool socks I gifted her last year on her birthday to keep her feet warm. Her shoulders and head shake as if she is dreaming, and she mumbles a ghostly whisper of words I can't understand.

Her sunken eyes move back and forth behind a skeletal layer of skin. I'm anxious watching her, and I might have to call the nurse in the next few seconds. But soon, my mother settles into a calming pose of serenity. The twitching movement in her left foot stops—a drowning gurgle in the back of her throat startles and shocks. I expel an unearthly gasp.

I look left and right along the hallway, about to yell for a nurse. They're all busy with other patients. Then, after a brief moment, all is crypt-quiet. My mother resumes breathing normally, her chest pumping up and down like a tire inflator. I take this moment to venture to the lounge for a soda.

When I return to the room, I sit in the stiff chair by the window, dividing my gaze between my mother and Eli's journal, which I remove from my knapsack. Using the dull overhead lighting, I turn to another passage in the book and start reading:

There was a time when I thought my life would end, not by choice but by a natural death. I never told you about my heart murmur. By the end of our one-year relationship, when things started to get rocky, I had developed an abnormal murmur. I never liked visiting the doctor for anything, as you know, especially a yearly checkup. I had no choice. I learned something was wrong. I woke up in the early morning hours with palpitations, shortness of breath, and gasping as if I'd dreamed horrible things. I thought I was having a heart attack.

I hid my anxieties from you because I didn't want to worry you. I never said anything, faced every day with hostility and fear because I didn't want to rope you into my craziness. I thought it was just anxiety. I've always had too many things to consider, issues that kept me awake most nights. There is nothing we could change, especially you.

Apologizing now seems trivial. Telling you in a journal instead of face-to-face detours from my style of dealing with these difficulties. But writing it down takes away some of the pressure. Believe me, Ralph, I didn't mean you any harm by withdrawing from us or being difficult during our relationship. I know I put you through a lot of shit, and we both know how much of an asshole I was, even on my good days. But I loved you. I still do. I'd have driven you to the moon and back if you wanted, but the horrors of my life distracted me from enjoying the small pleasures with the man I admired.

There are some secrets couples hide from each other. Not everything I did in our relationship was honest. That's not to say I didn't love, care, or want the best for you. I had problems, too many to mention.

I didn't want to rehash an old time between us. But I think if

I'm going to do it, now is the right time. It happened at the beginning of our relationship when you asked me if I was cheating on you. I was calm when you asked me why I came home late some nights. I told you I was working but knew you didn't believe me. I could see it on your face. You looked at me with those wide, little-boy eyes, an expression of pure resentment. You believed me nonetheless because you trusted and loved me and knew I wouldn't hurt you. I didn't want to have to lie, not then and not now—

I stop reading and close the journal in my lap, upset. Hostility sparks inside me like a grease fire. A nurse walks by the room, sees me crying, and pokes her head in. "Are you all right, Mr. Ashton?" She is older than Claire, with white hair and big hoop Dolly Parton earrings. She reminds me of my eighty-eight-year-old aunt, who is still kicking, dancing, and living life to the fullest. The nurse is Canadian, and I like it when she talks because I find her language lyrical and almost poetic.

I nod to hide the hurt I feel. I manage my emotions so I don't cry and wake and disturb Mom. The tall nurse strolls into the room and stands beside me. She looks to my mother, then to me. As she leans down, I get a whiff of her flowery body lotion: coconut and hibiscus. She whispers, "Can I do anything for you, sweetie?"

I shake my head, gripping Eli's journal.

"Don't hesitate if there's anything I can do for you." A light pat on the shoulder from her manicured hand feels reassuring.

She walks to my mother's bedside and checks her heart monitor to make sure everything is working. I mention the ghostly gasps from earlier. She tells me, "It's scary but normal. We'll keep an eye on her." I watch the nurse cover my mother's foot with the thin bedsheet, and as she turns to leave, she brushes a placating hand over my knee and smiles, assuring me that everything will be okay. Even though I know it won't.

She strides down the hall. I look over at my mother, dreaming, twitching, and moaning in her sleep.

Fighting to continue reading Eli's journal, I take a deep breath and turn to the drawn curtains behind me; the hypnotic sound of rain needles the window.

As I return to the room, my mother snores, drawing me out of my hopelessness. I wince at the airy, high-registered flute sounds she makes with each breath.

Finding the courage to return to the journal, I skim through the first few pages of the current entry. I want to know what happened to Eli the night he lied to me and left on bad terms. Is it the reason he was killed, I wonder? My imagination piqued, I turn my attention to the creased, coffee-stained pages before me, back to the mysterious life I led with a man I thought I knew.

> *What I knew then, I still wouldn't have told you if we were still together. The pain is too much to bear even as I write this. Either way, I feel better knowing that you didn't understand why I walked away. I didn't want you to get involved in my life—and those shady transactions.*

The mention of Eli's "shady transactions" in his mysterious past heightens my suspicions. I close the book with a thud. I admit there is nothing more I can do with the information, turning to my mother, snoring beside me.

I'm no good to her right now. I stand to stretch my legs and limp to the window. I slide the button to open the blinds and stare into an overcast afternoon. A mixed bag of sleet and rain hammers the asphalt between the brick buildings, and the world looks dismal and comatose. Leafless trees are asleep and naked in the long, harsh winter—snow piles in clumps in the side street leading to the ER entrance.

My mother's heart monitor is beeping, and I hear her snuffling and coughing. I turn around, but she is still asleep, dreaming and mumbling.

I check with Nurse Claire, sitting in front of a computer monitor at the nurses' station. She looks up at me with an exhausted gaze I know is all too real. I ask if I could sleep in my mother's room. "I want to be here if anything happens."

"Of course," she says, nodding, standing, and walking around the corner to my side. We stand side by side in the hall, out of earshot of other patients and hospital staff. "I think she'd like that," Claire says, a small smile stretching across her tired face. "Let me grab you a warm blanket and a cot."

"I appreciate it." Before she turns to fetch my bed for the night, I add, "There's one more thing."

She waits, staring at me blankly.

"Lee, my father," I say.

She hears the unhappiness and pain in my voice when I call Lee my father but urges me to continue my train of thought.

"I don't want him to know I'm here," I say. "We don't get along—" I wave my hand, dismissing him. "It's a long story, but I wouldn't feel comfortable with him knowing that I am sleeping here."

"I understand. But I don't think you'll have to worry. Today was the first time I'd seen Lee in a few days. He comes and goes."

Like alcohol, it's a bad habit—an ugly nightmare.

Panic and anger curl inside me at the thought of Lee at my mom's bedside. His narcissism riles me, and I want to punch him.

Claire sees my expression switch from gratitude to disgust in my balled-up fists coiled at my side and asks me if there is anything she can do to help.

"I'll be fine," I say. "But thanks."

"You shouldn't have to deal with these issues by yourself. It's exhausting and unhealthy, and eventually you'll have to talk to somebody," she says. "You can't go through life in pain."

I want to tell her that I am alone and everybody I love is gone or dying. "There's nobody to talk to," I say. "Not now. It's too late."

I think of Dr. Matheson. But what good can he do at this late stage of regression?

A light outside a room is blinking. It must be one of Claire's patients because she excuses herself and heads in its direction down the hall. "I'll bring that cot and blanket to your mother's room shortly."

I thank her and start heading in the other direction to the cafeteria to quell my hunger pains.

I order a chicken salad on whole wheat bread, fill a twelve-ounce paper cup with black coffee, and find a seat at the back of the room. Someone left a crumpled copy of the *Saranac Review* on the table. I thumb through it, but nothing important grabs my interest.

I read comics and my horoscope. I am a Cancer, and the horoscope tells me I am patient and a deeply sentimental, intuitive, and emotional person. *Let your mind wander*, it reads. *You have a few bumps in the road, but don't let them deter you from being the seeker that you are. Be a strong leader.*

The chicken salad sandwich is tasteless, so I only eat half of it, picking out moist chunks of meat and leaving the dry, brittle pieces on the edge of the plate.

As I leave the empty cafeteria, I toss the remains of my dinner into a nearby receptacle and head to the stairwell with my coffee. I walk down a long, empty hallway to the exit at the far end and exit through a side door for fresh air. I stand under a metal awning and listen to the urgent rain pelting me from the heavens. Vehicles speed along the interstate a few yards from the hospital grounds. A woman in high heels dashes in the dark to the edge of the sidewalk, a gust of wind tearing her umbrella from her hands as she slips into an idling Uber.

I wrap my fingers around the hot coffee cup to keep them warm. The wind brushes my face, and it feels like an intimate moment, a kiss on the mouth or a whisper in the air. Eli is talking to me, trying to contact me in his absence, and my face flushes with heat for intimacy, somebody to indulge my darkest thoughts. I miss Eli's closeness and intuitiveness, the way he touched me, comforted me, and made me feel needed.

Craving Eli's presence is lost on the thunder cracking through the night. I turn and go back inside, taking the long way back to my mother's room. I meander through the hospital's corridors as if searching for answers.

And hope.

Chapter Twenty-Three

MY MOTHER IS watching TV when I find myself in her room twenty minutes later. She is excited to see me, oddly ebullient with a feeble wave as I pass her bed, the volatile gestures of a small child. "Is it morning?" she asks.

"It's evening," I answer. "I went to the cafeteria to grab something to eat." I notice her dinner, chicken marinara with penne pasta in a basil sauce, congealing on her tray, untouched. I hover over her as if I am about to scold her for having a modest appetite. "Not hungry?"

She brushes her hand across her flat stomach. "The chemo made me nauseous today."

I forgot about her round of chemotherapy earlier this afternoon, hence her lack of eating. Depression weighs heavily in her cataract-dulled stare.

Pulling up a chair at her request, I hand her a medium-sized cup of tea I picked up from the cafeteria after my unplanned visit to the morgue.

"Thanks, dear, but I'm not interested in anything right now. My tastebuds are dead."

"I'll leave it here. I can always reheat it or get you a fresh cup."

She pats my arm. I smile at her craggy old face. Deep lines burrow around her forehead like a spider's web, etched with memories, sickness, and loss of time.

"What's wrong?" she asks.

"A lot on my mind. Nothing for you to worry about, though." I check the clock on the wall: 6:35. Darkness comes early and dreary these days, and I can still hear the constant rain pecking on the plate-glass window.

"How long have you been at the hospital?" she asks, licking her dry lips, eyes struggling to stay open.

I open the side drawer on the tray and rummage among toiletries, two different-sized hair combs, and a half-eaten bag of gummy Jolly Ranchers, looking for her beeswax lip balm. Standing over her emaciated body, I apply a generous amount of the raspberry-flavored gloss to her parched lips with my finger.

"That's nice," she muses, closing her eyes as if it is another day at the spa. "Just don't make me look like a clown." She smiles, but it is brief, a fast-moving light in the dark.

"I'm glad you haven't lost your sense of humor, Mom."

A murmur of soft voices from the TV emits through the intercom on the remote control. Static buzzes on the line.

She opens her eyes, and the playful earnestness in her compulsive, watery stare is charming but spooky, an apparition of my mother's younger self. She tells me she wants to sit up, genuflecting in her bow-hunched way. "My back hurts."

I help her with the control buttons and watch as the head and foot of the electric bed mold her into a snug, more practical posture. Letting out a long, dramatic exhale, she thanks me, aiming the remote control at the TV to shut it off. "I'd rather listen to you and the rain and the thunder than this hogwash."

Her spirits keep me hopeful of a better tomorrow, but she is wheezy and breathing hard, and I fear it might be a sign of a failing heart.

"What did you do today?" she asks, wincing as if in pain and swallowing hard.

"Do you want a drink, Mom?"

She nods and holds out a quivering hand. "I'll try the tea. What kind is it?"

"Chamomile."

I hold the cup to her mouth, and she sets her hand over mine. Her grasp is winter cold.

"Are you warm enough?" I ask, taking the cup from her and placing it back on the tray.

"Yeah. Fine. Why?"

"Your hand is cold."

"I've lost my circulation being in this fucking bed." It comes out harsh as her voice cracks. I am startled to hear my mother swearing because it is unlike her to use vulgar language. Always the proper one, she takes me off guard with her sudden brashness.

I want to protect her from her fears of death and disease and all the pain and hurt Lee inflicted over the years. "Do you want me to get you a blanket?"

"No. I need to pee."

"I'll get the nurse."

"The bedpan is on the chair," she says, gesturing to the nightstand. She presses the nurse's button before I get up, and yells into the intercom: "I need to pee. Can somebody please get in here before I soil the sheets?"

Panic sets in, and I get my first glimpse at my mother's worries and agitations, lying immobile as if trapped.

"I'll send somebody right in," a young female voice responds, and her tone is surprisingly calm for being yelled at. But it must come naturally to her in this environment.

A few minutes later, a young female college-age resident assistant named Ellen saunters into the room and walks by me to my mother's side. We share a glance as she busies herself with her evening duties. She tells me that they're understaffed, and she looks annoyed when she says it, her face pinched and unhappy.

I tell her it is okay and step out into the hallway to give my mother privacy. I close the door halfway behind me. Through the half-inch gap, I hear my mother crying and screaming from being touched and moved.

Her scared little girl voice coils inside me like dread, helplessness, and alarm. "I'm in fucking pain, you idiot! I hurt all over. I need something for it."

It is terrifying to listen to my mother in such agony, so I walk away and wander up and down the hallway, hearing and seeing other cancer patients in the same or sometimes worse conditions than my mother. Family members loiter outside their loved one's doorways, crying, talking on their iPhones, or sitting in the family lounge chatting amongst themselves. Others are hunched over in chairs in hospital rooms or staring fixedly up at the mindless TV screen, escaping the nightmare that has become their life. Perhaps a parallel of their future?

My mother's door is still closed when I return from walking a lap around the antiseptic-smelling corridors. I hear her and the nurse still talking or fighting, so I turn and head to the family lounge. I fall back into a chair by a window and feel the year's stress and anxieties draining from me. Shifting and sighing, I close my eyes and think of anything but hospitals and death and the bleak future that lies ahead.

Then, the inevitable questions arise when I am alone: What is the correct medical route for Mom? How does somebody live without a mother? Why is this happening to me?

I stand and pace around the quiet, empty room. I walk over to the window and stare at the dreary bleakness of late evening.

My mother's face flashes in the murky passages of my mind. Anger boils in me, like someone is holding a gun to my head, waiting for me to answer the list of questions about her dying. But I do not have a quick response.

I turn and stagger to the door, then head back to my mother's room, the long day unspooling like a tattered piece of thread.

When I return to my mother, the room is still; no yelling, moving, or talking, just the heart monitor beeping steadily in the corner. As I approach the bed, I don't know if she is asleep or just nodding off. Her eyes are closed, and I walk softly to my seat by the window. The chair's vinyl upholstery squeaks under me as I sit, stirring my mother awake. Her eyes open, and she asks, "Is that you, Ralph?"

"Yes. Do you need anything?"

She shakes her head. "Just glad you're here. Sorry for my bad attitude earlier."

"You're allowed," I say, smiling.

"It goes with the territory, I guess." She is weak, her voice slurred, sounding as if she's been pumped with morphine.

"Do you want to get some sleep?" I ask.

"Naw. I'll have plenty of time to sleep."

A quill of electricity stabs me at the sound of her voice. She knows what is coming. It must be frightening to see that you're going to die.

Then, something in her mood shifts, like a curtain blowing over her eyes. She is uncharacteristically cheerful, and I am concerned when she laughs. It is out of character and confusing. "I didn't want to wet the bed," she says. "I would've been embarrassed."

It becomes a rambling and messy conversation, and I fear she is experiencing signs of a stroke.

"Mom, are you feeling all right?"

She laughs. "Define all right."

I get up. "I'll be right back," I say, and head to the nurses' station. Nurse Claire is not in front of her computer, but Ellen is talking to another girl with a long dark ponytail and glasses. Ellen sees me standing in the hallway and holds up a hand to let me know that she'll be with me shortly.

I ask her if she can check on my mother when she comes over. "She's acting strangely. Her mood has changed, and she's mumbling incoherently. I can't understand her."

"She told me she was feeling anxious and that she had pain in her legs. It's a normal reaction in cancer patients. I gave her some codeine to alleviate some of the symptoms. She might be drowsy."

"I thought she was having a stroke."

"She's fine. She'll probably be asleep in the next half hour."

I tell Ellen I'm sleeping in my mother's room tonight and ask her about my cot and blankets. She says, "I'll page her nurse."

Chapter Twenty-Four

SOMETIME IN THE night, I am startled awake by my mother coughing, a phlegmy gasp. I throw the sheets off me, jump out of bed, and run to her side.

My presence surprises her, and she shakes awake, startled, her hands flying in the air, almost smacking me in the face.

I step back a few inches to dodge her violent thrashing—it is a means of defense; for me, she doesn't have an unkind bone in her body. "Mom, it's Ralph. Sorry. I felt scared. Do you want me to call the nurse?"

"Ralph." She closes her heavy eyes and sighs. "You scared me, son. No, no. I'm fine. It's just another coughing fit."

Her abrupt response jars me. I lean over the bed's railing and kiss her creased forehead, skin so spongy it feels like paste against my lips. "I'm sorry if I startled you."

"What are you still doing here?"

"I'm staying the night. Like old times."

She looks down at the rumpled sheets and blanket on the cot. She starts to cry. "A sleepover?"

A sad/happy smile uncurls the corners of my mouth.

"Like when you came over to stay with me at the house?"

I nod, knowing she can't see me in the dark, behind a veil of cloudy eyes. "Why are you crying?" I ask, wiping her tears with a gentle finger.

"I need something to drink," she says, diverting my question, being a brave mother.

Don't worry about me, she used to say. *A child should never have to take care of his parent.*

I hand her a paper cup of tepid tap water and help her sit up as she sips generously, emptying a third of the drink.

"I feel nauseous," she says. "And there's some pain in my stomach. I think the medication is wearing off. Can you ask the nurse if she can give me another pill?"

"Claire left for the night."

"What? Well, then, who's my nurse?"

"Diane."

She exhales and leans back into pillows that somehow make her look more substantial.

"Claire told me Diane is a great nurse," I tell her.

"Diane is the worst. She's condescending like your father. I don't like her."

"Let me go see if Diane is available."

"Find somebody else."

"Mom, if Diane's your nurse, I must ask her for help."

"There must be other nurses working the floor."

"There are. But they're not assigned to you."

Please, Ralph, dear. I dread Diane. She's a buffoon, the Dragon Lady, Frankenstein's wife."

"That's not nice," I say, patronizing and reprimanding my mother.

"When have I ever been nice?" she asks, a smirk on her nonexistent lips.

"All my life, as I recall."

"Goddamn it." There is humor in her impetuousness.

"Are you sure you're not mistaking Diane's rudeness for your anxiety?"

"Anxiety?" My mother hisses at the woman's credentials. "The only thing that concerns me about that rat-looking ferret is her clownish makeup and unpleasant bedside manners."

"What are you talking about?"

"Wait until you see her. She'll remind you of Ronald McDonald, Nurse Ratched, and Cruella De Vil, a crazy coot with a hot temper."

"Mom."

"Sorry. I meant Bozo the Clown."

Bewildered, somewhat amused, I stare at my mother in the bad silvery lighting above the bed. Her change of personality is bizarre. "What happened to my mother?" I bend over her, inhaling the fragrant raspberry lip balm I applied to her mouth earlier that evening. "Are you in there?"

Mom waves a dismissive hand at me, annoyed. I notice her bony foot poking out from beneath the blanket, tapping against the railing. She does not like confrontation after years of living with Lee. But, after a few minutes, she eases into a relaxing silence. Then, an onslaught of gunfire jokes continues. "Wait until you see the five-hundred-pound Godzilla," she says. "You thought King Kong had problems…"

"Mom."

"I'm not joking." She rises as if she's going to levitate and amplify her showmanship. "Nurse Diane is a scary woman, and she wears too much makeup."

"Someone's feeling opinionated."

"Belittling others makes me feel better."

"You've never been this way."

"I've never had a terrible disease either."

The room reels.

I reach for my mother's veiny hand. "We'll get through this together. I promise."

"Promises are for pussies," she says, looking at me for a reaction. When she doesn't get one, she adds, "Where's your father?"

"I don't know." I don't want to know, I tell myself. Nor do I care. Seeing him earlier was enough.

She turns her head to the white naked wall, and I hear her whisper, faintly but clear as day, "Like Nurse Diane, he's an asshole too." I grip her hand. She pumps it in response, turning to me, her eyes gleaming with tears. "I don't want to cry over spilled milk anymore."

"Some things are not worth crying for, especially him," I say.

She grins.

"Now, how about that pain pill?" I ask.

She winks. "Only if it comes from Nurse Claire."

Chapter Twenty-Five

MY MOTHER IS not joking about Nurse Diane. Diane is as large as she is tall, and her lavish application of makeup is colorful, eccentric, and hard on the eyes. But her polite personality makes up for all that off-Broadway brashness.

As she and I stand near my mother's bedside, I notice my mother holding her tongue and staring at the muted TV, pretending to watch a bake-off reality show as she eavesdrops on our one-way conversation. As I talk to Diane in theater whispers, I see my mother in my peripheral view, eyeing us suspiciously. She knows we're talking about her, and I feel her heavy gaze slicing through me like an old childhood scar.

I tell Diane that my mother has requested more drugs. "She says the pain is unbearable."

I'm in awe of Diane's stature. My mother wasn't joking when she pointed out her resemblance to Nurse Ratched from *One Flew Over the Cuckoo's Nest*. I'm sure she gets reminded of that occasionally by other patients as well.

Diane's modest, razor-thin grin stretches across apple-red lips, and her wide, rosy chipmunk cheeks have a unique personality. She waves me out into the hall to finish our talk as she leans to the side to glimpse my mother. "Doris, are you comfortable? How are you feeling?"

"I have a lot of pain," my mother answers, pulling her face into a grimace. "I need another pill." I scowl at her pitiful cry for help like she did to escape Lee's drunken besottedness from my childhood. I want to do everything I can to calm her.

"I'll see what I can do," Diane says, and she motions me to follow her into the hallway.

I turn to Mom. "Be right back." Before I leave, I ask her if she needs anything from the cafeteria, a hot cup of tea or a sandwich.

She is angry with me, and as she turns her attention back to the silent game show, I notice her eyes fill with melancholy. She works over-time not to raise her voice at me. Her hands tremble at her sides like a child's.

Diane and I stand ten feet from the door outside the room so my mother won't overhear us. I tell her that I've spoken with Nurse Claire about my mother's mood swings. "She wants to keep her as content and happy as possible during this transition."

Diane understands my concerns and advises me about the difficult road ahead. She talks about depression and suicide and the inevitable end. I cannot imagine a life without my mother, rock, mentor, and cheerleader.

"Claire and I talked about my mother's moods," I say. "She's happy one moment and a raging battle ax the next."

"Has Claire spoken to you about the antidepressants we're giving your mother?" Nurse Diane asks.

I nod.

Diane reiterates the other nurse's words verbatim, explaining the rocky path and choices I must make to keep my mother comfortable as the disease progresses and she becomes a prisoner in her own body.

She tells me everything is under control and that this is routine for cancer patients. "We want to keep the residents as comfortable as possible without administering too much medicine. We want to keep them lucid but pain-free. It is a slippery slope. But we're doing everything we can. I promise."

"I understand."

"Let me check your mother's chart and see what I can give her for the pain." She pauses, then adds, "While I'm at it, should I get you an ibuprofen for that swollen eye?"

"No." I wander to my mother's room. My bruised eye is the least of my problems. Inside, my mother sleeps. I turn my attention to Eli's journals to escape my current issues, only to be engulfed with other, much bigger mysteries.

Chapter Twenty-Six

Do you remember the night I came home from work, and you were sleeping on the couch? It was raining, and I was in a bad mood. The TV was on. And the neighbors were having a party next door.

I woke you because I needed to talk. You thought I was in trouble and jumped off the couch and wrapped your arms around me.

Do you remember?

You must've asked me over and over if I was hurt or in danger. It made me feel appreciated knowing someone cared for me as much as you did. I miss your voice and the supportive, gentle way you handled terrible situations. That night, you told me everything would be all right, even though I felt the world was ending.

I was angry about work and the stupid, senseless coworkers who wanted to see me leave because I wouldn't conform to their unprofessional ways.

Looking forward to going home to you was the highlight of my day. I wanted to close the blinds, shut out the rest of the world, pour us a glass of wine or slug down a beer, and spend the rest of our lives together—just us.

We fought like hell, and I wasn't always the most straightforward guy to live with. But at the end of the day, I didn't want to be anywhere or with anyone else but you.

I miss the old days. I miss us. I miss how you entered a room; it made me smile—waking up next to you and watching you knuckle sleep from your eyes or toss me one of your goofy grins.

I didn't have to say anything; you knew when I was having a bad day. I withdrew and became moody and preoccupied. You always knew how to reach inside me with happiness or a kiss and hug my heart. You knew the right thing to say. You learned how to talk to me without making me feel stupid. You spoke to me, not at me. Talking to you was like reading a book: I saw and heard things differently.

Not to sound cliché, but you were my rock, the anchor of our relationship. No other man would have stayed with me as long as you did. I frustrated you so many times, and you took it in stride. I saw in you what I wanted to be. Strong, compassionate, and wise. But my bad attitude and self-centered behavior broke the bond between us.

Relationships are tough. But I didn't invest in us as much as you did. I was selfish to think you could keep us afloat and happy, riding the wave until it crashed.

The challenging periods in our lives were the daily reminders why I loved you so much. Despite my misgivings and Jekyll-and-Hyde attitude, I wanted to fight for you. I never wanted us to separate. I wanted us to go on and grow old together (even though you never liked the word "old"—wink, wink).

Life was never the same for me after us. I knew it wouldn't be. I fell into the wrong crowd and did some nasty things. I wanted you to remember us the way we were together.

For the record, it was me who fucked up a good thing, not you. I don't blame you for anything. I never have. I was the problem, the uncontrollable live wire. I lost the best man I will ever meet in this life. I took you for granted.

When we went our separate ways, there wasn't a day that I

didn't think about you. I wanted to call you every day to beg you to return to me. I held the receiver in my hand, and every time the phone rang and rang and rang and the busy signal would beckon me to hang up, I had the phone to my ear, hoping to hear your voice.

Living alone was never in my cards. I felt hopeless and afraid. I'm not too fond of silence. It gives me the heebie-jeebies. I rarely slept or ate. I'd call out from work every week. I almost lost my job. Eventually, I quit and followed an uncertain path. I'll spare you the details. I intended not to hurt you, Ralph, but to enlighten you on the consequences I faced after leaving the most incredible thing in my past: you.

Thoughts of ending my life were significant and frequent in our post-life. But then I thought: I didn't want you to read about my death in the obituaries. Or the grotesque way I died. I didn't want to make you sad. I hurt you enough when I left.

One does not realize the importance of another human being until they're gone. Running away from your problems was never the right thing to do. But the only person to teach me how to deal with reality was gone.

I knew my life was over the moment I said goodbye.

Chapter Twenty-Seven

I SHUDDER AWAKE as a soft scream punctures the cold obscurity of the hospital room. I hear Eli's voice in the dark. "I wanted us to grow old and die together."

Who and what was Eli running from? What were his problems?

I sit up, clutching my chest, my mouth dry and gritty like sand. Sweat collects on my neck, and my T-shirt sticks to me like adhesive tape. I try to pull it off, but my hands are shaky, my palms damp and sticky. A wave of my stink wafts up from the warm recesses of my underarms and hits me square in the face. I wince.

I look to where my mother sleeps a few feet away, making gurgling noises in the back of her throat as if dreaming of horrible things. The frail outline of her body looks like cadaver remains, vacuum-sealed under the bedsheets.

A dull throb sets up home in my lower back and crawls down my leg. I reach for the armchair to stand. Woozy and unsteady on my feet, I am lightheaded. But I see and hear movement in the room. A shadow falls across the small gap in the doorway. Somebody is lingering in the corridor outside my mother's room.

A nurse? Lost patient?

Shuffling across the floor in my socks, I quicken my pace, grimacing against the needling prickle of heat in my knees and feet. I reach for the knob, my sudden movements startling the figure on the other side of the door.

I dash into the hallway, glimpsing a male figure running around the corner, his dirt-encrusted boots and Harley Davidson leather jacket the only distinctive attributes I recognize. A baseball cap covers his head and face.

I hurry after him, hobbling against the burning ache in my legs, and turn down a side hallway leading to the exit.

Shoving the door open, I dash into the stairwell, my breath labored, heart pounding. I hear the man's boots clamoring along the metal stairs and bouncing off the walls. I peer down two flights of stairs to the ground floor and briefly glimpse the dark outline of my night visitor escaping. It is when he reaches the bottom level that he peers up at me from beneath the baseball cap pulled snugly over his face, tufts of blond hair poking out from under it. He carries a white motorcycle helmet in his right hand. I reel from the familiar framework of the barbwire tattoo on the back of his neck. It is the young man from the ferry.

*

SHAKING OFF AN adrenaline rush, I race into the hallway and around the corner to the nurse's station. I ask for Nurse Diane.

A young nurse tells me she is with a patient. I meet her at the far end of the hall as she's coming out of a room. I ask her, "Did you notice a man hanging around my mother's room in the last ten or fifteen minutes?"

She looks at me, confused and alarmed, as she removes rubber gloves and tosses them into a biohazard waste bin nearby. "Your father?"

I shake my head. "No. Not Lee. A younger man carrying a motorcycle helmet. He had a distinctive tattoo on his neck."

"I'm sorry, Ralph. I've been on rounds for the past half an hour. Why do you ask? Is there something wrong?"

"I'm not sure. He just looked suspicious."

"Suspicious? How?"

"I woke up a few minutes ago and saw a shadowy figure standing outside my mother's room. When I came out, he took off into the stairwell."

"Do you want me to call security?"

"He's probably long gone by now. But I'd appreciate it if you'd keep an eye out for my mother."

"Of course. I'll let security know anyway."

I nod appreciatively and am about to ride the elevator down to the first floor and check the grounds outside for my mysterious visitor when she asks, "How are you holding up?"

"A bit shaken. Sorry, Diane. I gotta go."

Chapter Twenty-Eight

LOT A IS deserted except for a few people milling about smoking and talking. I stand under sodium vapor lampposts, staring across the twenty-two feet of parking space in the near darkness for the mysterious tattooed man.

Instead, I find Lee.

I hear llamas, alpacas, and peacocks shuffling in the enclosed cages adjacent to the parking lot and duck pond. I've been told that the llamas and alpacas are used as animal therapy for patients. Maybe my mother would benefit from it. Being an animal lover, she might find their presence warm and welcoming.

A door opens, and a mewling voice belonging to Lee stabs the night air. I see him struggling to get out of his white Honda Civic in a corner parking spot by the curb. He looks unsteady, drunk. This is his way of dealing with reality. Hit the bottle. Drown your problems.

He slams the door shut on his third attempt and almost falls on his ass, rocking back and forth, trying to catch his footing. There is nothing new from my perspective; Lee's middle name and favorite hobby is insobriety. It is challenging for me to watch, living in a violent and abusive household, growing up and hearing him stumbling home late at night, smelling of pot and booze.

He notices me, but I feign ignorance and stare around the parking lot for the mysterious intruder in the stairwell earlier. But Lee screams to snatch my attention and staggers toward me in an embarrassing gait. He taps his cane against the ground, favoring a limp in his right leg.

As he approaches, wobbling on his bad leg, the spicy scent of cigar smoke and body odor wafts like a brewing storm. My eyes start to water; my skin prickles against the chilly night and the unsettling sight of the man I loathe.

I am sickened by his intoxicated presence. "What do you want?" I ask, furious, my heart pounding and the rush of blood in my ears crashing like challenging waves.

"I need you," he says. "I don't wanna fight."

"You're right. You need help. But not from me."

He jabs a wandering finger my way, a listless gesture of failure and humiliation.

I swat his hand away from my face. "You're pathetic, Lee. Go home. Stay away from Mom. She can do much better than you." I turn to leave, looking left and right and behind me for the tattoo man.

Lee grabs my coat sleeve and tugs me backward.

I jerk away; the urge to hit him curls in my fists. I want to hit him. I turn to face him. Just the sight of him sickens me. Broken capillaries line his pointed nose and rosy cheeks. His eyes are glassy from drinking.

"Is this your idea of reality?" I scream at him. "Coming here and disrupting my mother's last days? You should be ashamed, but you're not. You're a poor excuse of a man, husband, and father."

He sways back and forth, his drunken gaze wandering to the ground, to me, then over my shoulders, to the foggy darkness behind us. He struggles to hold his head up. "You think you're better than me, boy?" he hisses.

"I've been present in Mom's life. You haven't. So, you tell me."

He laughs. "You sound foolish, boy."

From ten feet away, I can smell the stinging whiff of his sour stench. My stomach churns.

He stands next to a lamppost, leaning against it for support.

"You're an asshole," I say. "I don't know why you came back here."

He shakes his head. "You don't know me."

"I don't want to know you."

"Fool." He spits out the word, phlegmy saliva spraying the air in a soft mist.

"Mom is lying in a hospital bed, dying!" I scream. "You're three fucking sheets to the wind! Who's the fool?" Heat creeps into my face. I snarl like a rabid dog. My adrenaline boils as I rush across the parking lot and hover over the worst thing that has happened to my mother and me.

"You're a pathetic, violent drunk who wouldn't know a good thing if it slapped you in the face." I am frantic; both fists clenched at my sides, ready to throw the first punch. "I don't know what Mom ever saw in you, Lee. You're the reason why she's lying in that hospital bed dying."

"I've been there for you and your mother."

"You were never home! You were never with us."

"It's been years, boy. Why rehash things now?"

"Is that an apology? You're a bit late for that."

He jams his finger into my chest. "You've had a free ride living under our roof."

"Don't change the subject. And don't blame me for your problems."

"Most eighteen- and nineteen-year-old kids are more mature than you. They're more responsible than you'll ever be. They don't mooch off their parents like you did for nineteen years." He stumbles toward me, bull-legged, stooped with arthritis, his eyes wide and delighted. "If it was up to your mother, you would've lived with us longer and milked us for all we had."

"Growing up in that house was never easy. Most nineteen-year-olds don't have to listen to their fathers beating their mothers every night before bed or stumbling home in the early hours."

He curls his lips and buckles under the pressure of my tireless tone. I see the hate in his eyes and the way he tightens his fists as if he is going to take a swing at me. "I loved that woman."

"How can you say that?" My tone reels with sarcasm. "If Mom ever looked at you the wrong way or forgot to make dinner after you got home from work because she wasn't feeling well, you'd hit her. You'd beat her senseless. That doesn't sound like somebody who cares about his family."

"That's a lie!"

"Is it?" I approach him as the icy wind lifts the sides of my hair. "I'd wake up at night to the sounds of you two fighting downstairs. You don't know what that does to a child, to live in fear and hear his father hitting his mother. I was always worried about Mom's safety."

He scoffs and tweaks the end of his nose with a thumb, a troubling grin on his face. "You've always had a flair for the dramatics, Ralph."

"A nineteen-year-old shouldn't have to call the police on one of their parents. You gave me no choice."

"It was always two against one in that house."

I heave a sigh. "Jesus. I wonder why. Stop playing the fucking victim and own up to your mistakes."

"Everybody makes mistakes."

"Some people never repeat them."

"You always thought you were better than me."

I breathe deeply and roll my eyes. "I was a teenager, for Christ's sake."

"You're not now. Grow up."

"People who live in abusive households are scarred for life. People, especially children, never get over it. So, don't tell me to grow up." My fist is inches from his face, and with my flaring temper, moments away from hitting him. "I was the adult in that house. Not you. I had to take care of Mom to protect her from you. I didn't have friends because

I couldn't leave the house when you were home. Mom didn't want to be alone with you for fear that you'd give her a black eye or a bloody nose." I take a deep breath, my insides queasy. I keep a brave expression poised, maintaining eye contact. "A child shouldn't have to live in fear. Nobody should have to live that way. I did what I had to do to survive. I fought for Mom. Not you."

He is quiet.

"It was hell living in that house, Lee," I add. "Mom and I never knew when you'd come home drunk and start a fight. We'd go to bed hungry some nights because we were too anxious to eat. I'd watch you from the top of the stairs as you passed out on the couch in your work clothes. You made life unbearable for us. The only way to escape it all was to pretend that everything would get better. But it didn't. I knew it wouldn't. But I had to have hope. We had nowhere else to go. Mom wouldn't leave her because it was the house she grew up in with her parents. You were just a hanger-on, a fucking burden."

He looks ashamed but then says, "I didn't realize—"

"Listen to me! You didn't want anything to do with me when I told you that I was gay. Mom was my only support growing up. I felt hatred when you told me I would never succeed in this life as a gay man. You said that people would harass me, push me around, threaten my life, and that I should better watch my back because people in this redneck town wouldn't tolerate people like me." I pause to choke back tears. "You laughed at me, ridiculed me, and told nasty gay jokes with your bowling team friends when they came over to the house after the game. You did it to get a reaction from me and get under my skin."

He looks dumbfounded, staring at me with his familiar glossy-drunk gaze.

"You were a bully, and I hated you for it," I say. "I hate you now. You were never a parent, always picking and poking whenever you could, making me feel worthless, small, like a dumb child. I'll never forgive you, Lee. And I'll never call you father."

He is crying and whimpering like a kicked puppy, crouching on the ground by the lamppost, snot clinging to the untrimmed threads of his salt-and-pepper mustache.

"Go home," I tell him. "Sleep it off." I turn and walk away, leaving him to wallow in his self-pity.

*

NURSE DIANE STOPS me as I step off the elevator and tells me my mother is asleep. "I've talked to the doctor, and he's ordered blood tests and an X-ray for tomorrow afternoon. We'll know more then. I've also notified security regarding your earlier request. He's patrolling the hallways. All is clear and quiet."

All I can think to do is nod. Exhaustion settles over me like a damp, woolly blanket. "Thanks."

"You look tired," Diane says. "Why don't you go home and get some sleep? I'll call you if anything changes."

"I feel guilty leaving her."

"You need to take care of yourself. I'll call if anything changes," she promises. "You're not going to get any sleep around here."

She is right. I'll be awake for the rest of my five hours until dawn breaks through the bleak sky.

"I appreciate it," I say, releasing a long, ragged breath and heading to my mother's room to gather my belongings.

My knapsack slung over my shoulder, I stand in the room's cold shadows, watching and listening to my mother mumbling in her sleep. The uneven rise and fall of her chest unsettles me. Her breathing is strained and labored.

The constant beeping of the heart monitor rings in my ears, a lasting, sorrowful impression etched onto my mind as I walk out of the room, heaving a deep sigh and leaving my mother in complete darkness at the nurse's request.

Chapter Twenty-Nine

RETURNING TO MY apartment feels strange as if I don't belong here. I turn off the ignition and leave my car, staring at the obscure scrim of night outlining the massive apartment building. A sharp wind snags the yellow crime scene tape bordering ten feet by the river's edge as I get out of the car and pull my coat collar around my neck to ward off the biting cold.

I shiver from the misty rain hovering in the air as I walk toward the front doors of the building. I climb the stairs to the fifth floor.

When I reach my apartment, a wave of exhaustion assaults me. My legs feel spongy as I slide my key into the keyhole. Behind me, I hear a door creak open. I turn to see Mr. Williams staring out at me three doors down, his liver-spotted face poking around the chipped doorframe of his musty-smelling apartment.

"Mind your business," I say.

"You're in trouble," he says, then retreats into the shadowy sullenness of his sad life, muttering curse words at me and shutting the door with a thud. I hear him sliding the chain lock in place.

I step into my quiet surroundings and lock myself inside. I flip on the light switch to brighten the room. I reach into my backpack for Eli's journal and toss the bag onto an empty chair. Down the hall, I open the closet door and store the journal in a shoebox on the high shelf. I fold a blanket over it as if I am burying my past for good.

I stumble across the room, crawling out of my shoes and dirty clothes as I go, to the bathroom. I let the hot water in the shower run for ten minutes before I lose myself in the swirling steam. I close my eyes and raise my head upward to the showerhead. Eli's presence envelops me. His intoxicating smell settles in my nostrils. I breathe him in, wrapping my arms around myself and holding him as if he were here.

Tears flow, and I slide down the back wall of the shower, sitting hunched forward at the bottom of the tub. I pull my legs up to my chest. I cry, my head falling in my folded arms.

Fifteen minutes later, I dry off and climb into Eli's worn white T-shirt, the one he left behind before disappearing from my life again, and slip into a pair of my familiar briefs. I fall back onto the bed, curling up in a fetal position.

My bedsheets smell like Eli's light musk, and I imagine him next to me, our limbs tangled, our warm breath on each other's faces. I replay his kisses, his tongue wandering from my ear to my neck and the opening of my mouth.

I ball up a fistful of sheets and stuff my face with the smell of our damp, sweaty sex. A smile tugs at my lips from the heady scent of Eli's aftershave. A flooding rush of memories from the last forty-eight hours invades my thoughts like a childhood nightmare.

The weight of my exhaustion drives me into dreamland. It is only the afterthought of Eli's murder that keeps me from drowning, dying, and leaving this world.

Before long, sleep finds me, and I wake to more bad news when I stir in the blinding light of morning shining through bedroom windows.

*

A MIGRAINE DRILLS the back of my head, and a choking taste of morning breath sours my stomach. I am hungry but my gut grumbles against breakfast, warning me that a slice of dry toast isn't an option either.

Fumbling through the knot of tangled sheets and a prickling, dead weight of numbness in my arms, I try to sit up and throw my legs over the edge of the bed. Bowed at an awkward angle, a sharp, jagged pain cuts down my right leg. I wince, my breath catching in the back of my throat. I double over and fall backward, moaning.

A salvo of gunfire erupts in my head and I fear I am having a panic attack. I lie still because moving makes it difficult to breathe.

Closing my eyes helps keep me calm and centered.

Clenching a fistful of bedsheets in my sweaty palms, I yell out, but my voice is strangled and drowned by the words of Lee. "Faggot. Queer."

Then I hear movement in the hallway, somebody shuffling and doors closing, voices too low and incoherent to understand. I run a clammy hand over my face and take a deep breath. Another door opens and closes somewhere far off. Then everything goes quiet.

One. Two. Three. I start counting to myself. As I roll onto my side, my headache subsides. I stretch both legs out gradually, pulling myself up into a sitting position on the edge of the bed.

I am lightheaded. The relief doesn't last for long. Anxiety sets in, and I flee to the bathroom where I crouch over the toilet, dry heaving.

I stay hunched over the john for twenty minutes, wiping phlegm from my mouth with the back of my hand. When I pull myself up and glimpse the pale-white face staring back at me from the mirror, a fissure of capillaries spreading like a virus in both pupils and the ugly sight of my bruised eye, my unfamiliar face frightens me.

I lean over the sink and run the faucet until the water runs warm. I splash myself until color comes back into my face. I peel Eli's T-shirt and my briefs off and toss them in the corner of the room. I fill the tub with hot water and a handful of Epsom salt, submerging my tired body into the inviting heat.

The ceiling fan rattles and birdsong filters through the gap in the window. A car alarm somewhere near breaks the stillness of the morning—a neighboring dog barks. I hear a muffled voice trying to silence the dog and alarm.

An airplane rumbles across the sky, and a door slams in the hall, trying to block out all distractions.

When I come up for air, I hear the hateful warnings of Lee in my head, his fatherly advice lost in the fan's oscillating rattle and the incessant squawking of a car horn outside.

My skin is pink when I drain the tub ten minutes later and step out, dripping wet, grabbing a towel from the rack to ward off the chill in the air. I shake off the shiver.

I dry off and run the towel through my hair a few times, feeling semi-normal again. When I enter the bedroom to a ghostly emptiness, a wave of sadness overwhelms me. I see Eli in every corner of the room; the creepy presence of my former boyfriend circulates like the grating sound of dead noises coming from the fan. My neck hairs prick.

A ripple of fear clutches my chest. My gaze shifts from the bed where Eli and I slept and fucked, to the couch and fire escape. I hear him talking, his words too hard to understand. I shuffle closer to the window, his voice growing loud, angry, critical.

I hear him say: "Not here. No. Don't do this." His words start to string together from the night he disappeared. I hear the refrigerator door opening and slamming shut behind me, Eli grunting and grabbing a beer from the top shelf. I turn around. There's nobody there—a figment of my imagination.

That night, I wondered if there was somebody inside my apartment. Was Eli talking to somebody on the phone?

I pull on a clean white T-shirt, jeans, and a long-sleeved sweatshirt to ward off the chill. Scatterbrained, I walk over to my coat, dig inside for the key to Eli's apartment in Vermont and Dr. Matheson's business card, and stuff everything into my pants pocket.

I crawl under a warm blanket in a chair by the living room window and watch a steady rain beat amid a cold, overcast day. I stare out into a sleepless haze and think of my mother.

I call the hospital. After they transfer me to the third-floor nurses' station, I ask for Nurse Claire or Nurse Diane. I wait on hold for ten minutes, listening to sleepy elevator music, before Claire comes on the line. She sounds tired.

She apologizes for not getting in touch with me earlier. "It's been a busy morning." She tells me that my mother's blood and X-ray tests are on schedule and that she'll be out of her room between one and two o'clock.

I thank her for the update. "I'd like to stop by the hospital later this afternoon."

"That's fine. In the meantime, I'll call you if anything changes," she says, and we hang up.

I sit in front of the rain-streaked window, enjoying the peaceful silence, staring out at naked tree branches dancing in the wind. I stand to refresh my coffee and head to the bedroom, hoping to get a few hours of sleep. My eyes start to close as the weight of the last forty-eight hours blankets me. I lie on the unmade bed, slipping in and out of consciousness, my mind fuzzy and exhausted from not sleeping.

I hear noises. Raised voices, someone coming and going. A door opens and closes in the hallway.

I drift off to the faint sound of sirens and a branch scraping the windowpane. I fall deep into a dreamy forgetfulness. Death, murder, and a mirage of my dying mother yank me further into the dark vastness of my delusions.

Then, a loud, hard rap on the apartment door startles me and yanks me from the pitch-blackness of my staticky thoughts. It sounds like somebody is beating down my door with an ax. Dazed, I sit up, looking around the room, my gaze falling to my cell phone on the nightstand. Maybe there is an emergency at the hospital and Nurse Claire is calling with bad news.

The noise isn't coming from my phone. It's not ringing.

"Mr. Ashton! It's Officer Edwards. Open up!"

I leap off the bed.

"Mr. Ashton!"

My heart bangs hard. I am groggy and out of sorts.

I walk out of the room, down the hall, to the apartment door, staring at it. When the second rap of knuckles comes, hard and unannounced, the force of the impact knocks me backward.

"Mr. Ashton! If you're in there, open the door. It's the police."

An odd electricity vibrates through me. My hand trembling, I turn the knob and pull the door open.

Officer Edwards and his young deputy stare at me from beneath a dimly lit sconce in the hall.

"What is this about?" I ask.

"Mr. Ashton, you have the right to remain silent," Officer Edwards says.

My mouth falls open, face flushes, aghast. "What are you doing?"

The younger officer walks into my apartment and reaches behind me for both of my hands. He pats me down roughly, and I hear the clanking sound of handcuffs as he binds my wrists together.

Officer Edwards says, "We've uncovered further evidence in the death of Elijah Ray and found the murder weapon that killed him."

"What the hell is going on?" I struggle against Deputy Taylor's firm resolve. "I didn't kill Eli."

Officer Edwards holds up a piece of paper, waving it in my face.

I have to squint to read it.

It is a search warrant.

"Step aside, Mr. Ashton." Officer Edwards shoulders past me. His deputy holds me in his grip.

"What's going on?" I ask, almost begging.

I watch Officer Edwards rifling through my kitchen drawers, closets, and under my bed. He empties my sock and T-shirt drawer, tossing clothes over his shoulder.

"What is this about?" I scream. "What are you doing?"

Turning my apartment upside down, Officer Edwards continues reading me the Miranda Rights. His reed-thin, red-haired deputy shuts my apartment door behind us and escorts me to the set of elevators at the end of the corridor. I do not look in the faces of my next-door neighbors as I pass them, stumbling down the hall and hearing them whispering bigoted remarks at me as if I am a criminal.

I stand next to Officer Taylor, waiting to board the elevator. He smells of cigarette smoke and sweat. Officer Edwards stands off to the side, jotting furiously in his pocket-sized writing pad.

A bell dings, and the elevator doors stretch open like an accordion. We get in. The door closes.

We descend.

Chapter Thirty

WHEN I ARRIVE at the police station, I am frisked, booked, finger-printed, and photographed. I request a public defender even though I'm innocent.

Waiting in a holding cell across from two other detainees awaiting representation rattles me. My cement cell smells like a men's locker room, rank with piss, sweat, and dirty jockstraps. I lean against the bars, gazing at a long, empty hallway. Two ugly faces stare at me from across the fuzzily lit hall.

On my left, near the sink and toilet, sits my bed: a hard, white cot, no blanket.

Ten feet across the hall, a white guy with a Mohawk and a hand-made mess of tattoos scrawled up and down both of his gone-to-seed arms sneers, his mouth missing teeth. His eyes are wild and bloodshot.

He's withdrawing, coming off something shaky, seizing with nervous ticks, pacing like a caged animal. He wipes sweat from his face and forehead with a trembling hand. "Whadd'ya in for?" he asks, grinning.

I yell for Officer Edwards. "I need to go to the hospital. My mother's sick. She needs me."

The young man, probably in his late twenties, says, serenading me with a fretful threat, "You don't want trouble, do ya, boy? Whadd'ya in for?"

"Nothing," I say, glancing at him.

He opens his mouth to laugh, flicking his pierced tongue at me. He reminds me a lot of Eli—restless, erratic, troubled.

He turns and stares at an older man in the dark corner of his cell. I follow his gaze as he introduces me to his cellmate, Dirk. Big and fuzzy as a peach, Dirk sits against the wall on a cot, grumbling and moaning, shuffling and shifting his overweight mass. He grunts at me from the shadows, "From the looks of it, I'd say our little buddy here got himself into a nasty fight."

Fear feels like suicide inside this jail cell. I touch my left eye and cringe, yelling for an officer to let me out.

"You're in for the night, man," the strung-out young man hisses. "Don't waste your breath. Those pigs don't give a flying fuck about you."

More grumbling in the corner, and I get a whiff of shit and sweat drifting across the concrete corridor from my other cellmate. I glimpse the blimp-sized man sitting on the toilet, the outline of his colossal body silhouetted in shadows, unmoved by my presence. He mumbles as he talks, wiping his ass. His deep, rough voice is the result of too many drugs, I imagine.

Sweat drips down my cheek. I wipe it with a finger.

I think of my mother in the hospital, and anger swells like a metastasized tumor inside me. I grip the cell bars and scream. Nobody hears me. If they do, they don't answer—stony silence.

"The name's Pitman." It is the young man with the Mohawk. I lift my tired, heavy gaze to him and wonder how he screwed up his life getting in here. I peg him to be twenty-five or six at the most. He holds a bony hand through the bars as if showing off his homespun tattoos. Burn marks scar his hands. Slash marks line the length of his arm and wrists, the meticulous habit of self-cutting. The bruise on his right cheek suggests he's been in a recent brawl.

The toilet flushes. Dirk yanks up his big boy pants and wanders around the tight quarters of the cell, coming up behind Pitman and engulfing the skinny white boy in a looming shadow. Dirk strolls up to the bars next to Pitman.

I must look up to glimpse his double chin and rusty-brown eyes. His ragged beard is filthy and tied with a rubber band at the end. His stare is intense, hungry.

I turn to the closed door at the end of the hall. My heart beats faster. My knees feel soft like jelly. I don't know how much longer I can survive here. "Officer!"

"I'll tell you what's wrong with me if you tell me what you did," Dirk says.

"None of your business," I say.

"You're not in here for the hell of it, bro. Start talking."

I exhale. "I'm not your bro."

"Did you turn a trick?" Dirk asks, laughing, slapping his jail buddy on the back. The two of them snicker like schoolgirls.

I turn away, annoyed, my fingers curling around the bars.

"Did I hit a nerve?" Dirk asks.

"Stop talking," I say.

"It's going to be a long night if you don't make friends," he says.

"I'm not planning on staying," I say.

Dirk slaps the bars with his bear paw, curling his mitt into a fist, trying to torment me.

I look up at him and toss him a nasty look. "You don't scare me."

"Look at me," he says, his voice booming and echoing off the cell walls. "I can be your worst nightmare."

I smack the bars with an open palm and yell for Officer Edwards and his deputy.

The metal door opens and a broad-shouldered, middle-aged guard strides down the hall as if modeling his tight-fit uniform, heading in my direction. "Keep it down!"

"I need to get out of here," I say, pleading. "My mother is sick in the hospital. I need to see her."

"That ain't going to happen, son." He stands six foot tall, legs splayed, fingers intertwined under his leather utility belt. He glares at me with a bold, brute stare—facing off.

"You don't understand," I say. "I didn't do anything. I'm innocent."

"You'll have a chance to explain yourself. Right now, sit tight."

Frustrated, I yell, "I requested a solicitor. Where are they?" Then, after a brief pause, he adds, "I'm not a murderer!"

The guard sneers, turns, and saunters away, laughing.

"I knew you were in for something," Dirk says, meandering to the cot in the back of the cell. The box springs yowl like a cat in heat as he shifts, wrestling for the proper position.

Even from afar, his lurking presence is unsettling, staring at me as he rubs himself in the dark. Pitman snickers in the corner. He urges his cellmate to "Keep going. Beat that meat! Make our friend here uncomfortable."

I mutter a small prayer that I'm back in my apartment, lying in Eli's arms. "Please, God. This isn't happening. It's just a dream—"

"You religious, bro?" Dirk asks, and I wish he would stop talking to me.

I ignore him. Maybe he'll go away.

"I'm a seller," he goes on. "Marijuana."

"Good stuff," Pitman pipes up. "Got any on you now?"

I clench my teeth and tighten the grip on the bars.

"I've been a dealer for three years," Dirk says. "The best shit in town."

I lift my head. "Why are you telling me this? I don't care."

"Because I made many dumb mistakes, too many to list." He sits up and points a gnarly finger at me. "You seem like a half-decent dude. Don't fuck it up like I did." He rolls onto his side and the bedsprings ping under his weight.

Pitman sounds aroused, clapping with impulsive movements in the corner. "Great fucking speech, man. But it's as lame as a donkey dick."

"What are you jabbering about, Pit?" Dirk asks.

Pitman snickers. "Don't apologize, man. Drugs are cool. They make people feel good."

"You're an idiot," Dirk says, and I imagine a caring guy beneath that hard eggshell exterior.

"If I am, then that makes two of us," Pitman retorts.

"I'm trying to get my life back on track, asshole," Dirk says, standing, the ground shuddering under his weight.

"From the looks of it, you've got a long way to go." Pitman gestures with a jerk of his head to the claustrophobic surroundings where Dirk hovers in the semidarkness.

I imagine Dirk making both of Pitman's eyes a matching pair. I look over to see Pitman cowering in the corner, covering his face with his hands and backing away from Dirk as if the big man will hit him.

I slink away to the other end of my cell and sit on the cot, my back against the cold hard wall. I take a moment to collect my thoughts as my cellmates corral each other with physical, blasphemous threats.

The moment is fleeting when I hear determined footsteps clomp along the corridor to the edge of my cell, the metal door slamming shut behind whoever is approaching. I glimpse a skinny Black guard with a set of keys and a fat, bald man in a light-brown suit and a dark checkered tie, carrying a briefcase, standing under the fizzy fluorescent lights.

"Your solicitor is here, Mr. Ashton," the guard says.

Chapter Thirty-One

I SIT IN a small room the size of my apartment bathroom and stare across at the high forehead of my lawyer, his bald head glossy with beads of sweat. He shuffles papers, coughs, and sounds sick. With a big hand, he pulls a pink and white polka-dotted handkerchief out from the front of his coat pocket. He wipes his damp face and introduces himself as Leonard Weldon. His handshake is firm and clammy.

"Are you nervous?" I ask, breaking his concentration. "Ill?"

He stops ruffling through his stack of papers and looks up at me. "I'm warm in this suit."

I screw up my face and wonder how much trouble I am in.

He opens his briefcase, rifles through it, and rearranges folders and loose-leaf papers.

"I didn't kill Eli, Mr. Weldon," I say.

He closes his brown leather briefcase and folds his hands in front of his round belly, his short, stubby fingers barely touching. His stare is dodgy, eyes roving. He coughs and doesn't cover up the spray of germs blasting me in the face.

I grit my teeth. I don't like this guy.

He grumbles. "Tell me what happened the night"—he stops and searches through his notes for my ex-boyfriend's name—"Mr. Ray arrived and left your apartment."

My leg twitches. I shake my head. "My mother is dying in the hospital, Mr. Weldon. This entire charade is a fishing expedition. I need to go to the hospital and be with her."

"Please, answer my question."

I lean back in my metal chair and sigh.

"Maybe you can call her," he says. "After we finish here."

He gets my attention, and I lean forward. "Is everything I tell you confidential?"

"Depends."

"On what?"

"Whether or not you tell me the truth."

"The only truth I know is that I didn't kill my ex-boyfriend. I don't know what the fuck happened to him. I don't know why he left or where he went." Layers of lies.

"Do you have any idea who could have killed him?"

"How do I know you won't bail on me during these preliminaries?"

He sets his large hands across the table. "If I believe your story, I'll represent you. It's simple."

"We won't be here long because I'm innocent."

"Tell me what happened, then." He grips his expensive pen and catches my gaze. "First, how'd that happen to your eye?"

"Like I told the police on the way over here. I fell."

"You fell?"

"That's what I said."

Mr. Weldon coughs and clears his throat. "It doesn't look like a bruise from a fall."

"Jesus Christ. I fell and hit my head on the end table in my apartment."

"Don't get defensive, Mr. Ashton. I'm trying to understand what happened so I can help you."

I pick at an invisible piece of lint on my long-sleeved shirt.

"So, let's go back to the beginning," he says, refreshing his thoughts with his scads of notes. "What happened the night Mr. Ray arrived at your apartment?"

I give Mr. Weldon the play-by-play account of the night Eli waltzed back into my life after a year. "I woke up the next morning and realized Eli was gone. End of story."

"What was Mr. Ray's reason for being at your apartment? Why did he come back into your life now?"

"He told me that he wanted to see me. I'd been on his mind."

"Where was he coming from originally?"

"Vermont."

"Where in Vermont?"

I squirm in my chair.

"Answer my question, or this will be a long night."

"Why is it important to know where Eli lives?" I catch myself speaking in the present tense. Lives. As if Eli is alive and well. I close my eyes. "Lived."

"Is something wrong, Mr. Ashton?"

I detect a lisp in the man's speech. "No."

"You seem guarded."

I look away from him, agitated at Mr. Weldon's barrage of questions and innuendos.

"Why is it so difficult for you to answer a simple question?" he asks, his breathing heavy and difficult.

"South Hero." It comes out hurried, and I sound dishonest.

"All right. Do you know how long Mr. Ray lived in South Hero?"

"Two years."

"What does he do for a living? Sorry, what did he do for a living?"

"I honestly don't know." I think back to Eli's vague journal entries and wonder what activity he was involved in while we lived separate lives. I look up at the solicitor's damp, chubby face. He sweats profusely, his skin pallid and clammy. "I think we're wasting each other's time here."

"Why do you think that?"

"Because Eli and I were not in contact when we split up last year. I don't know his life before he drove into Grave Point."

"Okay." Mr. Weldon is exasperated as he sighs, jotting something in his notepad. He brushes a finger across his bushy brow. "Can you remember anything Mr. Ray might have said that could've tipped you off to his disappearance?"

I shake my head. "What do you mean?"

"What did you talk about when he arrived at your apartment?"

I need to clear my head. I can't think clearly of that night. Everything seems hazy. "I don't—"

"Can you describe his behavior?"

"He was normal-acting."

"What does that mean, normal?"

"He was himself."

"I don't know who Mr. Ray was; I never met him. You'll have to describe him to me."

"Kind. Moody, at times. Funny. Shy. Handsome."

"How was he the night he visited you?"

"All of the above."

"Did the two of you talk about what was going on in each other's lives?"

I think hard. Then, I say, "Eli told me he was taking some time off from life."

"What did he mean by that?"

I shrug. "I guess he was taking a break. Chilling."

"From work?"

"Possibly. I don't know. Eli was vague."

"Did you ask him what he meant?"

"No. It didn't seem relevant at the time."

"You said Mr. Ray was acting moody. Do you know if something was bothering him?"

"Come to think of it, he did seem distracted. Eli has always been enigmatic. It's part of his charm and mystery and handsomeness."

"Did he seem agitated about something or someone?"

"As I said, he seemed preoccupied, like something or somebody else was on his mind besides me."

"Can you elaborate?"

I move in my seat. My butt is numb from sitting too long. "When we talked on the couch, Eli seemed dodgy, like he didn't want to rehash our complicated past."

"What about your past?"

"The way we treated each other. Relationship stuff. It wasn't always hunky-dory or happy times or good sex."

"Was he happy to see you?"

I rake my hands through my hair. "I think so."

"You sound uncertain, Mr. Ashton."

"I mean…we didn't always see eye to eye."

"Would Mr. Ray ever hurt you?"

"No. Never. He was never abusive."

He waits a beat, then writes in his pad. "I'm trying to understand Mr. Ray's motivations to drive or ride the ferry from Vermont to Grave Point to see you."

One beat. Two. Then I say, "I don't know specifically, but—"

"But what?"

"All I can think of is that he missed me and wanted to reconnect. That's what he said."

"But you think differently?"

"Eli was mysterious. I couldn't read him sometimes or understand what he was thinking because he disliked talking about his feelings. But I felt something was wrong when he returned to Grave Point."

"Did he call you before he arrived?"

"No. He just showed up. It was a surprise."

"Does Eli have any enemies?" he asks, and the question puts me off. Then I think back to the journal. What was Eli hiding from me? Who was he running from?

I wonder whether I should share my former boyfriend's private musings with this strange man. "I don't think so," I finally say.

He scribbles in his pad.

"But you're not sure."

I shake my head.

"Did Mr. Ray ever talk to you about thoughts of suicide?"

I push away from the table. "Eli would never hurt himself."

"So, if what you're telling me is that he would never harm himself, and you didn't kill him, then someone must have had a vendetta against him. Right?"

The door to the room opens, and Deputy Taylor walks in.

Chapter Thirty-Two

THE YOUNG DEPUTY asks me to wait in Interrogation Room 2 with my solicitor. "Officer Edwards has more questions for you, Mr. Ashton. Sit still."

I raise my hands. "Where am I gonna go?"

He exits the room, shutting the door behind him. My lawyer and I sit for twenty minutes, mostly in silence, the temperature in the room stifling hot. Sweat pools in my armpits, and I want to peel off my long-sleeved jumpsuit and go rogue.

Mr. Weldon unbuttons his sweat-stained collar and twists his brown tie loose. His face is damp, and he blows his nose several times on his pocket handkerchief. He is wheezy.

The silence is aggravating, and Leonard's breathing worsens. He fills and empties his water glass three times in the half hour we wait.

When Officer Edwards finally enters the room with his freckle-faced deputy, both look annoyed as if we're keeping them from something more entertaining.

Both police officers look irritated. Deputy Taylor takes a seat across from my attorney. Officer Edwards remains standing behind his chair, glaring at me, his legs spread. He crosses his ropey, wiry arms over his big chest, an intimidating act.

Raising my hands to him, palms out, I say, "You're wasting both of our time. I didn't kill Eli."

"Where were you between midnight and one a.m. on the night Mr. Ray was murdered?"

"In bed. Alone."

"You're going to have to come up with a better alibi, Mr. Ashton."

I shake my head. "I don't have one."

"Your handprints are all over the murder weapon."

His cocky smirk annoys me. I look to my right to Mr. Weldon, then at Officer Edwards. "Whatever game you're playing, the joke's on you. I'm not worried because I didn't kill my ex-boyfriend."

"You should be worried, Mr. Ashton." Officer Edwards pulls out a chair and sits. "Maybe you should speak to your attorney privately about how to proceed with these allegations."

I cross my arms. "You've got nothing on me."

Mr. Weldon touches my arm to warn me that I am walking a tight-rope. I jerk away from him, keeping a steady gaze on Officer Edwards's stern poker face. "I know what you're doing. Trying to scare me and intimidate me, but it won't work. I didn't kill anybody."

"We've got your fingerprints," Officer Edwards reminds me.

"How do you have my client's fingerprints?" my solicitor asks the tall, confident to the point of cocky officer. Mr. Weldon, as close to me as his big belly will allow without wedging himself between the table and the small, tight space separating us, whispers in my ear, "Have you ever been arrested?"

I angle my head his way. "Nope."

Officer Edwards whispers to his deputy. The younger man pushes his chair out and stands. He leaves the room.

When he returns, he is carrying a clear plastic evidence bag. He drops the large bag on the table, and my stunned gaze falls onto the bloody tire iron it holds.

"What is this?" my lawyer asks.

"Do you recognize it, Mr. Ashton?" Officer Edwards asks, pushing the evidence bag across the table.

I stare at the blood-smeared tire iron encased in crinkled plastic in front of me. I do not answer him but say, "I'd like to make a phone call."

*

"I'M BEING SET up," I tell anybody in the interview room who will listen.

"Is that yours?" Officer Edwards asks again, pointing to the evidence bag.

The tension in my chest makes it difficult to breathe. "Yes, but—"

"Where were you between midnight and one a.m. the night Mr. Ray was murdered?"

I look up at the senior officer, my eyes crawling up to his rancorous glare. "I told you. I was home. In. Bed."

He points to the tire iron. "This bloody weapon tells me a different story."

Mr. Weldon is at my side, whispering and sounding like a chipmunk. His breath smells stale, like he's only just woken up. I shake my head at him as he mumbles for me to cooperate. He is persistent, telling Officer Edwards he wants to talk to me privately.

"I've still got a few questions," Officer Edwards says.

I sigh reluctantly, trying to block out both men, staring at the bare wall behind Officer Edwards' massive head. To the door, my last escape.

The police officer reaches for the evidence bag with the murder weapon and shoves it toward him. He grabs a pen out of his uniform front pocket and flips open his notepad. He squints at his pad, trying to focus, then looks up at me, refocusing his contemptuous stare.

"My mother is dying in the hospital," I tell him, groveling, trying to justify my actions, my voice trembling, almost stuttering. "I have to be with her."

Officer Edwards says, "I'm sorry about your mother, and I'll let you make your one phone call, but right now, I need you to answer my questions."

My fist comes down hard on the metal table. The officer sits back at my unexpected reaction. My attorney's cup of water spills across his paperwork to the table's edge, dripping into his lap. He grumbles and pushes away from the table, lunging for his briefcase, water pooling under his new leather briefcase.

"What the hell's wrong with you?" Mr. Weldon shoots me a hard stare. I feel, taste, and hear the exasperating rush of his breath in my face. "Control yourself."

I get up to jerk away from him.

Officer Edwards and his deputy stand in awe as if my solicitor and I put on a fabulous performance.

"Sit down," Officer Edwards says, the shape of his mouth turned downward, anger simmering on his pursed lips.

The door opens and a white-haired guard the size of my cellmate Dirk appears in the doorway. His face is hard and wrinkled, most likely from years of cigarettes and hard liquor. His blue eyes look faded and weak from age and time. "Officer Edwards, sir, you've got a phone call."

"Can you take a message?" he asks without turning and looking over his shoulder. He holds my gaze. "I'm in the middle of an interview."

The old guard says, "It's urgent, sir."

Officer Edwards grunts, sighs, and glares into his blank notepad. Wrestling with a nagging itch on the back of his head, he looks up at me with contempt, his eyes filling with hate. He turns to Deputy Taylor, and his words are lost in translation behind the young deputy's freckled face.

I am growing more impatient by the minute, my foot tapping the floor.

Officer Edwards slides out of his chair and stands. He heads to the door to join the older gentleman standing in the doorway. "I'll be right back," Edwards says, turning and jamming a finger at me. He mutters something under his breath and slams the door behind him.

After he is gone, I turn and vent to my lawyer, "This is bullshit. I need to get to the hospital. My mother is dying—"

He holds out a hand to me, fingers swollen from age, his fatty skin swallowing the ring's edges. He tries to calm me but without success. He looks to the young deputy, shakes his head as if embarrassed by me, and turns back to his opened briefcase, rummaging through the sheaf of loose-leaf papers, brushing beads of sweat from his face and forehead.

Minutes later, I hear determined footsteps approaching the room. I glance up when Officer Edwards enters, looking angrier and more agitated than before.

He hovers over the table and stares at me intensely, the flesh around his neck and cheek coloring as if from embarrassment or high blood pressure.

He paces the room, his hands on his waist. "Mr. Ashton. Mr. Ashton."

I force myself to look up at his pompous face. My heart bangs against my ribs. My leg trembles, my foot knocking. I pinch the inside of my palms with the ends of my sharp nails.

"I've got some good news," he says.

He baits me, keeping me in suspense. He pulls out a chair, sits, and shuffles unimportant papers in front of him. He says something only his deputy can hear and pulls away, snickering in an arrogant chuckle.

I feel my solicitor's eyes on me. He fiddles with a pen, clicking and unclicking it until I want to tear it out of his hand and slam it on the table.

I am boiling mad, my jaw tightening at the sight of Officer Edwards and my aggravating, useless public defender.

Officer Edwards stops pacing, turns to me, and asks, "Do you have a temper, Mr. Ashton?"

"What's the good news?" I retort, veering far from the issue of my unreasonably hot temper.

"My men have uncovered Mr. Ray's car," he says. A smile plays on his smug face.

Eli's car—this deepens the mystery of his whereabouts after he left my apartment the other night.

"Where'd you find it?" I ask.

"I ask the questions, Mr. Ashton."

"I have a right to know what's going on."

"When it's inconvenient for you, and you're not giving me the truth, is that it?" He grins. "That's not how this works."

"I haven't lied to you," I say.

"You haven't told me the complete truth either."

"Ask me anything."

"In due time." He takes pleasure in torturing me.

We sit silently as if we have all the time in the world.

"Mr. Ray's car was found on the rocky embankment by the water's edge, parked under a tree," Officer Edwards continues.

"Where?" I ask, my curiosity piqued, turning questions repeatedly in my head.

"Outside a place called Mac's Bar in South Hero, Vermont."

I am numb, unable to move. What was Eli doing parked down at the water's edge at Mac's Bar? Why not just leave the car in the lot?

"The investigation yielded useful information," Officer Edwards continues, his voice and demeanor cryptic and cold.

My solicitor mutters questions into my ear at gunfire speed. I shake him off and look Officer Edwards in the face. "What did you find?"

"Drugs. Cocaine. Heroin. Fentanyl."

"Eli didn't use drugs."

He shrugs. "I don't care."

"Do you know why the car was parked by the lake?" I ask.

"I thought you'd be able to tell me."

"How would I know?"

"What were you doing at a bar in South Hero the previous evening?"

"You've got me confused with somebody else." Playing coy is not my forte.

"Do you think this is funny, Mr. Ashton?"

"I'm not laughing."

"This isn't a game," Officer Edwards says. "This is a murder investigation. Don't lie to me."

"I'm not lying."

"Feigning ignorance will not help your case. Answer my question."

Mr. Weldon taps my arm, a rattlesnake ready to strike.

I ignore him and glance into Officer Edwards' stony gaze.

"One of my officers was on the phone with a witness at Mac's Bar," Edwards says. "According to that witness, you were seen snooping around the premises, asking questions about your friend Mr. Ray."

Who did Edwards speak to, I wonder. The bartender, or the drag queen, or the elderly neighbor across the hall from Eli's room.

"You've got some explaining to do," Edwards says.

I sit back in my chair, and the room goes disconcertingly quiet. Hairs on my arms prickle, and I stand up. "I don't know anything about drugs or my ex-boyfriend's car. But I do know those drugs don't belong to Eli."

"That's not how it looks from my perspective," Officer Edwards says.

"Eli was being set up."

"How do you know that?"

I swallow hard, but my mouth is so dry it hurts. "I know Eli. He didn't have anything to do with drugs."

"Was he dealing them?"

Dealing? My head is spinning. I try to recall the conversation with Eli's neighbors back at Mac's Bar. The old woman said something about hearing Eli's male visitors bullying him about drugs. Eli was in some trouble, I know. I shake my head at Edwards. "Eli would never deal."

Deputy Taylor coughs, breaking the stillness. I pick at a thin scab of skin on my right knuckle, and Mr. Weldon is murmuring in my ear again.

"What can you tell me about your visit to Vermont?" Officer Edwards asks.

I turn to my solicitor and mouth a conspicuous no, my mouth shaped into a wide O, when he asks me to tell Edwards the truth.

I can't. If I disclose my discovery of Eli's thoughts in the contexts of his brown leather journal, I'd be relinquishing the truth about a man whom I cared for and loved. I would not hurt him.

"Mr. Ashton?"

"I don't know anything," I say.

Officer Edwards leans against the table. I can see the reprimand in his eyes. "It will be a long night for you, Mr. Ashton."

Chapter Thirty-Three

I AM BACK in my cell across from scoundrels Pitman and Dirk.

"You promised me my phone call," I yell to Officer Edwards as he locks me back into my ten-by-twenty cement block. My request goes unanswered, my voice echoing down the long, empty corridor to nothingness.

Pitman snarls back. "Shut up."

"Fuck you!" I bang my hands against the bars, thrashing hard, until a nettling of pain shoots down my arm, my palms raw and sore. "Officer! I need to call the hospital. Now!"

Ceiling lights flicker and dim, and the hallway darkens.

Hopeless, I stop fighting, engulfed with fatigue. I doubt that I'll ever see my mother alive again. My arms fall to my sides. My head is swimming, delusional from lack of sleep. I stumble backward to the cold, hard cot in the corner of the room.

Falling onto the filthy mattress, I pull my knees up.

My eyes start to close, and I fall in and out of a dreamless sleep.

When I wake an hour later, a pear-shaped silhouette fills the cell's door. I knuckle my tired eyes and bite back the taste of bile rising in my throat. I am woozy, feeling drugged, hungover, or waking from a concussion.

Nauseated, I think I might vomit. The light is back on in the dingy hallway. I squint and groan against the intensity of the illumination.

"Ralph, you awake?" It is my solicitor, Mr. Leonard Weldon.

I mumble, "Go away."

"Ralph, we need to talk."

"Go away." I turn over and close my eyes to the wall.

"It's important you cooperate with Officer Edwards."

"I've got nothing to say."

"How about the truth?"

"I don't know what you're talking about. My mother—"

"I'll get you that phone call," he says. "Just kill the sarcasm. It's hurting your case."

The bedsprings pop and screech as I shift and turn my head halfway to see the large figure staring at me in the shadows on the other side of the bars.

"You're nothing if not persistent," I say.

Leonard sighs heavily, and it sounds like he is taking his last breath. "I can walk. You'll be on your own."

"Knock yourself out."

"Or I can spend my time helping you so you can see your mother."

I pause.

He says, "I believe in you, Ralph."

I swallow back the bitter taste of defeat. "I didn't kill Eli."

"I believe you. But it's not me who you have to convince."

I pull myself up and sit against the wall, my feet hanging over the narrow edge of the musty-smelling mattress. I try to hold steadfast, but the burden of the last twenty-four hours plummets me into a feeble state of restlessness. After a prolonged beat, I ask, "What must I do?"

Leonard heaves a sigh. "Answer me this: Did you find anything at Eli's apartment in Vermont relevant to this case?"

Confess or not confess? "Nothing," I finally say.

"Why'd you go there?"

"To see if I could find anything about what happened to Eli."

"Keeping silent doesn't make you look good."

"At this point, nothing I say will."

"Tell me again where you got that black eye. Who gave it to you?"

I fight the urge to follow the broken path of my repetitive past. "I told you. I fell and hit my face against the corner of my coffee table."

"How?"

"I was drunk. It's been a tough year."

Mr. Leonard judges me through determined persistence.

"You don't have to believe me," I say.

"It's not me—"

"Officer Edwards is a lost cause. It doesn't matter what I say. The man is so high on his fucking horse to believe anything I tell him."

"It's your bad boy attitude that will get you into trouble and keep you behind bars."

"I'm still here."

"Behind bars is not where you want to be, Ralph." He turns and looks down the long corridor. A light at the end of the hall flickers in the shadowy corner.

"I need to get out of here," I tell him. "Like tonight. I have to see my mother."

"With your long list of lies, I doubt you'll see the light for a week. Maybe longer."

"It's your job to get me out of here, Leonard."

"I can't help you if you're unwilling to cooperate with the police."

"I'm telling them everything I know."

"I don't believe that." There is a pause, then he asks, "Do you know anything about the drugs that authorities discovered in Mr. Ray's car?"

My head is heavy, and I close my eyes. "Eli never took drugs. At least, not when we were together." I open my eyes and look in Leonard's direction. "He wouldn't do it."

Leonard is quiet. He shuffles in his loafers. "Is there a possibility you didn't know everything about Mr. Ray and his goings-on when the two of you were separated?"

I don't want to know the whole truth, I tell myself. I want to remember Eli the way he was when we were together. I recall what I have read in his journal, and the idea that Eli could have been a drug dealer and involved in shady dealings with evil men is a real possibility, something I hope never to discover. "I don't know what to believe anymore."

"That may be true, but you must be real with me right now."

"You sound like Officer Edwards," I say. "Is that your idea of un-biased representation?"

"I want to help you, Ralph. But you're making it impossible for me to do my job."

"Then go ask Officer Edwards if I can make that phone call to the hospital. I need to get an update on my mother." I lean down and get a whiff of my smelly underarms. "I'm starting to stink like garbage. I need to get out of here, shower, and get on with my life. My mother needs me."

Leonard says, "I'll see what I can do."

I hear Pitman and Dirk whistling in their cell over the padding of my attorney's footfalls, heavy and indomitable, like a herd of elephants.

"How's Little Bo-Peep holding up?" Pitman jeers.

Closing my eyes, trying to block out his infuriating voice, I clench my fists at the irritating tone of his strangled whistles. When he laughs, he starts coughing. In my mind, I see my mother lying in the hospital, the horror of cancer eating at her slowly and voraciously.

Dirk warns his cellmate to shut up, or he'll "knock him out cold."

They grumble back and forth, and I hear a door open and someone walking toward us, the bottom of his shoes squeaking across the lino-leum.

Leonard is out of breath, his face flushed and sweaty with a rosacea-like redness. "I got Officer Edwards to allow you to make that call," he says.

I jump up. "Thanks."

"Now, look here, Ralph. I'm on your side."

"I know." *I think.*

"Then knock the chip off your shoulder. I'm trying to help you. I can walk away, no question."

I nod. "Fine. Thanks. I mean it."

*

"YOU'VE GOT FIVE minutes," Edwards says, telling me to hold out my hands through the bars so he can cuff me.

I follow him to a small windowless room off the central station. The walls are as white as clouds. It smells cleaner too. Disinfectants sting my nose and eyes.

A beer-bellied guard with a foul eighties haircut and stooping posture from years of slouching takes his position against the back wall.

"Ten minutes," he reminds me in his terse, old man's voice.

Mr. Weldon tells me he will be waiting for me in the hall.

I order him to go home. "I am going to be here all night, and there's nothing else you can do."

He refuses. I'm not in the mood to mince words. He is a trooper; I give him that, and despite my irritation with him, I am incredibly grateful and enormously thankful to have somebody fighting for me.

I stumble with the phone the first time, my hands bound so tightly that the handcuffs cut into my wrists. "Can you loosen these?" I ask the guard, but he shakes his head no, his tiny hands folded across his chest.

"You've got eight minutes," he says.

"Jesus," I mumble, reaching for the phone and struggling to steady my shaky hands.

I call County Hospital and ask the front desk receptionist to connect me with the third-floor nurse's station.

A young female nurse answers on the fourth ring and introduces herself as Tiffany. "May I please speak to my mother Doris Ashton's nurse, Claire?"

"Claire is making her rounds," she says. "She'll be a few minutes."

"It's an emergency," I say. "I don't have a lot of time to talk. I need to speak to her ASAP."

"Let me see what I can do." She sounds annoyed when she puts me on hold, and the line fills with elevator music.

Billy, the guard, reminds me that I have five minutes left.

"I'm on hold," I say over my shoulder.

"Five minutes." He smells of cigarettes. I get a whiff of him ten feet behind me.

I let out an exasperated sigh, and the chirpy sweet song changes three times before I hear Claire on the other end of the line, sounding miffed and tired. "Hello, Mr. Ashton." Her voice is grave.

Mr. Ashton. Not Ralph.

"I'm calling about my mother," I say, my voice frayed, weak, and frantic.

"It's best you come as soon as you can."

"What's happened?"

"It's that time."

I know what's coming. Woozy, I lean against the wall, my thoughts reeling, my gut clenching.

"Your mother has taken a turn for the worse." She sounds stressed.

"I was just there," I say. "My mother was talking and laughing and cracking jokes."

"Like I've explained to you before, cancer is unpredictable. We can never be certain how the patient—"

"So, now, my mother is just a patient to you?"

The guard hovers close behind me, and I smell the cloying scent of cigarettes. Maybe it's me, I think. Fear smells like death.

He taps me hard on my shoulder. I jerk forward and hold a finger to stall him for another minute.

"Your mother isn't reacting to the medication," Claire says in my ear, and her tone is gentler and more compassionate. "She's getting weaker."

"I can't believe it. I was just with my mother. She was bossing me around and being sarcastic like the old days. She was laughing." I am saying this more to myself than to Claire.

"Cancer is unpredictable," she says again, and this time, I weigh her words more seriously, and my eyes fill up. I fight the urge to cry over the phone. My throat tightens. My breath is rushed.

I hear Billy the guard shifting and grunting behind me, the impatient motherfucker. I shift to find a different position on my unsteady legs, pulling up my sloping shoulders; disconcertingly, my feet slide forward and backward under my chair.

I envision my mother lying in the hospital bed, unresponsive, her eyes closed to the world, to me. I cannot hear her honey-sweet laughter or see the light in her eyes. Her life is dimming and dying.

I can no longer control my emotions: My eyes are moist and misty, my cheeks burning with the salty sting of tears.

"Ralph?" Claire's tired voice pulls my thoughts back to the conversation. She tells me to come to the hospital now to be with my mother, but I lie to her and tell her that I'm out of town, visiting a friend.

"I didn't get to say everything I wanted to her," I tell Claire.

"Get here as soon as you can."

A lull, then I hear Billy telling me to hang up.

I wipe away a fat tear in my eyes and sniffle back a string of snot sneaking out from both of my nostrils.

"Claire?" I say and feel Billy's ghostly hand on the phone's handset.

"I'm still here," she says.

"Do me a favor."

She waits.

Before Billy yanks the phone out of my hand, I say, "Tell my mother that I love her."

Chapter Thirty-Four

IN MY CELL, I dream of Eli and pray for my mother.

I might never see or speak to Mom again.

Pitman's snoring is growing more aggravating, a sledgehammer bashing against my skull. I want to scream across the hall at the dirtbag and smother Pitman with a pillow. My hands tremble with palsy cramps, and I cover my ears to mask the noise.

Later, sometime in the dead hour, I wake to Officer Edwards aiming a flashlight in my face and the dark, fuzzy outline of my attorney Leonard Weldon standing next to him, waking me up with game-changing news.

My mouth is heavy and tastes stale and metallic, like dirty coins. I dig sleep out of my eyes and yawn, wincing against an intense pain building up like fire in my head.

"Mr. Ashton, you need to come with me," Officer Edwards says, rattling the bars with his keys.

"Is it my mother?" I ask groggily, sitting up.

"Come." It is my solicitor, his voice gravelly and demanding.

I run a hand through the knotty tangles in my hair. When I pull away, my fingers are filmy and greasy.

"I don't have all night," Officer Edwards says. "Chop-chop." He is impatient, determined, and authoritative.

"I want to know about my mother's prognosis," I say.

"My visit with you tonight is regarding your ongoing investigation, not your mother," he says, his tone grave and demanding.

"There's a shift in Mr. Ray's murder," my attorney says, and I catch Officer Edwards eyeing Mr. Weldon with disdain as if he's released a dirty little secret privy only to them.

"What does that mean?" I ask, standing.

"I can't discuss it here, Mr. Ashton," Edwards says. "You need to follow me."

I look to where Mr. Weldon stands in the inky shadows beside Edwards, antsy like a five-year-old child. As he nods, both of his double chins wobble in the overly bright fluorescents.

Following directions is outside my vocabulary, but I obey this time because the police officer sounds urgent. I walk to the bars and turn around to let Edwards bind my hands before he opens the door.

When the cell doors slide open, I shuffle down the hall behind him. My wrists prickle from the restraints. Dirk is awake on his bunk as I pass his cell, and Pitman grumbles like a bear in hibernation, snug like a bug with his knees pulled to his chest.

Officer Edwards opens the heavy metal door, and I glimpse his exhaustion, dark circles under his eyes and a cache of deep furrowed wrinkles lining his forehead and face.

In a room adjacent to the cell block, the officer orders me to take a seat. My attorney is at my side, his big hand on my back, ushering me into the airless room.

There is a window on the far wall, but it is too dark outside to see life passing by without me. "This again?" I say, pushing against my solicitor's hand to proceed into the cell. "I'm tired and all talked out. I've got nothing more to say. I don't know anything about Eli's death."

"You're going to want to hear what I have to say," Edwards says, his eyes reproachful and alert, squeezing himself through Leonard and the tight-fitting space of the doorframe. He stands in front of me, pointing a finger in my face. "Sit down."

There is a grumbling in the back of his throat, his expression obstinate and frightening. I fear the night hour is turning him into something otherworldly, so I sit and catch Mr. Weldon nodding furiously behind him, urging me to sit and listen, dabbing his damp face with the back of his hairy knuckles.

"I'll be right back," Officer Edwards says, leaving the room.

"What the hell is this about?" I ask my solicitor once the officer is gone.

Mr. Weldon waddles around the table, pulls out a chair, and sits beside me. He gives an unabridged explanation of tonight's wake-up call and the latest news. He sounds like a squirrel on speed.

"I don't understand a word you're saying," I say. He blinks back furiously, his long, spidery eyelashes fluttering. "Leonard, are you all right?"

Catching his breath, he says, "I'm fine. It's about your case."

"What about my case?"

He blinks a few times and swallows. "Officer Edwards told me not to say anything. He'd rather tell you."

"Why are you here?" I ask.

"For moral support."

"What time is it?"

He fingers the Rolex on his wrist and answers, "Four forty-five."

A sigh. "Jesus Christ. I need to see my mother."

Ten or fifteen minutes later, Officer Edwards enters the room and pulls out a chair. He sits and fiddles with an envelope in his hands. He opens it and rustles papers.

"What's going on?" I ask, seizing Officer Edwards with my watchful stare.

He pulls himself up straight and clears his throat. He looks like he's been through a few battles. He fidgets with the dog-eared corner of a white envelope.

"We got an anonymous call a few hours ago that your apartment was broken into."

"A few hours ago? Why am I being informed now? And what the fuck is going on?"

"You're still in police custody," Officer Edwards continues. "I've got a lot of questions to ask you."

I am wide awake, looking at my attorney and Officer Edwards. I am stunned, perplexed, speechless. My hands are shackled together in front of me, and I am asking all the essential questions: who, what, why, and when.

Edwards takes another breath. "My partner, Officer Taylor, took the call. We're still working on it."

"Do you have anybody in custody?" I ask.

He nods, and I see in his red-rimmed eyes that he is not telling me everything. Maybe he can't for legal reasons, but I ask if I can identify the asshole who broke into my apartment.

"Yes," he says, "but we've only apprehended two of the three suspects."

"There are *three* suspects?" I turn to Mr. Weldon for support.

He clamps a hand on my shoulder, reassuring me everything will be all right.

"When my officers got to the scene, they witnessed the third suspect escaping through a side window in the building. They lost him running through the woods and across the Saranac River."

I keep quiet.

"We've also uncovered drugs in a vehicle belonging to one of the suspects early this morning," he added.

I wait for him to continue.

"The drugs are similar to those we found in Mr. Ray's car in Vermont. We've also got part of a confession."

"A confession?" I say, shaking my head.

"To the murder of Mr. Ray."

"What did the suspect say?"

"I can't disclose that information during an ongoing investigation."

"What does this mean for me?" I ask.

"We're still interrogating the suspects, Mr. Ashton. It might be a while."

Time that I don't have.

"I didn't kill Eli," I say. "It wasn't me."

Edwards steeples his hands together in a tent on the table. "The pieces are coming together."

I spread my hand out in question, the chain rattling under my erratic movements. "What does that mean?"

"We're getting close to an arrest, but I've still got some questions to ask you."

"Ask away."

"In time."

"I don't have time, officer. I need to see my mother. She's dying." Tears fill my eyes, and my voice cracks, beaten and broken.

Edwards tidies his paperwork and closes the manila envelope, looking at me with a weary, complacent stare. His face is unreadable. He pulls away and hides his hand on his lap. "Given recent events, I'll get to work on the paperwork to have you released. But first—"

"I'd like to see the suspects," I say.

He is hesitant, and I'm not sure he will indulge my curiosity. He stays seated, rolling ideas back and forth in his tiny little head, picking at the corner of a piece of paper poking out from inside the envelope.

"Do you know what, if anything, the suspects were looking for in your apartment?" Officer Edwards asks.

I shrug. "Beats the fuck out of me."

"Wait here," he finally says and stands, opens the doors, and yells down the hall for another officer.

Officer Taylor, the tall, wet-behind-the-ears, freckle-faced redhead, rushes into the room, his pace and temperament both hurried. He looks more alert than Officer Edwards, but his face is blank, disquieting, and tired. He holds his hand at me and gestures for me to follow him. I stand and shuffle over to the edge of the door.

We walk along a quiet corridor, and my insides turn to liquid. My heart pumps hard, and my hands are greasy with sweat.

We stop at a closed door. As Officer Taylor grips the knob, turns a key into the slot, and swings the door open, I am met with a one-way mirror on the far wall. The young man gestures to me inside. I shuffle to the mirror and stand before it, my heart knocking like a jackhammer. I wait for the officer to open the curtain and reveal two faces.

My breath catches as he crosses in front of me to the corner of the room. He pulls on a cord, and the thin white curtain slides to the side.

I stand ramrod straight.

My neck is damp and sticky, prickly with fear and heat.

The curtain opens. Faces are revealed.

I gape, open-mouthed, at the two men staring straight back at me from the other side of the glass.

Holy shit!

Chapter Thirty-Five

"THAT'S HIM," I say.

"That's who?" Officer Taylor stands with his arms crossed.

I gently touch the one-way glass. "The man with the blond hair. I've seen him before." A shotgun warning comes out like a barrage of pellets.

"You've seen him before?" Officer Taylor is too close to me; I can smell his sweat infusing the small nook of space around us.

"The man with the blond curls and blue eyes," I say.

"Where did you see him?"

I stare at the man with a surfer dude physique, ripped in a tight white tank top and a bracket of rubber bracelets on both wrists. And that familiar tattoo on his neck.

"Mr. Ashton?" Taylor's young boy North Country drawl is barely a whisper, but it sounds like a grenade exploding in my head.

"He was at the hospital," I say.

"The hospital?"

"Yes!" I cringe at the rage and hate boiling in the depths of my gut. My lip quivers, and the heat of my anger curls the ends of my hands as I glare at the surfer guy's smug face.

"When was he at the hospital?" Officer Taylor asks.

"Last night."

"I'll let Officer Edwards know."

"Wait." I grab the deputy's arm as he skirts toward the door.

I see his befuddled reflection in the glass. "Mr. Ashton?" he says, piqued.

"He's been following me," I say, reflecting on the suspect's recent travels.

"Who?"

I point at the man with the blond hair. "I know where I've seen him before last night at the hospital."

It doesn't take long before Officer Edwards enters the interrogation room where I sit beside my solicitor and across from Deputy Taylor, both men looking chaotic and restless. Officer Edward holds a cup of coffee in his hand as he comes up beside me, asking me what I know about the suspects.

I block out his words and am thinking about my mother; her face blurred in the lines of time, half shrouded between here and there, earth and deadland, on the cusp of loss.

I don't want to believe that she is already gone. She'll be far off to the land of the dead before I can say a proper goodbye.

Officer Edwards is in my head again, asking what I know, spilling coffee on his shirt and tie, the dark-brown liquid staining the wrinkled creases of his pants.

He lets out a battered breath, and as he sets his coffee cup on the long table, I notice the slight tremor in his right hand. It's been shaking all night.

Edwards clears his throat and shuffles next to me, his cloying cologne smelling sweet like fresh-cut grass. He stands tall, rugged, and professional, like a man in charge. As a man in his position, he should, but I notice his vulnerability, and my mother's smile crosses my face, the air of bogus confidence we all wear as a mask when we leave the house.

"Tell me about the man on the left," Officer Edwards says, sliding photos across the table at me.

My breath shudders, and I'm not aware that he is speaking to me until he repeats his question louder, a forceful gale of words slipping off his tongue into my ear. "Mr. Ashton."

I swallow back the vile taste of animosity coating my mouth, my gaze glued on the man with blond curls in the glossy headshot. "I've seen him before."

"Where?" Officer Edwards sounds annoyed.

"On the ferry—" I stop mid-sentence and glance up at Edwards, half staring at him and the suspect. I feel the officer's heavy gaze on me, burrowing through me like a long-range red light.

I turn back to the man with muscles and menace. He watches me, straight-faced, unblinking. "He followed me on the ferry back and forth from Vermont," I tell Edwards. I pause to collect my thoughts. "He was riding a motorcycle."

Without taking my eyes off my mysterious fellow in the photo, I see Officer Taylor and Officer Edwards exchanging looks with each other. They bob their heads and shift, their boots squeaking on the waxy floor.

I say, "I've explained to Officer Taylor that I'd seen the same man with that distinctive tattoo at the hospital last night." I do not take my eyes off the beach-blond man.

"Do you know why this man would be at the hospital or your apartment earlier this evening?" Officer Edwards asks.

I shrug. "To scare me. Kill me. I don't know."

"To kill you? Why would you say that?"

I do not take my eyes off the guy's piercing blue eyes as I answer Officer Edwards, "If he's admitted to killing Eli, I have a feeling he was coming after me too."

Heat crawls into my neck at the mention of my ex-boyfriend. I want to smash through the one-way mirror and beat the two scoundrels senseless.

"Do you know the second suspect in the other room, Mr. Ashton?" Officer Edwards asks.

"I've never seen him before. Just the man on the motorcycle." I tap the face in the photo lying on the table.

"How do the suspects know where you live, Mr. Ashton?"

Another shrug. I'm so distracted and irritated from the last twenty-four hours. "They've been following me from Vermont. But I don't know how they'd know where I live." My throat is scratchy; my mouth is as dry as dust. My armpits itch from sweating so much. I need a long, hot bath to wash the stink and fatigue off me. A clammy stream of sweat trickles down my back.

My eyes are heavy and want to close.

"Have you seen any suspicious activity around your apartment lately?" Edwards asks.

I start to shake my head, but a niggling feeling stops me. I recall the night I was awakened by the sounds of Eli talking to someone on the phone. He had denied any such incident. Maybe it was one of these goons.

Then, the night before I was to leave on a trip to Vermont, the day after Eli's body was found, I remember a vehicle idling at the edge of the Saranac River, the sounds of a car horn blaring outside my bathroom window.

I share my thoughts with Officer Edwards.

"Why didn't you tell us about this earlier?" He rubs his neck, angles it, and cracks it.

"I didn't think it was important at the time," I say.

"Until now?"

I nod.

"I think you know more than you're letting on, Mr. Ashton."

Chapter Thirty-Six

I ASK OFFICER Edwards if talking here in the interrogation room would be all right. "I don't want to go back to my cell."

He nods. "Would you like something to drink?" he asks, his voice taking on a kinder tone.

"I'd like to get out of here. I want to see my mother."

"I'll release you soon, considering our suspects are in custody. But I'd like to get answers to those questions you just raised."

I force a weak nod and fight to keep my head up, eyes open, alert, and focused.

"Did you see the person inside the vehicle near your apartment?" he asks.

"No."

"What kind of vehicle was it?"

I shake my head. "I don't know. It was dark. It was hidden in shadows under trees by the river."

Officer Edwards leans forward on his elbows, deep wrinkles lining the middle-aged skin of his dog-tired face.

"Can I go?" I ask, almost pleading.

He finishes writing his last thoughts, caps his pen, and looks at me. "Let me get the paperwork ready for you to sign."

A weak smile spreads across my face briefly.

Officer Edwards pushes out of his chair and stands. He gathers his notebook and pen and stares down at me. "Where are you going to stay tonight?"

I have to think about it. "I don't know."

"I'm sorry to hear about your mother."

I suck in a deep breath as a flood of tears assaults me, and I lean on the tabletop and release all the built-up sadness.

Edwards lingers in the doorway. "Sorry about ransacking your apartment yesterday," he says.

I raise my head and wipe my face with my fingers. "You were just doing your job."

"It's probably not a good idea for you to return to your apartment tonight."

"I'll spend the night at the hospital."

"I can put you up at a motel for a few days if you'd like."

"Thanks, but I can take care of myself."

"Tell that to your black eye," he says.

I smile at Officer Edwards's cheap shot.

"I'll be right back." He opens the door and steps out into the hall, calling for his partner, a slight limp on his leg.

Fifteen minutes later, I sign a consent form with Officer Taylor at the front desk and gather the belongings confiscated from me when I first arrived. I thank my solicitor for his service, shake hands, and mince a few meaningless words.

I ask a sixtyish male officer sitting behind a glowing computer screen on my way out of the lobby to call me a taxi.

I sit on the curb for ten minutes, waiting. A female Asian driver picks me up and drops me off at the hospital. I pay the fare and race toward the automatic main entrance doors, then take the stairs to the third floor. My stomach sinks when the doors open, and I run out of the elevator, past the nurses' station. I don't see Claire or Diane anywhere. The hallways are eerily quiet.

My heart catches in my throat when I reach my mother's room. Behind the other side of the closed door is the end of my life. I say a silent prayer that my father isn't inside. I hear a voice behind me whispering my name. I turn around to see Claire lumbering toward me from down the hall. She looks the worse for wear. As she walks toward me, her face bears terrible news.

She extends her arms, embracing me. She pats my back and says, "I'm here if you need to talk to somebody."

I whisper a firm "thank you," wiping my eyes with the heel of my hand.

I take a deep breath and head inside my mother's hospital room.

*

IT IS THE sound of gasping that the nurse warns me about before I join my mother in her last moments. "The sounds may startle you, but your mother can't feel anything. It'll be more uncomfortable for you than her."

The room is unpleasantly quiet, except for my mother's wheezing.

This is the final curtain call.

I stand across the room and lean against the wall, frightened, angry, and sad. Tears fall fast and hard, my body shuddering.

My mother lies under a thin white sheet, her head propped on a pillow peppered with her delicate, dark hair. I can see her scalp.

She is emaciated, mummified, the bedsheet tucked firmly around the skeletal outline of her body. She is heavily medicated in a morphine coma. The nurse tells me that she can still hear me.

I watch her right shoulder lift and fall with each short gasp. It is startling because I think she is asleep, not dying.

I move around the side of the chair to the foot of my mother's bed. I hover like a stranger in the dark, watching the inevitable end of a wonderful mother slipping from me.

My shoulders start to somersault forward. I move closer to the portable table on the side of the bed, which lodges her hairbrush, paper cup of water, assorted pack of gummy Jolly Ranchers from the gift shop, and a stuffed purple monkey, the gift from me.

I slip my hand under her swollen fingers, skin bloated and spongy from the medication. I pull a chair out from the corner where she sat to eat her lunch on good days and move it closer to the edge of the bed.

"I'm sorry I couldn't be here sooner," I whisper, but my words are lost on the heart monitor beeping in the shadowy corner. "There are so many things I still want to tell you."

I lay my head across her arm. "Claire tells me you've been her best patient." Tears blur my vision; a fissure in my voice cracks. "She told me you made her nights very entertaining." I raise my head. "You were the center of my life, Mom. You made many sad days brighter. You made me laugh. Those were my happiest moments together."

My jaw trembles.

"You were my best friend, my teacher, and a damn good mother. I'm going to miss you." I sniffle and stare up at the gaunt, bony face of a woman I don't recognize anymore. I whisper, "I love you," as I hold her warm smile back in my mind.

I stand to kiss the top of her forehead. I wrap my arms gently around her cold, bony shoulders. "I don't want to let go," I say.

She smells like gingerbread, and my childhood days of baking with Mom in the kitchen appear in a white orb of light as if I am waking from a dream.

But it is not a dream.

I fall into the chair and sit with Mom; the last few hours are long and excruciating.

Close to midnight, my mother stops breathing. I jolt awake as if startled by a noise. I am holding her hand, sitting next to her in silence, as I envisioned it: Mom and me.

I wait for the night shift nurse, a young college intern named Chris with a pleasant bedside manner, to come into the room and listen to my mother's heart to pronounce her dead.

He checks the heartbeat in three different places, and on the third time, he lifts the stethoscope from her chest and wraps it around his scrawny neck. He turns to me sitting in the corner chair, my neck asleep and numb and prickling from resting on it at an awkward angle, and conveys his condolences. "I'm sorry for your loss."

He waits with me as I hold my mother's hand. I push out of the chair I'm sitting in and kiss her on the forehead. "I'm going to miss you, Mom. I love you." I stare at my mother for the last time.

Before the intern leaves the room, he asks me if I need anything. I tell him no and hug him. He pats me on the back and heads down the hall to the nurses' station.

I ask Claire about Lee, and she tells me she has not seen him in two days. "The last time we talked, he said to me that he couldn't stand to see your mother dying."

I make arrangements for my mother's body to be picked up by one of the local funeral homes.

We hug.

I stay with my mother for a few more hours.

Chapter Thirty-Seven

I HEAR OFFICER Edwards's voice in my head. "It's probably not a good idea for you to return to your apartment tonight."

I've got nowhere else to go, I tell myself, as I get out of the taxi and come around the driver's side door to pay the driver.

She backs up and drives away, and I turn, staring out at the Saranac River next to my apartment and the dusky outline of sunrise climbing over the distant horizon behind a bank of oaks, maples, and sycamores.

Crime scene tape flutters in the wind, tied loosely around the thick bark of trees.

The urgency in the wind ruffles my hair.

Hunched forward against a gusty wind, I walk to the front door and force myself to climb the stairs to my apartment on the fifth floor.

My legs feel rubbery when I reach the top.

Sliding the key into my door lock is useless. The door is ajar.

I hedge, pushing the door further open slowly with the tip of my boot and staring inside the semi-dark apartment. I notice overturned furniture and window curtains ripped off their rods. This is different from the work of Officer Edwards from earlier in the morning, but someone else, I presume. Behind me, I hear a chain lock sliding open and the raspy hinges of a door creaking open.

It is my neighbor down the hall—Mr. Williams. He pokes his head out into the hallway. He stares at me and dabs at his snowy mustache.

The florescent light pales his old-man features.

"Do you ever sleep?" I ask sarcastically. "Mind your business."

His response is a terse sigh.

I start to head into my ransacked apartment and feel assaulted as I step into my now safe place. But then I hear Mr. Williams mumble behind me, his voice low, stifled, almost inaudible. Something in his snappish tone seizes me.

"You've had company tonight," he says.

I lean half in/half out of my apartment. "What did you see?"

He jabs a shaky finger my way. "Not what. Who. You've had visitors."

"Who did this—?" Then it dawns on me. I start down the hall toward Mr. Williams. I stand before his apartment door, pondering my insomniac, nosy neighbor behind the giant owl-eyed bifocals and tufts of wiry, gray hair. His character hides in the folds of his leathery, worn face. He shrinks into the shadows of his apartment, gripping the door jamb, glaring at me as if I've interrupted his morning, frightened and cautious in cowering posture, measuring me in deep scrutiny. He tries to close the door in my face, and he should, given I haven't been the most outgoing of neighbors. I wedge my foot in the doorframe.

"You've had visitors," Mr. Williams reiterates.

I nod, my arms falling as if conceding to a long, hard battle. "Did you tip off the police earlier this morning about the break-in?"

"I was watching TV and couldn't sleep. I heard a noise and came out to see what was happening."

In the vestiges of my fatigue, I reach out to him. "You saved my life, old man."

He stares at me, then at my outstretched hand, looking at my peace-making gesture of gratitude and debating whether to reciprocate.

"Thanks anyway." I retract my sweaty hand and return to my apartment.

At my doorway, I turn to see Mr. Williams watching me from the dark corner of the corridor. He looks shifty, uncertain, and dodgy. He slinks back into the mothball stench of his environs.

At the sound of his door closing and the dead bolt sliding back into place, I head into my apartment. My first instinct beckons me to the closet, where Eli's journal lies under a scattering of blankets where I left it.

I dig around for it and clutch it to my chest as I stumble back into the bedroom where the most terrifying realization of my life becomes clear: I am in life-threatening trouble. Clothes and shoes and end tables lie in a heap on the floor, next to broken lamps and chinaware my mother gifted me.

My thoughts are numb, like a beer buzz. I feel violated, staring around the strange surroundings of my new dangerous life.

What were the intruders looking for? I wonder.

Angry, disoriented, and hopeless, I fall against the wall and slide to the floor, hugging Eli's journal against my chest as if it were a shield.

Fatigue crawls into my body like a snake shedding its skin, the invasive weight of the past seventy-two hours enveloping me in a boa-constrictor embrace. My eyes start to close. As I lean against the wall, I lose my grip on the journal, which lands with a thud next to me.

The muffled sound of a car door shutting wakes me. The stairwell door opens at the end of the hall. The carpeted corridor stifles approaching footsteps.

I turn my blurry gaze up, the bleak watercolor light spilling into the window above my head. The sky is the color of a fading campfire, and soon, the morning light burns bright and illuminates a new day. The sound of birdsong stimulates my weary spirits, and I drift off again, dreaming about my mother and Eli.

Tears prick my eyes and taste coppery in my mouth. I lick my lips and jolt out of my semi-consciousness to the sound of tires crunching along the snow in the parking lot below.

Through the closed windows, I hear a violent wind blowing off the river, the roaring gusts grumbling like nightmarish creatures.

I pull myself up and amble to the apartment door, rubbing my eyes. I turn the lock and head down the hall to the bathroom, sidestepping blankets, bath towels, and clothes strewn across my path.

In the bathroom, my gut clenches, and I feel sick. I hover over the toilet seat and a projectile spray of vomit gushes into the john. I stand, gripping the counter for support; I dry heave into the sink.

I am half sick from seeing my mother in her final hours, her plastic wrap image and papery skin.

A grousing ache in my stomach produces another period of dry heaving, and I am reeling with abandonment, furious when I turn to the sink to wash my face. The image staring back at me in the mirror is crestfallen. I drop my head to catch my breath, and as I clasp the edge of the sink to secure my dizziness, I hear hushed movement—shuffling—coming from the living room.

Outside the bathroom window, thunder clashes, and a burst of lightning brightens the morning horizon. The furious orange flames of the sunrise shift to a blood-red slash of crimson.

My heartbeat quickens. Sloughing off my listlessness, I pull myself up to my full height and wander to the door. I stare up and down the hallway, to the bedroom and living area, then to the kitchen in the opposite direction.

Nothing. Nobody.

Quiet as the dead.

A chill in the air tickles my skin like someone tapping me on the back with a cold finger.

A headache pulses in the back of my eyes, and the prickly heat of something threatening coils around my limbs, tightening and strangling and warning, keeping me in place.

The floorboards groan in the hall outside my apartment door. I reach the bedroom, frozen in fear, my breath catching in my throat.

Muscles tighten in my legs. I stand against the wall and do not move.

I watch the erratic movement of somebody pacing back and forth outside my door. Frantically, I look around the room for my cell phone. Then, I recall where I left it: on the living room table by the window.

As I turn and scramble through overturned obstacles in my way, panic grips me as the sound of the doorknob rattles behind me. I freeze mid-motion, turning around at the apartment door. My heart beats hard, my stomach clutching. I am lightheaded and nauseous again.

A strike of knuckles on the apartment door jars me, and I jerk back a few inches. The dogged force of the *knock-knock-knock* leaves me shuddered and unnerved.

Then, all goes quiet.

I imagine my next-door neighbor, Mr. Williams, stopping by to tell me he is sorry or offering me condolences he didn't before. But he would have called out to me, wouldn't he? And let me know if it was him on the other side of the door.

Frightened, I tiptoe across the room, closer to the door. I peek through the aperture. The hallway is empty.

I notice shadows moving in the corners of my fuzzy periphery, growing and receding from my view.

I back away from the door, but it is too late. Like a sucker punch, the impact of a foot slamming into the wood knocks me backward. I scream. The door hinges splinter and snap off the frame, and the chain lock disengages. Paint and wood chips shower the air. The apartment door flies open. The corner of it hits me in the face and knocks me to the floor. I smack my head against the corner of the overturned coffee table.

Glass shatters under my weight as I topple into it.

Reeling with pain and confusion, I scramble into fight or flight mode, kicking and screaming for somebody to hear me.

The man standing over me is massive, as tall and muscular as a cottonwood tree. My eyes can't focus as fear and panic surge through my veins. I crawl around the room, reaching for safety, behind furniture or out through a window. The sound of gunshots blasts past my head, missing me by inches, the bullet grazing and lodging into the back wall near the window's fire escape.

My exit, I think, as I stumble toward the window.

Behind me, out in the hall, I hear voices, raised and frightened, as all my dark nightmares swallow my thoughts. I fall and crouch behind the futon for protection.

My heart slams into my chest. I wriggle toward the window. Footsteps come up quickly behind me as if a stampede of wild boar rushes toward me in unison—closer, closer, closer.

As I reach the edge of the windowsill, crouching and yanking on the window to open it, a firm hand settles on my shoulder, pulling me back. I white-knuckle the windowsill with both hands, hanging halfway outside to freedom, my visitor and me playing tug of war with my life. Then a hand grabs the waist of my pants and, with one giant heave, hurls me in a backward somersault into the apartment.

"What the fuck? Who are you?" I scream, scrambling on my butt to the far wall and breathing heavily; I can barely talk.

The man is Hulk-strong, and I feel the weight of his giant grip in the way my button pops from my jeans, the zipper being pulled down with enough force I reel with adrenaline—a skin flick gone wrong.

My eyes swim with tears as he reaches for me and tosses me like a rag doll on my stomach. My face smacks the floor as the intruder sits on the lower lumbar area of my back. "What do you want?" He muffles my cries with his rough calloused hand.

"Elijah owes us," he grunts, thrusting himself harder into my buttocks. "I'm here to collect."

I pry his meaty fingers away from my mouth long enough to stammer, "I don't know what you're talking about."

With a rough hand, he shoves a cloth into my mouth that smells and tastes like stale, sweaty boxers, silencing my cries.

"I want my money," he growls into my ear. His breath is rank.

As he positions himself to reach into his back pants pocket for something to bind my hands, I manage to bring my leg up to his groin and connect hard enough that he releases a piercing moan and loosens his hold. He falls back, panting.

I yank the dirty cloth out of my mouth and gulp in a lungful of air. I flip onto my back and stare up at the worn face of my bald intruder, a woman's nylon stocking concealing his features. His neck is as thick and wide as a footballer's, his solid body mass the result of a religious workout.

I muster whatever strength I have to raise my knees into his midsection and take a cheap chop between his eyes. I hear bone or cartilage break, and the man falls back and off me, swearing in pain.

"Fuck! My nose is broken." Blood fountains everywhere like a failed fire hydrant, all over my face and neck and the floor.

I retreat toward the window, fumbling as if limbless, praying I reach safety.

As I turn my back, I hear the intruder lumbering toward me like a tackling linebacker. Along the way, I scramble off the path and dart for my cell phone, lying face down on the floor a few inches from me. I grip it, but in my urgency to exit the apartment through the window, I trip over the edge of the raised carpet, and the phone flies from my hand out onto the fire escape. I hear it clattering across four flights of metal stairs to the ground.

The male stranger is at my back, mumbling about killing me, his outstretched hand grazing the fabric of my T-shirt and yanking me half-way through the window.

Alarm and adrenaline fuel my next move as I tear away from him, yelling obscenities for him to "get the fuck off me!" My T-shirt rips in his grasp.

I pull away from him and scrape the skin on my arms and stomach as I fall forward against the metal edge of the windowsill. I shake off the stinging pain and bloody gashes in my arms and legs as I scramble to my feet and fly down the fire escape stairs at rapid speed, taking the steps three at a time.

On my way down, I notice movement from other tenants behind closed apartment windows. My breath catches in my throat, and a cold sweat pops out on my face and neck against the chilly morning air.

I see the safety of the ground halfway down the fire escape as I turn and look up at my apartment window.

The man is not gone.

I stop to take a deep breath. My heart hammers hard.

I turn and hurry down the last ladder of the metal stairs, my feet two steps ahead of me. I almost fall when I reach the bottom.

I look around for my cell in the snow when I touch the frozen ground. There, near the side wall of the building, close to the fire escape ladder, I see it. I run under the metal structure and scoop it out of a pile of ice and snow. I fumble with the weak connection to reach a single bar to call for help. A few seconds later, I punch my password into the keypad and call 9-1-1. I look around the parking lot to see if anyone is around. It is deserted, except for a big white truck parked off the path by the water's edge, a gun rack, and a confederate flag emblem covering the back window of the dirt-splattered vehicle.

I've seen that truck before, I recall, remembering the men's faces in those photos and back at the police station. A red flag warning flashes across my mind.

Hands trembling, I glance at my phone, having trouble focusing on the call. Is it ringing? Then, from behind, the side door of the apartment swings open, slamming onto the side of the building. My morning visitors run toward me. I run like hell in the opposite direction toward the highway. Someone tackles me.

My phone flies from my hand and slides across the snowy surface, skidding across a mound of ice.

I hit my head hard against a pack of snow, and something feels disconnected in my neck, my head at an unnatural angle. A warm heat crawls over me, then white-hot pain. I pierce the still morning air with a scream. One of the men presses hard on my back and shoves me face-first into the snow. Like déjà vu, he sits on me with dead weight. Blood trickles from his bent nose onto my cheek, and as he smears it into my skin like a keepsake, he threatens me in a guttural grunt, "You're dog meat, buddy boy."

I close my eyes. I can't move. He pins my arms down with his hands while his partner crouches next to me and spits in my face. "Give us what we want, and we won't hurt you."

"What do you want?" I plead.

"Our money," the shorter of the two says, his eyes big and frightening. They stare at me in different directions.

"I don't have any money," I say. "Just let me go."

"Your boyfriend owes us."

In a gauzy haze, he sneers at me with a toothless grin. His face is bruised and mangled from a recent fight. He rears back with a white-knuckled fist, his meathead muscle posture silhouetted against a campfire-orange-flame sky.

"Get the fuck off me!" I yell as my cell phone buzzes ten feet away in a pocket of icy snow.

As the hulking man comes down hard on the left side of my face with his curled fist, knocking me into semi-unconsciousness, I hear distant police sirens roaring along the interstate, drawing near.

Chapter Thirty-Eight

A week later

"I'M SORRY TO hear about your mother," Dr. Matheson says when I sit in his office a week after two of my favorite people abandoned me.

I fidget with a loose thread on the cuff of my only nice herringbone button-down pink dress shirt, a present from my mother three birthdays ago. I wear it to keep her close.

Dr. Matheson looks younger since I last saw him. A rosy glow of lamplight on his desk shadows his face. He stands and paces the edge of the room to the picture window overlooking the rocky Saranac River, then turns to me. During this visit, he seems content and much more personal, moving around the room, keeping eye contact, and finding a seat in the oversized chair opposite me.

His hair looks thin and without product, falling across his broad shoulders. My gaze falls across the stiff muscles of his chest and arms stretching beneath the fabric of his light-blue turtleneck. He's been working out from the looks of it.

There's something different today, a tad off, I observe. He looks terrific, his eyes a mysterious deep winter blue. His skin is an artificial bronze tan as if he's been lying dormant in a tanning booth in my absence.

"It's been strange and lonely," I say, switching mental gears and adding, "Most days, it's hard to get out of bed."

"When I read about the tragedy of your ex-boyfriend and the situation you've been through with your mother, I tried calling you," he says, surprising me, buoying my spirits, an inviting warmth settling into my face and neck.

"I haven't had time." I look away, staring down at the floor, shifting my feet. Nervous, I yank and unspool the stringy thread from the end of my shirt, twirling the fabric between my fingers. "Being behind bars is fucking scary," I say, changing the subject and gesturing an apology with a glib hand. "I'm sorry. It's just been a whirlwind of emotions lately."

"You don't need to apologize, Ralph. You can speak freely here. There are no judgments."

He stares at the blossoming bruise on my face where I touch the tender flesh under my eye. "A memento from a stranger," I say.

"Do you want to talk about it?" he asks.

I reach for the second glass of water on the table before me. I look at my watch and realize our hour together is ending. "Maybe another day."

Looking around, I notice most of the furniture in the room has been rearranged or removed entirely from my last session. The sofa chairs by the window are gone, as if he is downsizing.

I take a long drink, set the glass back on the chipped wooden coaster, and settle into the comfortable leather chair. I stifle a breath, but a dull ache thuds in my chest. I close my eyes against the pain of seeing my mother's face in the dark recesses of my drowning thoughts.

"Ralph?" Dr. Matheson touches my arm. Through my thin cotton shirt, I can feel the heat of his hands, his fingers kneading my arm reassuringly, waiting for a reaction.

His touch is supporting and stimulating, and I wonder whether he knows he is breaking patient/client boundaries. I don't react.

As he waits for me to respond, his light gaze drifts to the floor at the sound of my sneakers tapping against the hardwood floor. The Oriental carpet is gone too, I realize.

Dr. Matheson's eyes find mine.

I stare into his handsome, inquiring face, feeling him analyzing me, searching for answers through the dogged determination of his silence, which is strangely soothing.

"I never thought that my mother would die so young," I say, and the words drum like a mariachi band in my head. "I'm going to miss her. She was my best friend."

Dr. Matheson turns and shifts in his seat. He gives me his undivided attention, the leather upholstery cracking. "How old was your mom, if I may ask?"

"Sixty-five."

He nods, and as he slides his arresting grip off my arm and sets his hand on his lap as if pondering something monumental, I feel alone again. I peel at a sore hangnail of skin dangling from my finger.

"What about your father?" he asks.

As if I'm elbowed in the stomach, a sharp, low pain stabs my nether region. "What about him?" I sound sarcastic, angry, and defensive. I don't know why.

"Are you close with him?"

"As close as God is to the Devil," I answer.

He watches me and waits, his face a mask of wonder.

I add, "He's an abusive alcoholic. I don't want anything to do with him."

"Have you spoken to him since your mother's funeral?"

"No. I don't have anything to say to him."

"What did the two of you talk about at the funeral?"

I heave a sigh. I know why I hate Lee. "He thanked me for going as if my presence was a fucking surprise. Of course, I'd be there. She was my mother. I was there for her, always. He wasn't."

Dr. Matheson fingers the neat outline of his beard, thinking about his next question. "How long was she in the hospital?"

"A year is too long to suffer." I choke up at my own words.

"Take your time." His hand is back on my arm.

Another head shake. "I feel guilty for not being with her when she needed me the most."

"But you were with her in the hospital when she died."

"I wish I had stayed in contact with her during the last year. We drifted apart, I guess. I, uh, I could've been there for her in the beginning."

"What made the two of you drift away?"

"Him." Contemptuous. I can't say his name. "I was also scared of seeing her withering away. Now, her dying scares me. I have nobody."

"When did you hear that your mother was in the hospital?" Dr. Matheson asks.

"I got a call from the bastard—"

"Your father?"

I nod and continue. "I was on the ferry coming back from Vermont."

We sit in deepening silence.

I play with the fabric of my shirt when Dr. Matheson asks, "I notice it's difficult for you to say your father's name. Or even call him Dad."

"He was never in my life growing up. He brought me into the world, but that's it. I never expected anything from him. Maybe that's because he was never physically or emotionally involved in my life. No strings attached, you could say. He had other priorities. I wasn't one of them. Neither was Mom."

"What happened at the funeral?" he asks. "Before we started our session, you said something about a scene with your father at the church?"

"He was drinking. I could smell it on his breath. It's about him. Everything is about him. He didn't care about anything but himself—

selfish, sociopathic asshole." I raise my voice. "He wasn't even there when Mom died and when we had to put her house for sale on the market. I did all that for her—not Lee. My mother's nurse, Claire, told me he hadn't been in to see her in her final hours."

"Why do you think that is?"

"I just told you. Lee is a selfish prick."

"Do you think he was scared—like you—to see his wife in the last stages of her life?"

I shrug. "Are you defending him?"

"No."

"It sounds like an excuse. Lee should've been there for her."

"I'm not making any judgments or casting blame. I'm just asking questions and trying to understand what happened."

"Lee is too complicated to understand. I don't try to understand him anymore. He's a disgrace. Too much has happened in my life for me to forgive him."

"Like what, for example?"

I shrug. "Violence, so much of it. Emotional. Physical. Psychological."

"Did he ever hit you?"

I nod and notice I'm shaking. I hide my hands beneath my legs to stop them from trembling.

"What about your mother?" he asks. "Did he ever put his hands on her?"

"My mother received most of the abuse when Lee came home long after Mom and I had gone to bed. He'd wake her up to fight. I woke up to them yelling more times than I can remember." I shake my head. "I wanted to pack a bag many times and run away with my mom."

"Did either you or your mother press charges?"

"He would've beaten my mother senseless if either of us called the police. My ass would've been whipped." I glance out the window, turning away from the conversation to block it out.

"How's your personal life?" Dr. Matheson notices my discomfort and rearranges the subtleties of our tête-à-tête. "How are you coping?" He indulges me with an intelligent stare at the bruises marring my face. His hunched posture suggests a keen interest in my private proclivities.

I drink what is left of my water and stand to refill it from the glass pitcher sitting on a stainless-steel tray before us.

Dr. Matheson scoots to the edge of his seat and reaches for his water glass, our fingers brushing each other's. I pause and stare down at the barbell strength of his hands. It looks like he is beckoning me to hold his hand.

"I need to stretch my legs," I say and stroll to the picturesque and meditative winter scene outside the picture window. Dr. Matheson watches me from where he sits, legs crossed in gentlemanly fashion.

"Are you still living in your apartment?" he asks.

The ice water tastes refreshing, moistening my parched mouth and throat. "I've got nowhere else to go."

"Do you think it's safe to stay there after everything?" I hear the carefulness of his question, the tenderness in how he says the word safe, and the lilt of his accent, bringing a fleeting smile to my face.

"I have nowhere else to go," I repeat, sipping my water, closing my eyes, and envisioning a life without Eli or my mom.

"Can I help?" His question propels me to turn around and look at him.

"How?"

"I don't know. But if there's anything I can do—"

"I think I'll be fine," I cut him off. "But I appreciate it." I pause and stare into my water glass to buy time and rearrange my thoughts before I speak again. Then, I glimpse Dr. Matheson's steadfast stare. "All the men were arrested," I say, as if speaking it out loud lessens the pain and makes the situation meaningful.

"You almost lost your life a week ago," Dr. Matheson reminds me.

I recall the struggle with the tall, red-haired man pinning me to the floor, punching me in the face, and chasing me out of the fire escape of my apartment to the ground.

"I lost my life when Eli and my mother died," I say, and I turn around to the wintry wonderland outside.

I stand up taller at the sound of movement behind me. Dr. Matheson's hand rests on my shoulder.

"This past year feels like a dream." My voice is barely noticeable.

A firm pat on my back reassures me everything will be all right.

Dr. Matheson walks around the edges of his now unfurnished office to my side, and we both stare out into a steely, overcast day.

"There's so much I wanted to tell Eli," I say, and the jolting realization that my boyfriend is gone rattles me to the core. I try to rewind to when he was alive but replaying the moment between us in bed that night leaves me with goosebumps. Or when we kissed in the shower until our lips were raw and sore. "There's so much I wanted to know about him, like why he did the things he did, keeping me in the dark." I pause. "But it's too late."

"Do you know what the men were after, specifically?" Dr. Matheson asks.

"Money, I guess. But I still don't know what sort of trouble Eli was in." I hand Dr. Matheson my glass because I'm shaking too hard. I jam my hands into my pockets. My breathing is rigid, and he motions me to sit. I crouch forward in the window seat, rocking back and forth. I ask, "How does somebody live without a parent?"

Dr. Matheson pulls a vinyl stool from the corner and sits before me.

I do not look away from his handsome face. His eyes sparkle, even in the dimly lit room. They're gentle and beautiful.

He answers, "You'll think about them daily, but it will be fine. You'll get through it."

I struggle to fight back tears, wrestling to get through the next hour without falling apart.

"I don't know if I want to go on without them." I hate the sound of my voice, the weakness in it. I am at a crossroads with life and death.

"What do you mean?" Dr. Matheson leans forward. So close I can taste his cologne in the back of my throat. Cloying. Friendly. Intoxicating.

Breathing hurts. My nerves churn like a helicopter's propeller.

His shoulders rise and fall as he takes in a breath himself. I watch him exhale and let it out slowly. He studies me as I study him, observing like a great work of art.

"Death is everywhere," I say, turning sideways and staring at a watery sun slicing through the silver lining in the sky. "I thought I was going to die when that man broke into my room and assaulted me. I thought I would join my mother and Eli in the clouds."

"But you didn't," he says.

I clear my throat. "Maybe I should thank Mr. Williams for saving my life."

Dr. Matheson looks at me to continue. "Who's Mr. Williams?"

"My next-door neighbor. He's called the police. Twice."

"It looks like an angel was watching over you."

"He's an old busybody," I say.

"A busybody who saved your life."

Dr. Matheson reaches out a hand to me, palm up. High five? Handshake? I look at his outspread hand, then up to his face, nonplussed. He nods for me to take it.

I pull my left hand out of my pocket, my skin sweaty from my body heat, and place it on top of Dr. Matheson's. He says, "I'll listen, day or night."

I slide my hand back into my pocket.

Turning back to the window and the gunmetal grey morning, I sense Dr. Matheson has more to say. He sighs and sets the glass on the narrow windowsill. We stand side by side, watching blackbirds, carefree and unruffled, soaring in the big open sky.

After a few seconds, Dr. Matheson unsettles the peace and says, "I've got a few changes happening in my life."

His abrupt announcement yanks me out of my daydream. A triggering of gunshots fires inside my head. He looks around the barren room and back at me, his unfazed gaze falling across my face. Do I look alarmed? I wonder.

"This will be my last year practicing therapy," he says. "I'm retiring in the fall."

Waylaid, I reel with lightheadedness and disappointment, a sucker punch to the gut. I open my mouth to say something, demand answers, and express my anger in bad words, but Dr. Matheson quickly adds, "I'm moving to the city. New York."

I gather the courage to ask, "Why are you retiring?" I wrestle and obsess over losing somebody else.

"My sister is in town and heading back to New York for work and family. I'm moving to be closer to her."

I turn around. "Wait? What? What will you do with all that free time?" I ask, overstepping.

He says, "I'd like to return to a leisurely lifestyle. Tennis. Cooking. Maybe reestablish my green thumb." I hear the joy in his voice and am stabbed with guilt, worry, and too many regrets to name.

"I won't be able to talk to anybody else," I say.

"Why not?"

"It'll be different."

"You need to keep talking about your feelings, especially now. I don't think you should stop therapy cold turkey."

"I wouldn't be comfortable with another therapist."

"My decision to leave the practice should not reflect your needs to continue therapy and taking care of yourself."

"Where in New York?" I ask, removing my clammy hands from my pockets and wiping them off on my pants. I notice Dr. Matheson's body language changing, one leg over the other, a hand resting on his knee as he sits on his stool in front of me. I've violated patient/therapist boundaries.

"Upper East Side," he answers.

"Fancy." I smile at my cheekiness.

"Change will be difficult, but I need it too."

"Are you leaving because of me?" I ask. "Was I too challenging?"

"Of course not, Ralph. My reason for retiring is strictly personal. It's got nothing to do with my patients."

His smile is flirty, and I imagine him taking me to the city.

I turn to the sliver of sunshine, peering between the stodgy framework of clouds and trees in the distance, beyond the tip of the picturesque Adirondack Mountains.

"I'm worried about you," he says.

I turn to see the unease in his eyes. "I appreciate the concern. But I'll be fine."

"We all need support. That's part of what makes us human."

I say, "I'll survive."

"You've lost two important people," he says as if I've forgotten.

"I know."

"How do you feel about adopting a dog?"

"Like a therapy dog?"

He angles his head and nods.

"I don't have time for a dog. I'm never home. It wouldn't be fair to it."

"He or she could help you with your anxieties."

I stare around the bare-boned room, knowing I'll miss our talks. "How's this? I'll think about it."

Dr. Matheson seems satisfied with my answer as he folds his hands on his lap and smiles, his dimples deepening on both sides of his face. "Do you have my number?" he asks.

I recall the business card he handed me during our last session. I skim my fingers beneath the opening of my jacket pocket and feel around for the card inside. I don't go anywhere without it. "I do."

"You can call me day or night."

"I thought you were retiring?" I stare at him, grinning.

A glint in his eye conceals a secret. "You're the exception."

"I should get going. I've got somewhere to be."

He stands and envelops me in a firm handshake.

I don't want to pull away. I lean into him and close my eyes, controlling my impulses, inhaling his pleasant, woodsy, robust smell.

"I wish you the best, Ralph."

I rush across the room to gather my coat from the rack behind the door and climb into it. I watch Dr. Matheson walk toward me with a confident stride that makes me dizzy.

"Will you call me if you want to talk?" he asks, standing at arm's length, still holding my water glass.

I nod, turn, and reach for the doorknob in the outer office.

His following words stop me in my tracks. "Promise me you'll keep in touch," he says. It is a request, not a statement.

I whirl around and lick the brittle skin on my lips. "Thanks for everything."

"Take care of yourself, Ralph."

"You as well."

And I leave, ending another meaningful chapter in my life.

Chapter Thirty-Nine

A month later

DEATH CHANGES EVERYTHING.

I kneel on a hard bed of frozen ground, staring down at my mother's small tombstone.

My hands shake from a chill in the wintery air as snow swirls through the bare limbs of maples, oaks, and hemlocks in Pine Woods Cemetery on the outskirts of town.

A brisk wind crinkles the cellophane-wrapped lavender and chrysanthemums I lay on the snowy lot before the gravestone.

My eyes tear up from the razor-sharp cold breeze. I wipe my face with a closed fist.

Slipping into a dead zone, I hear the approaching whispers in the wind. My mother's laugh, a distant, familiar sound from childhood. Her smile is catching, innocent, and spirited.

I set my hand on the flowers and glimpse my mother in her garden at home, pruning and weeding her beloved hibiscus and honeysuckle beds. "Gardening teaches patience," she once told me when I was young and curious about how she occupied her time.

Now, her death is like a scar that never fades.

I stand to stretch my legs. My knees pop like gunfire under me.

Saying my goodbyes, at least for today, I shoulder through a biting wind to my car parked at the wrought-iron front gates.

"I'll see you tomorrow," I whisper, but the wind carries my cries across the river.

I think of Eli and smile as his face flashes across the snow-swept morning. As I open the door to get in, I turn to glimpse my mother's grave, fifty feet in the distance. A mournful feeling of loss and sadness clings to me. "I'll be back same time tomorrow."

In my mind's eye, I squeeze her hand to tell her I love her.

I get in the car and sit behind the steering wheel, staring out onto a blanket of powdery snow, the fragments of my life dispersing like ashes.

I look out onto the wide-open yard of the snow-dusted cemetery. A man walks his golden retriever through a shortcut in the woods, along a bike path by the water's edge.

I watch man's best friend and owner disappear into a knot of pine trees at the far end of the stone bridge.

The sight makes my decision for me. I turn the key in the ignition, drive to the wrought-iron gates, and brake to adjust the rearview mirror. Tears come fast and hard as I stare along the snowy path to my mother's final resting place.

I wipe my eyes and look for any oncoming traffic. The road is empty at this pre-dawn hour. I signal left and drive toward town, heading for the local animal shelter.

About the Author

Thomas Grant Bruso knew at an early age he wanted to be a writer. He has been a voracious reader of genre fiction since he was a kid.

His literary inspirations are Dean Koontz, Stephen King, Ellen Hart, Jim Grimsley, Karin Fossum, Sam J. Miller, Joyce Carol Oates, and John Connolly.

Bruso loves animals, book-reading, writing fiction, prefers Sudoku to crossword puzzles.

In another life, he was a freelance writer and wrote for magazines and newspapers. In college, he was a winner of the Hermon H. Doh Sonnet Competition. Now, he writes book reviews for his hometown newspaper, *The Press Republican.*

Facebook
www.facebook.com/thomasgrantbruso

Twitter
@thomgrantbruso

Other NineStar books by this author

Eye Of the Beholder
Summer Storms
Prayers for the Undead
The Lost Child
V is for Valentine

CONNECT WITH NINESTAR PRESS

WEBSITE: NINESTARPRESS.COM

FACEBOOK: NINESTARPRESS

X: @NINESTARPRESS

INSTAGRAM: NINESTARPRESS

BLUESKY: NINESTARPRESS

THREADS: @NINESTARPRESS